THE
ECHO
WIFE

S A R A H

THE
ECHO
WIFE

G A I L E Y

HODDER &
STOUGHTON

First published in Great Britain in 2021 by Hodder & Stoughton
An Hachette UK company

1

A CIP catalogue record for this title is available from the British Library

Hardback ISBN 9781529354492
Trade Paperback ISBN 978 1 529 35450 8
eBook ISBN 978 1 529 3545 22
Audio ISBN 978 1 529 35453 9

Printed and bound in Great Britain by Clays Ltd, Elcograf S.p.A.

Hodder & Stoughton policy is to use papers that are natural, renewable and recyclable products
and made from wood grown in sustainable forests. The logging and manufacturing processes
are expected to conform to the environmental regulations of the country of origin.

Hodder & Stoughton Ltd
Carmelite House
50 Victoria Embankment
London EC4Y 0DZ

www.hodder.co.uk

THE
ECHO
WIFE

CHAPTER
ONE

My gown was beautiful. It was the kind of garment that looks precisely as expensive as it is. I did not hate it, because it was beautiful, and I did not love it, because it was cruel. I wore it because wearing it was the thing this night demanded of me.

I bought it six months before the Neufmann Banquet, and, miracle of miracles, it still fit me exactly as well as it had when I'd tried it on the first time. Everything had changed in those six months. Everything except for my body. That, at least, was the same.

Still, I nearly dislocated my shoulder trying to get the buttons on the damn thing done up. Fifteen minutes of trying not to swear, fifteen minutes to do something that would have taken ten seconds if someone else had been there to do it for me. But I did it on my own, in the end. The help would have been convenient, but I didn't need it.

Twice in my life, now, I have buried myself in finery. Twice I have arranged myself within a great complication of fabric to prove that I understand the importance of a moment. It's clothing as contrition, a performance of beauty I have put on to pay penance to the people gathered to acknowledge me. They are here to see me, and I must apologize for requesting their attention, must make up for the weight of my demand by ensuring that looking at me will be a pleasant thing. Never mind the suffocation of the outfit, never mind the expense, never mind the impracticality. The transaction must be made: my efforts at beauty in exchange for their regard. And so, twice in my life, I have worn the cost of that recognition.

The process of defeating the buttons distracted me, and so it was only after I had my shoes on that I realized I had no way to see whether I'd achieved enough loveliness to satisfy the demands of the occasion. I used a kitchen knife to cut the packing tape away from my full-length mirror, feeling at once foolish and resourceful. After I'd peeled the layers of protective plastic wrap from the glass, there I was.

I allowed myself a breath of satisfaction: it was enough.

The gown was black silk. The skirt fell perfectly, the darts at my waist making the fabric bell over my hips before draping into crisp pleats. I, inside the silk, was the same person I always was, but the gown was a costume that gave me the right to be notable. It justified the evening I was about to face.

I tilted my head to see that my earrings weren't too much, ran my fingers across the high bateau neckline.

The task was accomplished. The result was good.

By the time I turned away from the mirror, it was six o'clock. My car was due in four minutes. I turned the lights off in my house and walked into the gray light of early evening to wait.

My wedding gown had also been beautiful, and expensive. It had been nothing at all like my gown for the Neufmann Banquet. Satin instead of silk, and suffocatingly tight. It had been white, gently cut, with a low neckline trimmed in Alençon lace. It had been aggressively soft, determined to be hopeful.

It had been vulnerable, where my Neufmann gown was severe. It had been tender, where my Neufmann gown was pitiless.

On the day that I had worn the kinder of the two gowns, Nathan had snuck into the suite where I was dressing. He walked in with exaggerated stealth, his tuxedo shoes squeaking as he minced pizzicato across the waxed wood floor. He gave me a velvet box with a necklace in it. The pendant floated perfectly above the dip of the lace. He wasn't supposed to see me—he'd bought the necklace to give me after the ceremony, but he said he just couldn't wait. He'd wanted me to have it sooner.

He clasped it behind my neck and kissed my cheek and fled

before I could scold him for breaking the rules. Before I could bring up the traditions that neither of us cared about, but that both of us had been so determined to follow. When I walked down the aisle, the sapphire of the pendant caught an errant sunbeam and refracted light across the arm of Nathan's father's suit.

After the ceremony was over, Nathan touched the hollow of my throat and smiled, a small secret smile that was just for me.

I can't remember ever wearing that necklace again. It had been a ridiculous extravagance. When would I ever wear a sapphire?

But I watched for that smile. I watched for it every time I dressed up for a date or an event, every time I came home from a conference, every time we made up after a fight. I filled my pockets with that smile. I tucked it away for later, to get me through the lean times when we couldn't look at each other.

Even then, I think I knew I'd need it.

———

Three and a half hours after I put the Neufmann gown on, I was ready to be finished wearing it. The silk was fitted closely through my ribs and waist, flattering enough, but as uncompromising as an ethics committee. I couldn't seem to get a deep enough breath. The banquet hall was full of people, all of them looking at me or talking about me or thinking about me. Or worse: not thinking about me at all. I kept catching people's eyes by mistake, flashing smiles that felt raw and strange on my face.

I wondered if there was enough oxygen for everyone present. I wondered if maybe there was some problem with the ventilation system, and whether the carbon dioxide levels in the room were rising. Everyone in the room exhaled once every few seconds. There was no avoiding that. They had to respire.

Every time they did, I felt the air grow a little heavier.

People were talking to me, endlessly talking to me, and I knew that there were hours still to come, hours and hours of people looking at me and moving their mouths and raising their eyebrows and waiting for me to say things back that would satisfy their vision of the person I was supposed to be. Hours of their opinions and compliments and complicated insults. Hours of smiling.

There were seven other people seated at my banquet table, their wineglasses kept in a perpetual state of half-emptiness by a series of bored waiters. The man seated to my left was a senior jurist from the selection committee. He was talking to me, just like everyone else, and I arranged my face into a shape that would seem pleasant and interested. He was important. I should have known his name.

David? No. Daniel?

"I've been terribly impressed," the man was saying, "by the finesse your technique displays. I've never seen such singular control of the acute hormonal mode of neuropsychological conditioning." I smiled and nodded, pretended to take a bite of risotto as though I could possibly have swallowed it. It rested on my tongue like a pill. It tasted like nothing at all, like the flesh of the roof of my mouth, like the edge of the wineglass in front of me. I could not eat it. I had to eat it. The man on my left (Douglas?) was looking at me, waiting for me to accept his compliment.

There were hours still to go.

After much too long, the risotto slid down my throat and the name appeared fully formed in my mind. "Thank you . . . Dietrich," I replied. "It's been a team effort, of course—"

"Nonsense," he said, and my throat clenched the way it always did when a man in my field interrupted me with that word. "You have a fantastic research team, there can be no doubt of that— but no, Dr. Caldwell, this is about your work. Your legacy. You get the credit, yes? *You* are the pioneer of the Caldwell Method. It's all right to bask in it, at least for tonight."

He lifted his glass. I obligingly raised mine to meet it, because *don't be a bitch, Evelyn*. The movement caught the eyes of others around the table, and soon, everyone held their glasses aloft, their faces expectant. Dietrich led them in a toast. "To Dr. Evelyn Caldwell, changing the world."

Federlauer, his last name came to me at last, Dietrich *Feder-lauer,* how could I have forgotten? Stupid, stupid.

Six people repeated my name, and they touched their glasses together, and the heavy air rang crystalline. The woman across from me exhaled as she drank, the glass near her nostrils fogging. She caught my eye and smiled, and I looked away before I could even try to make myself smile back.

The lights in the room began to dim. A spotlight illuminated the podium at the front of the room.

The air was so heavy.

I held my breath for a few seconds before swallowing my mouthful of wine, willed my heartbeat to slow down. There was no reason to be nervous. There were no surprises coming to get me. That silver helix up on the podium had my name engraved on it. The speeches that would take up the next hour were already written, were about me and my work. My face was the one on the posters lining the banquet hall. *An evening to honor and celebrate Dr. Evelyn Caldwell,* that's what had been on the engraved invitations.

Everything was good. Everything was already decided. Everything was for me.

Nothing would go wrong.

Your legacy, Federlauer had said. This, tonight, this would be what I was remembered for. This would be the focus of my eulogy. Not the other thing, not the shameful disaster that my life had briefly become thanks to Nathan. No one would be talking about that—about Nathan and his weakness. It would be this, just this, my work and my research and my success.

I lifted a hand to tuck a strand of hair behind my ear, then arrested my arm in the middle of the movement, Nathan's voice ringing through my memory. *Don't fidget. You look exactly like your mother when you fidget.*

He'd been right. He'd been cruel about it, cruel on purpose, but he'd been right to remind me. I already looked so much like my mother that, in my graduate program, the jokes wrote themselves.

Wow, it looks like the cloning research is going well! It was bad enough to have the same colorless hair, the same dishwater-gray eyes, the same thin mouth as that woman. I wouldn't act like her too.

I'd left that behind long ago—being anything like her, doing the things she did to get to the end of each day intact. I'd left that behind and I'd never looked back.

Poise, that was the way. No twitching. No fidgeting. Poise.

I lowered my hand to my lap, curled it into a fist and nested it inside my other palm. No one would be able to see me clenching that fist, digging my nails into the soft valleys of flesh between the tendons of my hand. Even to the forgettable Federlauer, I would seem composed.

The room was full of eyes, and I reminded myself that I could hide from every single one of them. I knew how to walk quietly. I knew how to slip by unnoticed. I knew how to be the thing they wanted to see, the thing they wanted me to be.

I knew how to hide when I needed to.

I had gotten through the previous year of impossibly hellish obstacles. I had survived the discovery and the betrayal and the fallout. I could handle this banquet.

On stage, a woman I'd never met was talking about my early research. She clutched the microphone in a white-knuckled stage-fright grip, and described the initial stages of my work in glowing terms. It was, quite frankly, mortifying. Neuropsychology, neurobiology, hormonal conditioning—it seemed so entry-level now, so sophomoric. At the time, it had seemed like the biggest thing in the world. It had seemed worth every late night in the lab, eating takeout with Nathan while samples spun in the gravity centrifuge.

The woman onstage called that work brilliant, and I choked back a startled laugh. We were so young then, balancing notebooks full of handwritten lab notes on our knees, trying not to spill noodles on the pages. Falling in love. We had dreamed of a night like this: me in a ball gown, him in a tuxedo. Two names engraved on a silver double helix.

A legacy.

I caught myself balling up my napkin in my fist, reflexively clutching at the fabric. I smoothed it out, creased it carefully, and set it next to my plate. I folded my hands. *Poise, Evelyn,* I repeated to myself. *Poise.*

This banquet was supposed to be my night. It was not a night for regret; it was a night for *satisfaction.* After everything that had happened, didn't I deserve that much?

I crossed my legs, drank my wine, arranged my face into a gracious smile, and pointed my chin at the podium. There was no point in dwelling on the things that the Evelyn of a decade ago had wanted. I told myself that I had been a different person then, practically a child, with a different life. Different goals.

Things change.

Things die.

And now, here was a banquet hall filled with intellectual luminaries. Wine and waiters and flowers and programs. Rented gowns and uncomfortable shoes, speeches and seating charts, all to celebrate me. All for me.

I did not allow my hands to tremble. I did not grit my teeth. I did not climb up onto my chair and tear the silk from my ribs and scream at the top of my lungs about everything that was wrong and broken and missing.

There was nothing to feel upset about. Not a single thing.

CHAPTER
TWO

I tried to pace myself at the reception, but glasses of champagne kept appearing before me, pressed into my hands by people I'd never met, but who seemed to know me. Everyone wanted to be the one to give me a fresh glass, everyone wanted to hold the award, everyone wanted to talk to me. It had been hours and there was so long still to go. There were at least a hundred rented tuxedos standing between me and the door. The end of the night was well beyond the horizon. There were too many people, thousands, it felt like, and I couldn't possibly keep up, so I sipped champagne and smiled at all of them and tried to let myself feel swept away instead of half-drowned.

"Isn't that thing heavy?"

"What will you be working on next?"

"I have a question about your use of cognitive mapping in the developmental process."

"How on earth did you come up with the idea to sidestep the Mohr Dilemma?"

"Where's Nathan?"

This last question snagged me like an errant briar; I only just caught my smile before it faltered. It was Lorna van Struppe asking—and, yes, handing me yet another glass of champagne, my half-drunk one whisked away already.

Lorna was my old mentor, the woman who had developed the practice of telomere financing to extend the lives of research subjects. She was also the one who showed me how to gracefully deflect academic misogyny. Lorna was tall and brawny and intellectually terrifying to most of her peers. She had always reminded me of a darker-complected Julia Child. Her resonant voice cut easily through the hum of congratulations, and the swarm of men whose names I would never remember fell quiet before her. They always did that when Lorna started talking.

Normally, their silence would be a relief—a safe harbor created by Lorna's overwhelming presence. But her question hung in the void, stark and obvious, and I absolutely could not answer it. I raised my glass to her and deflected as hard as I knew how, forcing bright affection into my voice. "Thank you for this. The other one was almost ten seconds old! The bubbles were nearly elliptical already." It was an old joke from the first time Lorna and I had drunk champagne together, celebrating a publication. We'd gotten silly, started laughing about the bubbles going flat; champagne in two dimensions, we called it. Not funny unless you were drunk and giddy, which we had been, and so the memory of our laughter had fueled that joke in the intervening years.

But the deflection didn't work. Lorna was as intent as ever, infuriatingly focused on the one question I didn't want anyone asking. The question I was sure everyone was whispering about when I was out of earshot.

"Where's Nathan?" She was so loud, heads were turning, people were listening, and if they weren't already wondering they would start to, and they would talk about it. *Damn you, damn you, damn you, Lorna.* "I haven't been able to spot him all night, and I want to have a word with him about the research assistant he sent me last quarter. Nowhere near the caliber I'd expect, don't know what he was thinking—" Lorna craned her neck and looked around, not one to be caught up in praising me when there was an opportunity to excoriate Nathan on the table. As she listed the defects of the research assistant, more than a few members of our audience lost interest, thank God.

"He's not here," I said. The seam of my dress dug into my skin, merciless. "He's probably at home with his fiancée."

"His what? Oh," Lorna said, catching on and looking at me with deep, sudden concern. "I see. Tell me, do we hate him now?"

"No, no, of course not." I let my grip tighten on the silver double helix just a little, just enough to keep my voice steady. I couldn't tell if I was drunk or not. I wanted to be drunk. I wanted to be extremely drunk. "Very amicable."

Lorna raised one wild-haired white eyebrow. "I'll be taking you out for coffee later this week, and you can give me all the details. In the meantime, I'll commence hating him just a *little*, in case I need material to seed hating him a lot."

"I'd love to get coffee, yes," I said, my cheeks numb, and before I could add something about *really, though, there's no need to hate him, things just didn't go as we planned,* a hand was on my elbow. I endured an urgent introduction, another fresh glass of champagne. By the time I turned back, Lorna was talking to someone else.

It was a mercy, in a way. The whirlwind of the evening had kept too many people from asking about Nathan. I didn't think I could have stomached defending him, not to Lorna. Even if it was the right thing to do, professionally. It wouldn't have been good for me to be seen bringing my personal life into my professional circles, damaging Nathan's reputation in his academic ones. It would have been *justified,* but justification didn't matter in situations like this; no, I needed to be careful.

I had seen it a hundred times in the field that we'd chosen. I knew who always bore the weight of divorce. Nathan could afford all of this, would come out unscathed regardless of how clearly the entire situation was his fault. And no matter how obviously I was the wronged party, it would haunt me for the rest of my career if I slipped at all, even once, if I ever seemed hurt or angry or sad. I needed to maintain the moral high ground, which meant that if I was asked, I needed to insist that everything was fine. I was fine. Nathan and I were fine. *Amicable.*

I did not want to be asked. The internal battle between doing the right thing and doing the honest thing and doing the *tempting* thing was an ongoing one, and I just wanted a break from it, just for one night. I wanted to hide.

And there were so many hiding places in that crowd.

Any other night, my story of the development of synthetic amniotic fluid alone could hold the right audience rapt for an hour at a stretch—but of course, this crowd didn't want to hear about amniotic fluid, nor about the process of accelerating bone growth in nascent specimens without damaging skeletal integrity. No, this crowd knew about that work, had heard it all before. They wanted something different, something remarkable. They wanted to know about the work that had won me the Neufmann Prize.

The process of taking an adult clone and writing their personality into their neurological framework: It was mine. All mine.

Sleepless nights, research mishaps, hours and hours in the lab alone. Nobody cares about those solitary, devastating failures. They don't want to hear about that—they'd rather hear the story of the eureka moment. And mine was good. "I was making eggs for breakfast," I would tell them, "and I was watching the way they started cooking from the bottom up, and that's when I figured it out: the key is to begin programming before the tissues of the hypothalamic nuclei have solidified. I ran to write down my breakthrough . . . and I completely forgot that the eggs were still on the stove. They burned so badly that we had to throw out the pan."

Things I never added to the story: the fact that Nathan had been the one to throw the pan into the trash, had been the one to open the kitchen windows to let the smoke out, had come into my study red-faced and shouting. The way he stormed out of the house without listening to my breakthrough. The way he didn't come home for days. Was I supposed to use the word "husband" or "ex-husband" for that part of the story? I could never decide, so I always told the story as though I'd been making breakfast for myself.

It was my breakthrough. It was my legacy, not ours. Nathan was already nostril-deep in academia then. It was all mine.

The Caldwell Method had never been a thing we shared.

"But aren't you concerned about the developmental mottling of the limbic system in early stages?" This question from a man in rimless glasses and a wrinkled suit, another person I'd never met before. I fielded the question as if I didn't chafe at the implications of such a basic objection to my methods. *No, you asshole,* I did not say, *it* never *occurred to me to keep an eye on the fucking* limbic *system, what a breakthrough, here, take my grant money.*

Poise. Patience. Be nice, Evelyn.

I answered questions, worked the crowd, took photographs. Someone asked me to sign a program, and I did, feeling ridiculous. I kept thinking that I wanted to go home, and then remembering that "home" didn't really exist anymore. I just wanted to escape. Right up until the moment when it was time to do just that. That's when I realized that leaving the suffocating press of the crowd would be the very worst thing in the world.

But there was no choice. The night was finally over, and home was waiting. I climbed into the back of a black car with my award in one hand and my tiny, useless clutch purse in the other. I leaned my head against the window. Behind my eyes, the champagne-hum was already turning into a headache that would be devastating come morning. The streetlights that passed were blurry, haloed by the winter air. I tried to remember why that happened—ice crystals in the atmosphere? No, that was the thing that put a ring around the moon. Maybe it was something wrong in my own eyes, something that I should have recognized as a warning sign. *Should have known,* I'd say later. *No one else ever mentioned halos around streetlights.*

It was past two o'clock in the morning by the time I walked in through the backyard of the little town house I'd rented, letting the gate slam shut behind me. I kicked my shoes off next to the sliding glass door and made an involuntary noise at the relief of standing flat-footed. The carpet was new, installed just before I signed the lease, and it was a mercy to curl my toes into something soft. I put the silver double helix down on my newly assembled flat-pack dining-room table.

I'd put the table together just that morning, half an hour with an Allen wrench and an illustrated manual. It existed for the express purpose of holding two items: my award, and an inch-thick stack of papers bristling with sticky-note flags.

Finding out what Nathan was doing should have been so much easier than it was. Once I started looking right at things, it was obvious. He had gone to no great lengths to hide her from me. His nightstand was littered with receipts—for clothes and jewelry that never made it to our house, and meals at restaurants I'd never had time to eat at. He didn't bother to make excuses for late nights out, for strange bruises on his shoulders and scratches on his back. Was there ever lipstick on his collar? Did I ever pay close enough attention to find out?

I don't know if he thought I was too stupid to see what he was doing, or if it just didn't matter to him that I might catch him.

Now, I padded across the unfamiliar dining-room tile to the open galley-style kitchen and filled a coffee mug with water. Drank the whole thing, yes, must be responsible about hydration, then refilled it and took the mug back with me to the table. My belly sloshed uncomfortably with water.

Now was as good a time as any, I figured. I'd sign the papers while I was still a little buzzed and riding high on the ego-flush of the evening. I'd get it over with, and in the morning, I probably wouldn't even remember doing it.

I fished a pen out of my leather shoulder bag, the one I took to work with me every day. It was big enough to fit a few shirts, a few pairs of underwear, a pair of slacks, a toothbrush. It was small enough that no one noticed I was living out of it, the week after I'd found out about Nathan. It wasn't unusual for me to stay in the lab for a couple of hours after everyone else was gone, and no one commented on the way I was there before anyone else in the morning. No one had needed to know that I was sleeping in my office during that terrible week.

I pressed the tip of my pen to the bottom of the first page, above the first yellow sticky flag, a line with my name on it. My married name. My name for good, since all my publications were under it. My doctorate had been issued to that name, even. I was so young when I married Nathan, so sure that he was good enough, that he was what I wanted. So sure that we'd go on to conquer the world together. So ready to give up the name I shared with my mother and my father. So ready to become someone new.

My award glinted in my peripheral vision, the silver double helix shining in the fluorescent light from the kitchen. I put it on top of the thick stack of divorce papers and let the weight of it compress the pile.

"Worth it," I whispered to myself. I let the pen in my hand fall to the ground. I could sign the papers in the morning, with coffee and aspirin and whatever headache was waiting for me. I decided that I would lean right into the misery of it, make it a whole pathetic tableau.

I walked upstairs and wilted onto my bed, on top of the covers. I yanked at my gown until I felt the buttons between my shoulder blades pop off. I tugged the silk over my head and gasped at the feeling of freedom, my ribs expanding further than they'd been able to for hours.

I could breathe. I could finally breathe.

CHAPTER
THREE

The weekend gave way to Monday like fog dissolving in sunlight. I drove to the lab with too much gratitude, embarrassingly relieved to be out of the little house I'd never wanted. The lab, by contrast, was something I'd wanted with the kind of mania some women reserve for childbearing.

It had been an incredibly hard win. The Artemis Corporation hadn't initially wanted to give me my own space for my research—they'd claimed that, without military contracts, my work was too controversial to be profitable. It took years of fighting to convince them that my work could have other applications, the kinds of applications that would bring in immeasurable profit from private sources. Years of measuring out the size of the waves I could afford to make. Waves just big enough to keep the conversation going, but not so big as to make me into a *problem*. Years of sharing my space with people who could never begin to understand the kind of work I was doing. Except for Seyed, of course. He always understood the work. He always understood me.

But then, one day, the fighting was over, and the lab was built. Tempered glass tubes filled with artificial amniotic fluid, tables made of tungsten instead of steel or aluminum, a fume hood big enough to fit an adult specimen if necessary. I still had to fight over funding every year, of course, but maybe the Neufmann would change that. Maybe *results* would change that.

Either way. My lab felt more like *home* than any iteration of *home* ever had.

"Did you bring it?" Seyed never greeted me with a "hello." He considered that kind of formality a waste of time. It was part of why I'd hired him in the first place.

Seyed was already waist-deep in the fume hood. I couldn't see him until after I went through the airlock, positive-pressure ventilation pulling a few strands of my hair loose—but I could, as usual, still hear him. He always started talking as soon as he heard the affirmative *beeps* of my entry code.

Now, his muffled voice reverberated through the vents of the hood as I walked into my lab. "Of course I brought it," I said, setting the Neufmann on a bare patch of lab table. "You'd quit if I didn't."

Seyed emerged from the fume hood, scrub brush raised high, and yanked off the respirator that covered the lower half of his face. He was small, rail-thin but with a round face that made him look like an undergrad. A soul patch sat in the center of his chin, groomed with the great pride a man shows the only facial hair he can reliably produce. He stared at the silver double helix with a critical eye. "It's smaller than I expected," he said.

I dropped my things on my desk and told him to get used to it. "You'll have ten of them someday, if you keep practicing your fume hood maintenance." He saluted me with a finger, pulled his respirator back on, and vanished into the fume hood again. "What are you doing in there, anyway?" I asked. "Did something explode?"

"No," he said, "not technically. Don't worry about it, I ordered the replacement parts already."

I didn't worry about it. I never worried about anything that Seyed told me not to worry about. Some of my colleagues would flinch at the idea of trusting an assistant the way I trusted Seyed, but he'd earned it. He was smart, sure, but anyone could be *smart*. I would never take on an assistant who wasn't *smart*. I demanded more than smart—brilliance was the bare minimum required to keep up in my lab, and *not* keeping up wasn't an option. Not keeping up was dangerous.

Seyed was more than just brilliant. He was competent, independent, and fearless on a level that matched me pace for pace. I spotted it in him for the first time when Nathan brought him home for dinner, when he was a graduate student threatening to become Nathan's protégé. The questions he asked me about my research that night went well beyond polite interest. His teeth were sharp and he was hungry, too hungry to be satisfied by the kind of growth Nathan could offer him.

I told him so, that night, and then I offered him a job where he could flourish, and that was that. I don't remember if Nathan was upset or not. I suppose that, by then, I'd stopped paying attention to that kind of thing.

Most of the time, it was just the two of us working together, and it was easily the best working partnership I'd ever been half of. I trusted Seyed's judgment like I trusted my own. I trusted him without question.

So I didn't bother looking into the fume hood to see what he was doing. Instead, I grabbed a clipboard from the side of a specimen tank and started reviewing nutrient updates, as recorded by the weekend intern I'd never wanted to hire. I hated trusting data collection to someone other than Seyed or myself, but there were labor laws to consider.

The subject in the tank, 4896-T, was eight days into the growth process and was already recognizable as an adult humanoid. She appeared to be progressing well, but her HGH levels were uneven, which was concerning. I eyed the major muscle groups on the subject's thighs, looking for signs of atrophy—the only visible indicator of the compartment syndrome that would result from the subject's muscle growth outpacing the flexibility of her other tissues.

Of course, if there was atrophy, it was already too late to fix the problem. If there wasn't atrophy, it would be tough to tell if there was any compartment syndrome at all without getting involved in some seriously invasive diagnostic procedures. Those procedures would interfere with the programming process

significantly enough to make the subject useless for research pur-
poses, and the waste would be a nightmare to justify when I was
trying to get my budget for the next year locked down. I tapped
my pen against my clipboard, mentally flipping through options.

It was a habit Nathan hated——the way I drummed out a beat
while I was thinking. It was an indulgence I allowed myself only in
my own lab, now, where he had never once set foot. It felt like a stolen luxury, a finger dragged through the frosting on an uncut cake.

"You missed a call," Seyed said, interrupting my rhythm. I
tamped down irritation: it wasn't his fault that I hadn't found
the answer to the HGH problem before he finished his work. I
didn't bother to school my face to stillness as I turned toward
him, though. I didn't have to do that with Seyed. He would commence giving a shit about my emotions the moment I raised them
as a subject of concern, and not a second sooner. Inside my lab, I
could afford to frown.

"Congratulations, I suppose? I won't be returning those calls,"
I said.

Seyed emerged from the fume hood with a bundle of rags. He
held the rags at arms' length, walked them to the red biohazard
bin next to the autoclave, and dropped them in along with his
elbow-length gloves. With his bare hands he removed his respirator and, after a moment's consideration, dropped it into the bin
too. "Someone named 'Martine.'"

The metal edges of the clipboard dug into the soft meat of my
fingers.

I forced myself to loosen my grip. I replaced the clipboard,
carefully threading the hole in the metal tab over the plastic hook
that was affixed to the glass of the tank. The clipboard clicked
against the glass, and the specimen in the tube twitched. I flinched.
"Seyed, please do me a favor and line each clipboard in this lab
with felt. Any neutral color. Back and edges."

"You got it," Seyed said, scrubbing his hands to the elbows
with antimicrobial soap. "Deadline?"

"End of day," I called over my shoulder, not looking back for confirmation.

I walked to the lab phone. There was a trash can on the floor next to it, which held messages—one of the many ways in which Seyed had streamlined the systems in the lab since I hired him. The legal pad next to the phone was dominated by a running tally of who had last ordered takeout. S, E, S, E, S, S, S, E, E, S, E. Next to the column of letters, Seyed had written the name "Martine" and a phone number. His handwriting was architect-tidy. "Did she say what she wanted?"

"No," Seyed called back. "She just asked if I would pass along her regards and her 'request for a return call at your earliest convenience.' What kind of person talks like that?"

No kind of person talked like that.

My mother talked like that.

Martine talked like that.

I thanked Seyed, and my voice must have given something away, because he asked if I was okay. He never asked if I was okay, never. He would only have asked if I sounded truly broken. I swallowed another flash of anger as I told him that I was fine. "I mean, I'm not fine, but I'm fine," I added, hating everything about the conversation already.

"Right, sure," he said, his voice as steady as if I'd said something normal. As if he believed me.

That, I think, is the thing that made me tell him the truth. I hadn't planned to say anything, but Seyed sounded like he believed me, like he thought it possible that I could be fine at a time like this one. "Martine is Nathan's fiancée."

I didn't like to talk about Nathan. Especially not at work. Especially not with Seyed, whose connection to Nathan I'd so effectively severed. But there it was, in the room, right there where Seyed could hear it: *Martine is Nathan's fiancée.* It was the first time I'd ever said that exact sentence out loud, and it stayed on my tongue with an aftertaste, like tin and brine.

Seyed sucked his teeth. "He's engaged already? Shit, I'm sorry, that's fucking terrible."

"Yeah." He was right. It was oddly satisfying to hear someone put it that way, because yeah. It *was* fucking terrible. "They've been together for a while now. I haven't really talked to her beyond the bare minimum." I shook my head. "I don't know why she'd call me here."

Seyed paused, his eyedropper of iodine hovering over a slide. "You're listed in the staff directory." He was being careful, staying neutral, trying not to step wrong. It didn't suit him at all. "It was probably the only polite way she could figure out to contact you."

A headache was spreading through my temples. I couldn't tell if it was new, or the lingering remnants of my champagne hangover. "Right, no, I mean I don't know why she'd call me *at all*."

"One way to find out," Seyed singsonged.

I glared at him, but he didn't look up from his work, and after a few seconds the glare felt more like theater than anything else. I tore off the part of the legal pad with the phone number on it and tucked it into my breast pocket. It could wait.

Nothing Martine had to say to me could possibly be urgent.

Putting off the unpleasant business of returning Martine's call was easy enough. The lab was full of work that urgently needed doing—assessing Seyed's tissue samples, adjusting fluid levels in the specimen tanks, taking and testing new fluid samples from 4896-T, writing up a plan to level out the hormone ranges of several struggling specimens. I owed the lab director an expenditures report, and I needed to figure out how to massage the numbers in the report to justify a slow increase in costs. We were running through supplies faster than we could afford them, and the only solution was money.

Procrastination would have been easy enough, if not for the crinkle of paper in my pocket and the little blinking light in my brain: *Martine called. Martine called. Martine called.*

Why on earth would Martine call?

CHAPTER
FOUR

Late in the afternoon, Seyed sat on a lab stool next to me and eased my pencil out of my hand. "Hey, Evelyn?" He ducked his head and looked at me with his wide, patient brown eyes.

"Yeah?"

"You're driving me fucking crazy." He drummed the pencil on the side of my clipboard in a staccato rhythm. It was loud, uneven, and deeply irritating. He twisted in his chair, looked at the lab phone, looked back at the clipboard, tapped it with the pencil again. "You've been doing this shit all day," he said. "Call Martine already."

A flush of shame. *Fidgeting.* "You're right. I don't know why I've been—ugh. I'll do it soon, okay?" I almost apologized, but I stopped myself just in time. It was one of my rules, a rule that my father branded into me when I was a child. It was a rule that had gotten me through grad school and internships and the endless fight for respect and recognition. Never apologize in the lab. Never apologize in the workplace.

Never apologize.

"C'mon, boss." Seyed gave me an encouraging smile. It stung like cautery. "You're Evelyn Goddamn Caldwell. You just won a Neufmann Honor. This lady's got nothing on you."

I grimaced, but nodded. Seyed calling me "boss," the sign of a serious pep-talk attempt.

He was doing his best.

He couldn't help what he didn't know.

I've never been an optimist.

I've never had cause to expect a positive outcome when all the signs point to a negative one.

Except once.

I bowed to optimism one time, and it was a mistake.

I had been at the museum, enduring an ill-advised attempt at connecting with Lorna's other research assistant. He was a man who rode his bicycle to the lab every day and ate raw vegetables for lunch. He was tall, stringy, an array of tendons loosely hung on a wire framework. He seemed like a good way for me to practice networking, if not actual friendship. I can't even remember his name now—Chris, probably, or Ben.

Nathan had found me while I was waiting for my colleague to return from an eternal trip to the lavatory. He sidled up to me at a display of collider schematics. He had long hair then, past his shirt collar, and wore it tied back into a low ponytail. I remember noticing the ponytail and rolling my eyes before he even spoke to me. Later, just before our wedding, he cut it off, and I cried myself to sleep missing it.

"You don't look like you're having fun on your date." That was the first thing he said, his voice pitched low enough that I didn't immediately recognize that he was talking to me. When I glanced over, Nathan was looking at me sidelong, his mouth crooked up into a dimpled half-smile.

"It's not a date," I snapped. "We just work together."

"He seems to think that it's a date," he'd said. "Poor guy's under the impression that you think it's a date too. He keeps trying to grab your hand." I looked at him with alarm, and he held up his hands, took a step away from me. "I haven't been watching you or following you or anything, we've just—we've been in the same exhibits a couple of times, and I noticed. Sorry."

He started to walk away, hands in his pockets, but I stopped him. "It's not a date," I said, not bothering to keep my voice down.

"He knows it's not a date. We're just colleagues." My non-date came out of the bathroom then, looked around, spotted me. He started to cross the gallery, and I panicked. "In fact," I said, "you should give me your phone number. Right now." He grinned and took my phone, sent himself a message from it. *Hi, it's Nathan, rescuing you from an awkward situation.*

By the time he'd finished, my colleague had reached us. I gave Nathan a wink, trying to come across as flirtatious, as bold. He would later tell me that I'd looked panicked.

"Give me a call," he'd said, glancing between me and poor Chris, or Ben, or whatever his name was.

I'd gotten what I needed—a way to make sure my colleague knew that the thing he had hoped for was never going to happen. I told him brightly about getting asked out, said something about how we should do coworker outings more often. I pretended not to notice the way his face fell.

I never had any intention of calling Nathan.

But I did call him. I didn't have a good reason to, didn't have any data to support the decision. I took a chance on him.

I had hoped for the best.

———

Martine answered the phone on the second ring. Her voice was high, light, warm. Nonthreatening. Hearing it was like swallowing a cheekful of venom.

"Hello, this is the Caldwell residence, Martine speaking."

I forced myself to look past the fact that she'd used Nathan's last name, as if it belonged to her. As if she were a Caldwell. As if she got to have a name at all. I unconsciously slipped into the low, brusque tone I used when speaking at conferences. "It's Evelyn. My lab assistant gave me your message." I didn't ask any questions, didn't let any uncertainty through. Authoritative. Unapologetic. *Don't fidget. Don't apologize.*

She was more than polite. Excited, even. She sounded like she was talking to an old friend, instead of to the woman whose

husband she'd stolen. *That's not fair,* I mentally chastised myself.
It's not her fault. I told her that I couldn't talk long, tried to sound
like there was a reason I had to go, instead of like I was running
away.

"Oh, before I forget—I understand congratulations are in order," Martine said, her voice easy. I couldn't help admiring the
way she navigated conversation, the infinite finesse of it. She was
showing me mercy: by interrupting, she kept me from having to
commit the rudeness of admitting I didn't want to stay on the
phone. The faux pas of her interruption rescued me from feeling awkward. It absorbed discomfort on my behalf. The ultimate
mannerly posture.

I recognized the maneuver. It was directly out of my mother's
playbook.

Martine asked me if I would consider getting a cup of tea with
her. I paused long enough that she asked if I was still on the line.
"Yes. I'm here." I cleared my throat. "Why do you want to get tea
with me, Martine?"

Martine laughed, a light, tinkling laugh, one designed to make
people feel fun at parties. That was also my mother's. "Oh, I'm
so sorry if I've worried you at all, Evelyn. I just wanted to get tea
so we could get to know each other a little. I know that things
with Nathan aren't ideal, but I don't want there to be any troubled water between us. Don't you think it would be better if we
could be friends?"

I choked back a laugh. "Friends?"

"I would love to get to know you," Martine said, as though this
were a perfectly reasonable request. I was the woman who had
been married to Nathan, the woman whose life Martine's existence had blown to pieces, and she wanted to get to know me. Of
course she did. Why wouldn't she?

She asked again, and this time, a note of pleading entered her
voice. "Just tea. An hour. That's all. Please?"

I didn't ask for his opinion, but of course Seyed told me not to
do it.

"I have to. I said I would."

"Don't get coffee with this lady, it's weird. You know this is weird, right?"

You have no idea *how weird this is,* I thought. "She asked me to get tea, not coffee. And I have to go."

Seyed looked up from the felt he was gluing to a clipboard. "Why do you owe her anything? It's not like *you're* the homewrecker here."

"She's——it's complicated, Sy. And besides, I already said I'd go."

"When are you doing this objectively insane thing?"

"Tomorrow morning. So I'll need you to handle the fluid sampling."

He raised an eyebrow. "You mean I'm covering your workload while you do the thing you know you shouldn't do."

"Yes," I said. "Please."

"Great." He walked the clipboard back to the tank it belonged to, returned it, and grabbed an un-felted clipboard from the next tank over. "Perfect. Because I didn't have enough to do."

He was irritated with me, and rightly so. I debated telling him everything—telling him why I couldn't say *no* to Martine, what I owed to her, why I needed to see her. But it was too much already, him knowing who Martine was. Him knowing Nathan had been unfaithful.

The idea of telling Seyed who Martine really was caused my entire mind to recoil. "I'll be in by ten," I said.

"Have you ever seen this woman in person before?" he asked. "What if she's, like, a murderer?"

I grimaced at the memory of my knuckles on the red-painted front door of Nathan's second, secret house. The knob turning. Martine's face, smiling out at me, eyes blank and polite in the few seconds before recognition struck us both. "I've seen her before," I said. "She's very sane."

Seyed shook his head, cutting a strip of felt. "I still don't think you should do this to yourself," he said softly. "Not that my opinion matters."

That last part wasn't a barb—it was an apology. He knew he was intruding, knew he was speaking out of turn. And he also knew that his opinion did matter, mattered when no one else's did. He was allowed to question me. He was allowed to offer opinions. He was allowed to speak during oversight meetings, even when my funding was at risk, even when the meeting was really a battle for survival.

I respected Seyed. He could keep up with me. He was one of the only people who was allowed to have an opinion at all.

"I know I shouldn't do it, Sy," I replied, watching him apply glue to the back of the clipboard. "But I'm going to anyway."

I couldn't turn my back on Martine.

I couldn't escape her, any more than I could escape myself.

CHAPTER
FIVE

The tea shop Martine had chosen was cute. It was small, with mismatched furniture and clumsy velvet couches and a hand-chalked menu behind the counter. Tea-filled jars lined the shelves behind the register. The place smelled like steam and wood polish. There was a bulletin board covered in handwritten fliers for babysitting, yoga classes, free furniture.

It was almost exactly halfway between our houses. A bell over the door announced my entrance, bright and brassy. I tried not to look for her, but I failed, and there she was.

She was already seated, her hands around a steaming mug, her eyes on a book. She didn't look up, didn't notice me standing there—too engrossed in her reading. The air in the coffee shop seemed thin. My breath came too fast. I took my time at the coat-rack, unwinding my scarf, shrugging out of my coat, watching the way Martine moved. Watching her tuck a finger under the page she was reading for a few seconds before turning it. Watching her blow on her tea before taking a tentative sip.

It was hypnotic. Martine moved in ways that I didn't, in ways that I had consciously, effortfully trained myself out of. Tucking-in of my arms and legs, ways of making myself smaller, less obtrusive. Delicate flutters that might imply indecision. Little hesitations that could make my colleagues think they had permission to doubt me.

And then there were the similarities. I knew, without having to think about it, that I chewed my lip in that same way when I was reading a sentence that challenged my assumptions about something. I knew that I took the same care when setting a glass on a table. I knew that my chin drifted toward whatever I was paying attention to.

When I went to the counter to order a tea, the server did a double take. He kept glancing up at me as he took my order. Just when I thought I might scream, he shook his head and apologized. "Sorry," he said, "it's just—are you here meeting someone?"

"Yes. Her." I pointed to Martine's back, anticipating the follow-up question.

"Are you guys twins?" the server asked, pouring hot water into a mug to warm it. "It's uncanny."

"Yes, twins." The lie was easy. "Can you bring that to the table when it's ready?"

"It'll just be another minute," he said. But I was already walking away, my skin jumping.

Twins. Sure.

———

It was stupid, stupider than anything in the world, the way I'd caught Nathan. A cliche: I'd found a hair.

My own hair is watery, the kind of blonde that doesn't catch the light, that vanishes at my temples and makes my forehead look Tudor-high. My mother's hair.

The level of coincidence that led to me finding the *other* hair was absurd.

It was the kind of thing that couldn't have happened if I'd remembered just a minute earlier or a minute later. I wouldn't have known. I wouldn't have had a clue.

I'd been on the way out the door, headed to work, and I realized at the last moment that I needed a hair to demonstrate a sampling technique to some visiting grad students who would try to leave résumés on my desk. I let the lab send me a batch of them a few times a year, a show of goodwill on my part, and this was a technique I could let them see without worrying that anyone would faint. The method I was going to demonstrate could make use of old, dead tissues, and a hair was perfect for the task— small, annoying to keep track of, difficult to manipulate.

It was midsummer and my hair was up, tucked away from my face and off my neck so it wouldn't stick to me in the humidity. But I spotted one of my loose strands on Nathan's coat as I was leaving the house, and I grabbed it, pleased to not have to go upstairs and harvest one from my hairbrush. I'd folded it into a receipt from my own pocket, a receipt for butter and brussels sprouts and cotton swabs.

When I demonstrated the sampling technique to the wide-eyed students, I noticed that something was wrong. My sequencing result showed the trademark Seyed and I used to flag specimens, a goofy line of code that, when translated, spelled out *it's alive*. Our little joke. Our little signature.

I wish I could say that I'd felt even a moment of knee-jerk denial, that any part of me had insisted it couldn't be so—but no, that would be a lie.

I knew. I knew right away, like knowing the doctor has bad news to share. I remember the way my stomach dropped, the way heat flooded my throat.

This is bad, I thought, and I wasn't wrong.

I didn't try to pretend. I just verified. Once the students were gone, I sequenced the sample again. There was plenty of the hair left to use. I sequenced it three times, and the third time, I showed it to Seyed to check my own observation. He immediately spotted the signature line.

I sat back in my chair and let out a long, slow breath. "Well, this is awkward, Seyed," I said, my voice shaking. "But I don't think this is my hair."

What had followed—a private investigator, an envelope full of photographs of Nathan walking into a strange house, late nights spent scrolling through his text messages and emails looking for something, anything, a name, a reason—was less crisp in my memory. It all blurred together into a frenzy of bitter anger and determination.

What stayed sharp was the confrontation: the moment when I knocked on the door of the strange house.

The moment when the *other woman* answered the door, and the observable data confirmed my hypothesis.

The moment when I was faced with a mirror image of myself, wearing a strand of pearls and a blank, welcoming smile.

———

I sat down across from Martine without saying "hello" first. I repeated *never apologize* over and over again in my head.

Martine looked up, smiled, closed her book without even marking the page. She tucked the book into her purse before I could see the title.

"Evelyn, I'm so glad you had time for me. I know you're terribly busy."

I clenched a fist under the table. "Terribly busy" felt like code for "too involved in work to save your marriage." That wasn't what she meant. Of course I was overreacting. But then, it was Martine. Wasn't I entitled to overreact? I bit back everything I wanted to say. "Of course," I replied. "It's the least I could do."

Martine rested her wrists on the edge of the table to hold her mug. Not her elbows. Elbows would be rude, but wrists, those were fine. I recognized the posture, and I sat up a little straighter, felt my lips purse with distaste. She didn't seem to notice, smiling up at the server as he delivered my drink. She thanked him for me. He looked between the two of us for a moment before leaving.

I took a sip of my drink. It was too hot. I took another sip, letting it scald my throat.

"I wanted to ask you some things," Martine said, then looked down into her mug. "But first, I hope you'll forgive me if I step away for a moment? I got here a bit early and my tea has just run right through me."

I was about to say that I didn't mind. I was thinking that of course I didn't mind, that Martine could get up and leave whenever she wanted, that Martine could take a running leap off a high bridge for all I cared. But before I had the chance to say anything, Martine pushed away from the table and stood, and the sight of her standing up stole my breath from my throat.

Martine gave me a small smile, then walked off to the restroom, one hand smoothing her blouse over her slightly rounded belly.

I finally managed a soft "Oh."

So that's what she wanted to talk about.

CHAPTER
SIX

Martine was not the cause of my worst fight with Nathan.

That fight, the worst one we ever had, happened years before she existed. Before Nathan and I were married, even. We had been working together, then, for two years, and had been dating for three. We already shared a home, a research lab, and—I thought—a dream.

Then I got pregnant, and I found out how wrong I'd been.

He didn't go with me to the clinic, not because he didn't want to, but because I didn't tell him I was going. I can own that mistake: I should have told him that I wasn't going to keep the baby, should have made it explicit. We had been working together for long enough that I knew Nathan struggled to grasp obvious concepts, and I should have applied that knowledge to myself the same way I applied it to pipette distribution and sensible glove disposal.

I suppose, on some level, I hoped that I wouldn't have to tell him every little thing all the time—I suppose I hoped that there would be something, anything, that he would understand without me spelling it out.

But somehow, Nathan didn't understand that a baby would destroy our dreams, would ruin the career that we had been building. Even though he'd known me for three years, even though he'd seen my endless hours of work, even though he knew how close I was to making a name for myself in the field—in spite of all that, he failed to see that I would never keep that baby. He failed to see that my career was all the legacy I would ever need.

I got home from the clinic, unsteady on my feet and nauseated, to find him waiting with a bottle of sparkling cider. He told me his good news: He'd accepted a job as an assistant professor on an accelerated tenure track. He told me he would be able to support our family, that I could *put work on hold for a couple of years.*

The fight was endless, cruel on both sides. He blamed me for his decision to throw away his own ambition in favor of "stability." I told him that he was a coward, seeking refuge in the comfort of a child who would admire him without question, and colleagues who would never know how sloppy and useless his labwork was, how limited his dreams were. He yelled at me, knocked over a chair, clenched his fists and looked at me like he was going to put them to use.

I vomited a thin stream of yellow bile onto the kitchen table, my head swimming, my vision spotted with white sparks.

He threw a roll of paper towels into my lap, called me selfish. I threw them back at his head, calling him naïve.

It was awful.

The fight itself was bad enough, but the timing was catastrophic. I could barely hold my own after the day I'd had. Part of me wanted him to hit me, wanted him to make it the worst it could be—but instead he stormed outside for a cigarette. I waited for half an hour before I realized he wasn't coming back.

By the time he came home, I'd cleaned off the kitchen table, taken a scalding shower, and gone to bed. He woke me by turning on the lamp on my nightstand and saying my name.

"Evelyn, wake up," he said, his voice soft and calm, his hand gentle on my back. I remember the way my skull throbbed, his scotch-and-cigarette stink seeming to pulse in time with the pain in my temples.

Nathan told me that he was sorry.

If I had been in better condition, or maybe if I hadn't been so recently asleep, that apology would have started our fight afresh. Nathan always apologized to try to make me feel guilty for having been angry with him, or to make me back down from a point.

It was cowardly, his apology, and if I'd been myself I would have told him so.

But I didn't tell him so, and in that silent space where my hornet's sting should have gone, he told me that he loved me. He set a ring down on the nightstand—no box, just the ring, pinched between his thumb and middle finger. He put it down with a tiny *click* of metal on wood, then walked out of the room without saying a word about it.

I heard the squeal of the bathroom tap, the hiss of the shower running. I tried the ring on as I listened to the water rushing through the old pipes in the walls of our tiny apartment. The narrow band was yellow gold, set with two emeralds, and it was not so tight that I could say it didn't fit.

I fell asleep with the ring on. In the morning, I startled at the way it caught the light.

The worst fight we ever had, and it ended with our engagement.

After that, Nathan and I never really argued over whether or not to have children. We stopped arguing all together; arguing would have required me to engage in conversation beyond the word "no."

He started agitating anew for a baby shortly before he got tenure, and I told him that I didn't intend to put my career aside just because he was bored by his, and that was the end of that. It never came up again.

We had agreed.

Or at least, that's what I thought, until that day in the tea shop.

———

I waited until Martine was out of sight before allowing myself to collapse into a parenthesis. But I only gave myself a few seconds to slump in my chair before straightening; it wouldn't do to have Martine see me in a posture of defeat.

It wasn't possible.

Martine was pregnant. Not *very* pregnant, but definitely, absolutely pregnant. Impossible, completely impossible, there was simply no way—but it was right there in the soft swell of her belly.

Martine couldn't be pregnant.

Martine was pregnant.

Later, I would kick myself for losing my composure. I should have kept it together. But when Martine came back and sat down, it was still the first thing I said.

"This is impossible."

She offered me an opportunity to repair the moment, acting as though I hadn't said anything, trying to pick up the conversation where we had left off.

"As I said—"

But I cut her off. "It isn't *possible*," I repeated. I knew that I was speaking too loudly, but I couldn't stop myself. I leaned across the table, gripped by feral disbelief. "You can't get pregnant, you can't, it's not—" I cut myself off midsentence, lost in my own indignation.

Martine's cheeks lifted into a Mona Lisa smile as she rested a palm on her solar plexus. "I am. So, I suppose that I can."

I shook my head, staring openly at Martine's midsection. "It's impossible," I whispered. "It's impossible." I ran numbers in my head, reviewed data, tried to find the place where I'd failed, but I couldn't find the hole that had let this through. How? How? *How?*

Martine's face didn't harden, not exactly. It set, though, just like an egg yolk firming from easy to medium. She was still open, still welcoming, but I was spending her goodwill at a rapid pace, and it showed.

"I wanted to ask you some questions," she started again, but I held up a hand. I couldn't do questions. I couldn't do anything until I figured out how this had happened—where my work had unraveled. How she had undermined it so thoroughly.

"You don't understand," I said, trying to buy time.

"I understand perfectly," Martine said, her voice one degree above cool.

"No," I snapped, as impatient with her as I ever got with the incompetent assistants I'd run through before Seyed. "You don't understand. Nathan could go to prison. *I* could go to prison. This is—this is *highly* unethical, this is *illegal,* this is—"

"A miracle," Martine said. Her smile was beatific. She was glowing. I wanted to incinerate her.

"No," I hissed, looking around the room. "You can't be pregnant. Clones can't *get* pregnant."

Martine smoothed her blouse over her belly again. "It would seem," she said, her smile fading, "that we can."

CHAPTER
SEVEN

The remainder of my tea date with Martine had not gone well. I've never liked the idea of "needing" a drink—it made me feel too much like my father—but if there was any time that felt like the right time to bend to "needing" a drink, it was now.

I jabbed a pair of scissors into the packing tape sealing a cardboard box, three layers of it. The scissors sank through the packing tape and into the tissue paper inside with a satisfying finality. There was something absolute in the sensation of driving the blade into the box, something primal and honest. I sliced through the tape, then yanked at the cardboard, tearing some of it with the strength of my grip. All around me, other boxes labeled KITCHEN were half-dissected, paper and bubble wrap streaming out of their open tops.

When it became clear that Nathan was going to stay with Martine, I had hired a service to pack up my things. The service was cheap, but it had labeled the boxes by room, which was useful. The movers hadn't made any small talk, hadn't asked any questions; they'd just come in and wrapped everything I owned in gray paper, sealed up the boxes with what seemed like too much tape, and taken a check from me without any fanfare at all.

I plunged my arm down into the nest of packing paper and felt the thrill of victory as my fingers met with cool, thick glass. *Finally.* I withdrew my arm, my fist clasped tight around the neck of a dark-green wine bottle. I twisted my elbow to read the label. It wasn't a special bottle of wine, wasn't one I'd been saving for any kind of occasion. It was just the first one I found in the mountain of still-packed kitchen things, which meant that it was perfect. Another dive into the same box surfaced a corkscrew with a folding knife attached to cut through the foil on the neck of the bottle, and I uncorked the wine with savage urgency.

In hindsight, I don't know why I ever thought he wouldn't choose her. She was perfect—everything he wanted. He made her that way. He must have thought he'd never have to decide between us, but when it came down to it, she was the thing he wanted.

It wasn't just that Martine was pregnant. That was hard to take in, sure, but it would have been hard no matter what, even if she'd just been some woman Nathan had run off with. Even if she'd been a fling he'd had, the pregnancy would have stung—the permanence of it, the undeniable evidence of his betrayal.

But it wasn't that.

Martine shouldn't have been able to get pregnant.

It shouldn't have been possible.

Nathan had somehow found a way to circumvent the sterility that was built in to the entire framework of duplicative cloning. It was one of the things that made my work legal and ethical: each duplicative clone was an island, incapable of reproduction, isolated and, ultimately, disposable. It was bedrock.

Clones don't have families.

But somehow, Nathan—Nathan, the coward, the failure, who had abandoned industry for academia nearly a decade before, who shouldn't have been able to even approach the level of work I was doing—somehow, Nathan had found a way to undermine that principle. To undermine *my* principles.

If only it could have just been those things. If it had just been those things, I could have kept my composure. If it had just been those things, I wouldn't have said what I said.

But no. It was everything, all of it together, all at once. None of this was happening to me suddenly, but it still felt like a slap. I poured wine into the same mug I'd been hand-washing and reusing for the week prior. I didn't bother putting the cork back into the bottle—I just sat down on the floor with the mug full of wine clutched in both hands.

I drank fast, not registering the taste. A text message to Seyed—*not feeling well, be home the rest of today, see you tomorrow*—and another drink, slower this time. I set my phone on the floor next to my knee, leaned my head back against the wall, and forced myself to look the thing right in the face.

What broke me ran deeper than the professional insult, deeper than the knowledge that Nathan had gotten Martine pregnant while we were still living under the same roof. What broke me was the knowledge that, as it turned out, he hadn't just created Martine to exercise a fantasy. He hadn't just created her to be an easier version of his wife, a version who had the time and patience for him that I didn't have.

I'd known that part already, the part about how Martine was a more navigable rendition of me. I'd absorbed that blow months before, when I first found her, during the screaming sobbing fights that defined the end of my marriage. But now, this new facet: Apparently, Nathan had created Martine to do what I wouldn't do for him. What I'd refused outright, what I'd gone to great lengths to prevent. What I thought he'd stopped wanting a long time ago, when I'd made it clear that I wasn't going to budge.

Nathan had created Martine so that he could have a family.

I thought he'd given up on all that. But as it turned out, he hadn't given up on that dream at all. He had just given up on *me*.

I drank wine down like medicine and I tried not to regret the things I'd said to Martine. I tried not to feel the cruelty of my words. It had been wrong to say the things I said, I knew that, but it had felt good in the way that vomiting felt good sometimes. It had felt right, getting that poison out of my belly.

You're not even a real person.

You're just a science experiment.

You're just a declawed version of me.

Martine had looked hurt. Shocked, even. It probably wasn't in her framework to say things that were cruel just for the sake of saying them. Nathan wouldn't have put that into her patterning. It was one of the things he'd always hated about me. My "needless venom," he'd called it. "You're like a hornet," he'd told me dozens of times, "stinging just because you can."

After I left Martine at the tea shop, I sat on the floor of my condo with only that wine bottle for company, digging deep into the bruise.

I could have turned away from it, but I was feeling flattened and sad, and, masochistically, I wanted to feel sadder. I wanted to get all the way to the bottom of the hurt, to let the weight of it crush the breath from my lungs. So I let myself curl up around it.

I thought that if I could just cry, maybe I could let go of the anger that had driven me to say such awful things to Martine. I meant the things I said, that was the worst part. Even the cruelest thing, the thing I knew I'd said only because I couldn't bite it back in time: *Why do you think you exist? What are you even for?*

Martine had rested her hands on her belly, taking the stream of abuse with placid neutrality, until that last one. Her face had crumpled, and I stormed out, not wanting to see my clone shed the tears that I hadn't been able to muster.

Toward the end of our marriage, Nathan had switched from calling me a hornet to the simpler, more straightforward mode of calling me a bitch. The former stuck with me more than the latter. Partly because it was more unique: I'd been called a bitch any number of times, occasionally for good reason.

Nathan hadn't been calling me a bitch for any good reason—he had been calling me a bitch the way a cornered dog growls, hoping it will seem bigger if it makes a noise.

I'm embarrassed, still, by how long it took me to notice. Everything was right there in the open, right there in front of me, but it still took me so long to see the person I had married.

It took me so long to hate him.

Now, I pressed the bruise again and again—the way Martine's chin buckled, the way her forehead had ruched into an expression of bewildered hurt. The way her hands had flown from her stomach and settled on the table.

Shame. That's the thing I had wanted Martine to feel in that moment, and I succeeded. I watched shame sink into the furrows of a face that was exactly, precisely my own, and I felt satisfaction.

The tears still wouldn't come. It was the same emptiness I'd been trying to work with since I first felt that twist in my belly, staring at my own signature on the sequencing result I got from her errant hair.

My eyes burned, and a pit yawned open at the hollow of my throat, but the tears wouldn't spill over.

I ran a hand through my hair and let out a long, slow breath. I needed to cry, but every time I got close, something old and deep in my bones echoed a familiar refrain: *Quit crying, or I'll give you something to cry about.*

I couldn't overcome that directive, no matter how hard I tried.

Another failure.

My phone, still on the floor where I'd left it after texting Seyed, lit up. *Nathan Caldwell,* the screen said. I knew that if I didn't answer, I would have to listen to one of his long, rambling voicemails later—no matter how many times I'd told him to just text me, he insisted on leaving messages that were needlessly descriptive and detailed. If I didn't pick up, I would have to delete it later, would have to decide whether or not to call him back. I clenched my jaw and answered.

The first thing I heard was heavy breathing, wet and ragged. A cough on the other end, a whining intake of breath. This was not Nathan. This was something else. "Who is this?"

"Evelyn?" The voice was not light, was not airy and nonthreatening. It was hoarse, almost a growl. "It's me. It's Martine."

"Are you okay?" I said it automatically—the raw edge of Martine's voice wicked concern up out of me unbidden.

"Something's happened. At the house. I need you to come here, please. Now. It's——it's an emergency. Please."

I tried to ask what happened, but Martine had already hung up.

I stared at the phone in my hand, at the open wine bottle on the counter. I didn't have to go. What right did Martine have to call on me? What right did Martine have to anything? She wasn't even legally a human being, much less a *friend*. But then, I thought, Martine had called me. Even after everything I'd said, Martine had called me.

Which meant Martine was alone, too.

I called a car, and by the time I'd gotten my shoes on, it was waiting outside. The afternoon had been freezing. As I stepped out into the thin, pale light of the waning day, sobriety hit me hard in the temple. Not the kind of sobriety that would render me safe behind the wheel of my own car, no——rather, the kind of sobriety that nearly stopped me in my tracks with the weight of reality. It was like waking from a dream, except that the dream and the reality were the exact same thing. *Yes*, I told myself, forcing my feet to take me to the waiting car. *You are walking out of your new town house in order to help the pregnant clone your husband made to replace you. Yes, this is real. Yes, you are doing this.*

The car had complimentary bottled water in the backseat. I drank one fast, trying not to notice the taste of the plastic. I rolled down my window and let the cold slap my cheeks, clenched my jaw to keep my teeth from chattering. It was a twenty-minute drive, just long enough for me to feel stupid. I was reading too much into Martine's tone of voice, I told myself. I didn't need to go——it was a bad idea to set a precedent like this, that my clone could call me and I would come running. Besides, I told myself, if Martine has an emergency, she should call Nathan. He's the one who opened that can of worms. It was uncharitable to think of Martine as a can of worms, but it was the truth. If the clone had problems, they were Nathan's problems. And if Nathan had problems, they were his own. That was the whole point of the divorce.

By the time I tipped my driver, I was mentally composing a

speech to give Martine. Something about how I regretted losing my temper at the café, a gentle apology for my behavior. Something acknowledging how that had been wrong of me, but also emphasizing the fact that Martine and I simply could not have a relationship. *I would prefer if you live your life and I live mine,* I rehearsed in my head. *It isn't healthy for the two of us to know each other, and I don't think it's a good idea for you to call me again.*

My father's voice echoed in my memory. *There will be no further discussion of this matter.* It was the last thing he'd ever said in front of me.

I kept rehearsing as I walked up the paved path that bisected the dew-shining lawn. *It isn't healthy.* I took in the house, a lovely gingerbread-looking thing with leaded windows and climbing ivy and a porch swing. It was one story tall, brick and shingles, an English cottage nestled into an immaculate American lawn. *I would prefer if.* The house was exactly nothing like the home I'd shared with Nathan, which had been modern and easy to clean and then shockingly easy to leave. This was a house for children to play in, for Martine to work hard at keeping clean. *I don't think it's a good idea.* The front porch was wide enough for jack-o'-lanterns to line up on, and the big bay window right in the front would have made a perfect frame for an enormous Douglas fir, whether or not Nathan had decided to start celebrating Christmas.

I walked up onto that broad, well-swept porch, my speech pressing against the backs of my teeth. I raised my fist to knock on the richly grained wood of the front door. But before I could land a blow on the house, the door swung open. Martine's face stared out at me, just like the last time I had visited this place.

This time, it was not a blank, welcoming smile she wore.

Martine was gray-faced and trembling and she stared right at me, looking into my eyes with an animal intensity. Her hair hung around her face, one wild tendril swinging a loose bobby pin. A livid bloom of reddish purple mottled her throat. Her right hand gripped the door as though it were the only timber left of her storm-sunk ship.

Her left hand gripped the rosewood handle of a chef's knife.

I had to look down, if only for an instant. That was all it took for me to verify what I knew I'd see: the skirt of Martine's dress, which clung wet and red to her legs. An arc of blood swung high across her waist and breasts; it had already begun to dry on her calves and ankles. But the skirt—that was saturated.

When I met Martine's gaze again, I saw blank horror there, and I knew that I had been right to come to the house after all.

"Thank you for coming," Martine said in a throaty whisper, her words coming slow. She cleared her throat, wincing as though it were painful to do so. "Something terrible has happened."

CHAPTER
EIGHT

The conditioning of a clone is a process that requires some fortitude.

The duplicative cloning process is, of course, based on genetics. One hundred days from sample to sentience, and every building block is based on the DNA of the original. Each specimen emerges from amniocentesis at the state of telomeric decay established by the source material: The clone is the exact same age as the original, give or take a handful of weeks. Telomere financing means the clones don't age at the same rate as the original—clone tissues simply decay quite a bit slower than standard tissues—but no clone is in use for more than a few months at a time, so it isn't an issue.

At the end of one hundred days, a perfect double of any human can exist in my lab. It's all genetics. It's all growth.

The problem with the process is that, without intervention, the clone develops according to ideal conditions.

Humans rarely develop according to ideal conditions. My work, for the most part, has been focused on truly duplicative clones—ones that will look exactly like their originals. A body double for a politician, for example, must be convincing enough to attract a bullet, otherwise the expense involved in creating that double is unjustifiable. The expense in developing the process *at all* becomes unjustifiable.

Thus, conditioning is necessary. Nutrient levels during development must be carefully controlled. Light exposure, allergen introduction, heavy metal exposure: all are crucial during the nascent stages of growth and maturation.

But there are other factors at play. The original subject might have a crooked nose from a poorly healed fracture, or a distinctive burn scar, or a missing limb. A limp from a broken leg that never set quite right. A cracked tooth from a bar fight or a mugging.

This is the conditioning that necessitates a sense of remove, a steady hand, and a strong stomach.

Clones aren't people, legally speaking. They don't have rights. They're specimens. They're body doubles, or organ farms, or research subjects. They're temporary, and when they stop being useful, they become biomedical waste. They are disposable. With the right mindset, conditioning a clone feels like any other research project. It feels like implanting stem cells under the skin of a mouse's back, or clipping the wings of a crow so it can't fly inside a controlled space. There's blood, yes, and there's some discomfort, but it's necessary for the work.

By the time I knocked on Martine's front door, I had been conditioning adult duplicative clones for several years. I had been disposing of specimens, both failed and successful, for even longer than that.

I couldn't afford to be squeamish. "What happened?" I asked, because I had to say something. I couldn't just stand there forever. Time would only begin to advance again once I imposed motion. Action was imperative.

"We had a fight," Martine rasped.

There was so much blood.

"He was angry," Martine said. "I told him about getting tea with you, and I asked him about the thing you said. About what I was made for."

I started to say something—not an apology, never that, only an admission that I'd perhaps spoken too harshly—but she didn't let me get a word in.

"No," she interrupted. "You were right. I was made for something, and I've never even wondered about it. I was never *asked* if I wanted this." She gestured to her belly. "So I asked Nathan about it. I said . . ." She swallowed hard, lifted a hand to her throat as she did so. "What if I wanted something different? What if I didn't want to be a mother? That's what I asked him." She darted a quick glance at me, her eyes fierce. "I do want to be a mother. I want this. More than anything. I just wanted to know whether I had a say or not."

I believed her. Nathan would have programmed her, after all, to want this more than anything. But then, he also should have programmed her to not ask questions like "what if." At least, that's what I would have done, if I was going to build a perfect, docile version of myself. I couldn't help but feel a twitch of satisfaction: Of course Nathan would cut that corner. He always was sloppy. "And what did he say?"

"He got so angry. He kept talking about his failure, saying that he'd overlooked my flaws. I was cooking dinner, and I turned to get a knife from the block, and it wasn't there, and then I looked over and he was holding it, and." She stopped talking midsentence and looked down at the knife in her hand. "Oh," she said, and dropped it as though it had suddenly sprouted thorns. "Oh no, oh no, oh no," she repeated in an increasingly frantic pitch. "Oh no, he—he came at me with the knife, and I screamed and I knocked it out of his hand, and he put his hands on my throat, and—"

I clapped my hands once, hard and loud, and Martine startled into silence. "Take a deep breath, Martine," I said in a low voice. "I can put the rest together, you don't have to tell me. Just take a deep breath, that's good. Eyes on me. Don't look at the floor, look at me." I was not being gentle with Martine. This wasn't a moment for gentleness. The trick of the thing was to crush her rising panic. I had done it with a dozen rejected lab assistants, the ones who couldn't handle the process of conditioning live specimens. "Now, take three steps toward me." Martine followed my instructions without question, her unblinking eyes locked on mine.

I took her by the arm. Her skin was tacky with half-dried blood. I led her farther into the house. "Where's your bathroom?"

"Down the hall," Martine whispered.

"Good. We're going there." I kept my voice authoritative. Let Martine think someone was in control of the situation. Let that someone be me. *Forward.*

We walked into the bathroom, decorated in muted tones of lavender and sage, all the soaps in decorative glass bottles with brushed aluminum pumps. I spun the knobs in the tub, turned the shower on, and undressed Martine while the water got warm.

It was like handling a doll. Martine was mute, pale-lipped. Her eyes stared right through the wall in front of her. I unzipped the blood-soaked dress and let it fall to the floor, a stiff puddle around Martine's ankles. Her underwear was nice, obviously expensive: black lace with white stitching. I heard the echo of my own voice in the tea shop: *What are you for?*

I eased Martine's lingerie off, touching her skin as little as possible in the process. I tried not to look at the gentle swell of her belly, or the way her nipples were the kind of dark and full that comes with pregnancy. I led my clone by the arm, helped her step over the lip of the tub, and guided her under the spray. She shivered, and I turned the hot water a little higher.

"There," I said, watching the water around Martine's feet turn pink, ignoring the water that was soaking my own shirtsleeves. My vision narrowed to the swirl of blood around the drain. I blinked hard. "That's better. Can you wash?"

She nodded silently, but she didn't move until I handed her a bottle of exfoliating soap. She scrubbed at herself mechanically, the dark brown of drying blood giving way to pink skin.

She didn't have any of the freckles or scars that I did. Her skin was smooth, unblemished, hairless. She didn't even have stretch marks.

I stared at the woman my husband had wanted, and I saw all the ways in which she was nothing like me. Another corner cut: Nathan had neglected her conditioning.

But then, maybe that wasn't an accident. Why would he want a wife with a scar on her knee, when he could have a wife without one? Why would he take the time and care to break her wrist and splint it just a little crooked? It wasn't another *me* that he was after. Martine was something—someone—else altogether.

She was the woman Nathan had been looking for. Had he been looking for her all along? Had I been a rough draft?

She didn't stop scrubbing until I reached in and laid a hand on her wrist. "That's enough. You're all done."

Martine turned once in the water, rinsing the last of the soap from her arms and face. She reached down to turn off the tap, her arms and hands moving slowly, her grip weak.

I wrapped her in a purple towel. She shivered in my arms, trembling under the terry cloth with her eyes squeezed shut tight.

"I do want this," she was whispering. "More than anything. I just wanted to know if it was my choice. That's all. I swear."

"I know," I murmured, using a foot to shove Martine's blood-soaked clothes behind the toilet and out of sight. They left a faint pink smear across the tile. "I believe you."

"I swear," she said again. "I swear."

I left Martine sitting on the edge of her bed wrapped in the towel, staring at her hands. I needed to leave before the crying began. I could deal with a lot of things, but I didn't have the patience for her tears.

Martine would need to weep alone.

When I got to the kitchen, Nathan was still dead.

I looked at his unmoving back, and I didn't see the person I'd slept beside for the better part of a decade. So long as he was face-down, he could have been any corpse at all.

I stepped around the blood on the floor and took it in, the scene somehow absurdly small and simple: an onion next to the cutting board, stripped of its papery skin, waiting for a knife. A plastic-wrapped package of chicken thighs next to the stove. The knife block on its side, knocked over in what must have been Nathan's haste to stab Martine. And then, of course, the blood.

When I'm training lab assistants on conditioning, I make them watch as I throw a vial of blood on the ground. Ten cc's—less than a tablespoon—but when it's on the floor, it looks catastrophic. I teach them not to freeze at what seems to be a high volume of blood. I teach them how much blood a specimen can lose during conditioning before they should start to worry. I inoculate them to the panic that comes naturally at the sight of blood spreading across cloth, across tile, across steel.

I've spent a lot of time thinking about blood volume in the course of my research. The numbers are always at the front of my mind. Nathan was an adult man: he had twelve pints in him, give or take. He was dead, not just unconscious. Dead, which meant that there were at least six pints on the kitchen floor. Maybe more.

I thought of the many nights we'd spent at our favorite dive bar in the early days of our relationship, downing pitchers of weak beer and playing darts and talking about the future we were going to shape together. The conversions came so reflexively that they were almost comforting: Six pints on the ground. Three and three-quarters pints in a pitcher. A little less than two pitchers of blood on the ground, then. It doesn't seem like so much, put that way. Not even two full pitchers.

Still. He looked so small. He was so empty.

I looked at him, and at the blood, and I waited for grief to strike me down. I was sure that it would hit me at some point. For all that I was furious at him—for all that I hated what he'd done and who he'd become—he was still my husband. I had stood across from him on a Saturday afternoon, in front of all of our friends and all of his family, wearing a dress and the jewelry he'd given me. I had tied my life to his. I could smell my own grief, distant, like the first hint of smoke on the wind.

But it wasn't on me yet. All I could see was his back, and his blood, and the only thing I needed to feel just then was the weight of the task ahead.

I couldn't call the police. That much was obvious; the consequences would have been ruinous. At a minimum, my research funding would be frozen while an ethics committee investigated the fact that the impregnable clone model had been undermined. And I would be publicly humiliated. The scientific community would forget that I had ever been a luminary of the industry, a pioneer, a genius.

They would instead remember me as the woman whose husband had used her own research to make a better version of her.

Aside from that, there was the sheer impossibility of proving what had happened. If Martine decided to lie, there was no way for an investigation to show beyond a doubt that she was the one who had murdered Nathan. We had the same DNA. *And who,* a small voice in my mind asked, *has the obvious motive to kill him? Who took a car here? Which of you is crying because he's dead, and which one is cleaning up?*

No. Turning Martine over to the authorities simply wasn't a viable option.

I threw the chicken into the trash—who knew how long it had been sitting out?—and returned the onion to the crisper drawer in the refrigerator, considering my options.

At the lab, specimens were cremated along with the medical waste, but oversight was too intense down in Disposals for me to toss in an extra corpse. I tried to remember things I'd seen in crime dramas on television, and the mistakes people made in novels, the drunken late-night conversations I'd had with friends about the best way to hide a body. People always brought up the idea of feeding the body to pigs, as though there were a pig farm on every goddamn corner.

I left him lying on his face as I discarded possible solutions. There was no reason to turn him over. Not until it was time. I was scrubbing the knife when Martine came in.

"You're still here." She stood in the doorway. Her hair was tucked under a kerchief. It made her look more like me. "I thought you'd gone."

I blinked at her a few times. It hadn't even occurred to me. She had called—I had answered. I was here.

My gut twisted with something that was a cousin to grief, and it took me a moment to recognize it as guilt. It had been there, dull and aching and low enough to ignore, but the naked gratitude on Martine's face honed it to a razor's edge and I couldn't pretend it wasn't there anymore.

I hadn't left because this was, ultimately, my fault.

If I hadn't been such a hornet (such a *bitch,* my memory helpfully echoed), Nathan would be alive now. If I hadn't been so focused on my own research, he wouldn't have been able to slip away from our marriage so easily. And without my research, Martine would never have existed for him to slip away to.

I could leave the house and the blood and my fucking clone behind, but I would never be able to walk away from the truth: It was my fault that Nathan was dead.

So I smiled at her.

"Of course I'm still here," I said. "I wouldn't make you do this alone."

I watched Martine believe me——believe the best of me, believe in my kindness. I made myself memorize the trust in her eyes, and then I turned away. I grabbed Nathan by the ankles, lifted my hips, and gave an experimental tug.

The floor was well polished.

Dragging him across it wasn't hard at all.

CHAPTER
NINE

My mother was a gardener.

She spent hours in the garden, kneeling on a special pad that stood between her clothes and the soil. It wouldn't do for her to have dirty clothes, any more than it would be acceptable for her to have an unkempt garden. She wore gloves to keep her hands soft and her fingernails clean. She moved carefully in the garden, directing the paths of wild-growing things with a kind of precise authority she never displayed elsewhere. Her fluttering hands grew steady as she gripped rosebush stems, slid them deftly between the blades of her shears, and cut them short.

When I was young enough that I still wanted to understand her, I followed her into the garden and asked questions as she worked. Why did this plant get water, but that plant didn't? Why did we hate snails but love praying mantises? The thing that perplexed me most was the pruning. Her grapevines and roses and rhododendrons all looked healthy, happy. They grew full and lush, their blooms and branches spreading wide. Why, I asked her, would you cut those off? Why would you ever cut the blooms off the rosebush?

It was one of the only truly useful things she ever taught me: Stress stimulates growth. Sometimes, in order to make something develop in the right direction, you have to hurt it. She put the shears in my hand and pointed to a few places on a lilac plant. She showed me which flowers were fading. She told me that if I didn't remove the still-pretty flowers now, there wouldn't be any next year.

She waited patiently for me to take action.

I cut off every bloom she pointed to.

I put them into a cup of water to give to my father when he got home. By the time he did, my mother had already arranged them in a vase. When I woke the next morning, the flowers were in the trash—the blooms had wilted in the night, and my mother had fluttered them into the garbage before my father could see.

Martine's garden was as beautiful as my mother's had been. Birch trees, lavender shrubs, climbing grapes. A trellis with vines just starting to wrap their tendrils around the bottom few rungs of white-painted wood. Strawberries for ground cover. The entire thing was well-tended and precise. It was manicured rather than lush, careful rather than abundant. Everything was arranged to be pleasing, and so I was pleased, but there was nothing stirring about the fruits of Martine's labor in that garden.

My own labor in Martine's garden was stirring, in a way. But there was no beauty in it.

The rain that pattered the soil under my shoes that night was convenient, if uncomfortably cold. It was a fine rain, barely heavier than mist. The soil in Martine's backyard was loosely packed, well tilled for gardening, and it was even easier to move the soil as it grew damp. Digging the pit wasn't easy work by any stretch of the imagination, but I put the full force of my shoulders into the shovel, and it wasn't long before I stopped noticing the gentle tap of falling water on my hair.

A few feet away from me, the blanket wrapped around Nathan's corpse collected the water, a soaking dew that would have ruined the quilt, even if it hadn't been for the dead man leaking blood into the cotton.

Inside the house, Martine was baptizing the kitchen floor with bleach. Turning Nathan over in the kitchen in order to roll him onto the blanket had been an ordeal. At the sight of his still-open eyes, Martine had raced to the bathroom to vomit. I hadn't been ill, but it had been harder than I expected, seeing his empty stare. I knew better than to try lowering his eyelids, movie-hero style.

They would simply open again, so he could stare unblinking at whatever was in front of him.

I had left Martine the work of cleaning up the blood, telling myself it was an easier task than digging. If I thought too much about it, I wouldn't have been able to decide which job was actually easier. I knew which I preferred, though, and I'd decided it was selfless to give her the indoor cleanup. A simple job, straightforward, with an obvious endpoint: Make the floor look like it did before Nathan spilled his life out onto it.

I leaned the shovel against the side of the hole and shook out my hands, willing some warmth into my stiff fingers. I was only halfway done with the hole and my hands were already sore. In a way, it was gratifying: a physical manifestation of penance. I tried to tell myself that I had not a single thing to repent, beyond my cruel words to Martine—still some grim part of me was satisfied by the pain. I was hip-deep in dirt and my shoulders were screaming and I was freezing and drenched, and it was fine.

It's fine, it's fine. I kept repeating it to myself, but as I dug I couldn't help pressing the bruise of my guilt over and over again. The fact that Martine existed at all was a direct expression of all my failures, all the ways Nathan had decided that our relationship wasn't enough. All the ways he'd decided that I wasn't enough.

I used the back of one wrist to push a hank of wet hair out of my eyes, and I bit down hard on the blame until it foamed through me like a poison. *He's dead because you couldn't make yourself give him a baby,* I told myself. *He's dead because you were selfish. It's your fault, all your fault. If you had just been the wife he wanted—*

"How deep are you going to go?"

I looked toward the house. Martine stood under the tiny overhang that projected past the back door, arms wrapped around a bundle of pink-tinged fabric. I recognized the gingham check of a sleeve: Nathan's dress shirts. A shock of respect jolted me as I realized the practicality of what Martine had done, using Nathan's shirts to clean up the bleach and blood from the kitchen floor. No rags would be wasted in service of eliminating the evidence. The shirts would need to be disposed of anyway, eventually. There was a terrible, tidy efficiency in it.

My mother's voice drifted up from my memory. *Waste not, want not.*

"I think I'm about there," I said. I was chin-deep in the pit now. It was an ugly ellipse, uneven at the edges with a ragged slope to the center. But it didn't need to be pretty. It just needed to hold a body.

Martine peered over the edge, then opened her arms and let the blood-soaked dress shirts fall into the hole. It was an oddly child-like gesture: there was something innocent in the way she held her arms out straight, elbows stiff, and watched the shirts slap into the damp soil. Then she knelt in the earth at the edge of the hole and held an arm toward me. A fog of bleach-stink rose off her. Her fingers were white with cold, pruned from scrubbing the kitchen floor. I stared at them blankly for a few seconds before coming to my senses and gripping Martine's wrist. My shoes scrabbled at the dirt as my clone hauled me out of the grave I'd made.

Nathan was not heavy, not with the two of us lifting together, but it was tricky to maneuver his deadweight with the wet blanket wrapped around him. Neither of us suggested removing the blanket, though. It was better to have him covered up and awkward to handle than to see his bare, blank face staring into the rain.

I did not pause to look at him after we dumped him in on top of his ruined shirts. I didn't want to see him, small and still in the bottom of the hole. But when I went to grab the shovel to start the process of burying him, Martine asked me to wait.

"What is it?" I asked. Martine held up a hand, looking down into the grave, and I suppressed a spark of irritation. If she wanted a moment with him, she should have taken it before I arrived, before his body cooled. I couldn't help but think that she should have thought of "goodbye" before she murdered him.

This was no time for sentiment. The work needed to be done.

I tried to figure out how to tell Martine to hurry up her farewell without sounding like a pitiless monster—but before I could say a word, Martine jumped into the grave. The motion was graceless, foreign, and it struck me as strange that she would even think to do such a thing. I asked what she thought she was doing, whispering as loudly as I could, but either she couldn't hear me or she chose to ignore me.

Down in the hole, she knelt over Nathan's corpse. It was just barely too dark for me to see what she was doing. I assumed that she was saying something to him, a final farewell—but then she straightened, and she had the rain-heavy blanket in her fists. She gave it a wrenching yank and it came free from Nathan, his corpse tumbling into the soil. She dropped the blanket next to him in a heap. Then, without my help, she climbed up out of the grave, digging her hands into the soil at the side of the hole and pulling herself up onto the edge. Muddied and panting, she strode across the yard to the garden shed.

She pulled the doors open, leaving streaks of mud on the aluminum siding. The inside of the shed was dark, littered with bags and tools. Along one wall, white boxes were stacked from floor to ceiling.

"This will help," she said, not bothering to whisper as she returned with a white box in each hand. She handed one to me, her fingers leaving dark streaks along the sides of the box, and tore the lid of her own box open. I looked at the label on the box. *Organic Gardening Lime.*

"Why do you have so much lime?" I asked, tearing my own box open and shaking the contents into the grave, absurdly reminded of feeding my classroom's fish when I was in fourth grade.

"The roses like an acidic environment," Martine said, gesturing with her free hand to a row of four rosebushes under the kitchen window. She shook wide arcs of white over Nathan's corpse. I looked pointedly at the shed, at the stacks of white boxes, more than anyone could possibly need to tend a half-dozen rosebushes. "The soil is very alkaline here," Martine said placidly, throwing her empty box into the hole.

I tossed mine in after it, then grabbed the shovel. The rain fell softly, steadily onto the lime, turning the white powder to a paste. As I tossed the first shovelful of soil over Nathan—aiming somewhat deliberately to cover his face—Martine returned to the garden shed.

"Does it really work?" I called after Martine's back. In the dying light, I could only just make out Martine's answering shrug.

She returned holding a second shovel, smaller than the one in my hands. "I don't know if it works, but I saw it on a show once," she said. "And it can't hurt, right?"

The idea of her watching television startled me. It shouldn't have. She was a clone, not a robot. She didn't just sit dormant whenever Nathan wasn't looking at her. But it felt strange, somehow—the thought of her sitting and enjoying a show, something I might have watched on a bored weeknight, something with a hidden body and a virtuous-yet-troubled investigator. I pictured her with her feet tucked up, a blanket over her lap, a glass of wine. Nathan's arm over her shoulder.

We buried him together, in a silence that was enhanced by the cocoon of steady rainfall. By the time we were slapping our shovels over the last of the soil, the rain was coming down harder. Both of us were shivering, dripping, and we walked inside stiff and numb.

CHAPTER
TEN

The air in the house was harsh with bleach; I caught myself reflexively taking shallow breaths. I pulled my limp hair off my neck and, turning, saw that Martine was doing the exact same thing—both our elbows angled up into the air as we gathered our hair away from ourselves, both our necks ranging forward to avoid the discomfort of a damp cling. It gave me a moment of vertigo, looking at a mirror image of myself out of the corner of my eye.

I did not like knowing that she and I could fall into the same patterns. I did not like that at all.

I looked away. "We should wash up," I said, my voice strange and tight to my own ears.

"You should take the hall bathroom," Martine answered, slipping out of her mud-caked shoes. Her voice was soft and genial again, painfully courteous. "That shower is bigger. I'll be fine in the master bath. I already took a shower today anyway."

I paused in the middle of taking off my own shoes. This was programming at work—Martine had been designed to be a perfect hostess, self-sacrificing and polite to a fault. Even now, after burying her husband, she was putting herself last.

"Thanks," I said, not arguing with Martine's sacrifice, because I was not like her. I wanted the bigger shower. I wanted to be warm. I wanted to use that fragrant vanilla soap, wanted to wrap myself in a sage-green towel. I wanted it, and I did not care if she might also want it. I was going to have it.

Nathan used to call me selfish. Maybe he was right.

But, I thought as I closed the bathroom door and clicked the button-lock on the knob, whether or not he had been right was irrelevant now. It was that simple. His opinion stopped mattering the moment he stopped breathing.

Disposable.

Just like any specimen.

That's what I told myself, over and over, willing myself to believe it.

I tucked my hands under my arms, waiting for them to stop shaking.

It was the cold, I told myself, breathing slowly. That, and fatigue. Digging the grave had been hard work. It had been a long day. I was just tired. A shower and a good night's sleep, that was all I needed, and then this whole thing would be behind me for good.

I turned on the water. I didn't climb under it until the steam was too thick for me to see my reflection in the tap. I closed my eyes and leaned into the spray, and I let the water scald me until I was numb.

Never apologize.

Never look back.

Forward, Evelyn. Forward. That's the way.

———

When I walked into the kitchen, my hair dripping onto the shoulders of the shirt I'd borrowed from Martine's closet, an open bottle of wine was waiting on the counter next to a single glass. A chardonnay, the name of the winery debossed in gold lettering onto the cream label. Condensation frosted the thick green glass, but did not dew enough to drip onto the countertop.

I filled the wineglass well past the point of a single measure.

Martine was waiting for me in the living room. She was sitting on the blue couch that Nathan had claimed in the separation, her back to the door. A low chignon was perched at the nape of her neck, just a breath away from the top of her pajama collar.

Her head turned slightly as I approached, as though she'd been listening for footfalls.

I felt nine years old again, like I'd snuck out of bed to discover my mother waiting up for my father in the wee hours. She never went to bed before he was home, and on the nights when his work kept him out until dawn, she stayed awake. My mother was a woman in a perpetual state of waiting.

On those late nights that bled into early mornings, she'd hear my sock feet padding on the hardwood, just as quiet as I could tread, and she'd turn her head just like that—enough to let me know that she'd heard me, but not so far that she could see me. Just enough to let me know that I should sneak back to my bed.

My ears rang with how similar the movement was. I felt a flash of childish rebellion: Martine couldn't make me go back to bed. She couldn't make me go anywhere. It was absurd, of course— she'd left a glass out for me, she'd been waiting for me to join her.

Still.

I perched on the arm of the couch, feeling aggressive and somehow in the way. It was strange to see that couch in this living room—the feeling was a close cousin to the sensation of running into an elementary school teacher at the grocery store. The context of the thing was all wrong, and it was unnerving in a way I was ill-prepared to process.

That couch was the first thing Nathan and I bought together. It followed us from our first tiny studio apartment, to our first place with doors, to our house. It was a part of our life, part of our home. It was where we fought and ate and laughed for years. It was where I slept when Nathan was too angry at me to let me into the bedroom, when the fights were bad, before he gave up and took to pretending things were fine while he built this new life for himself.

In this place it was almost unrecognizable. It wasn't the couch where I slept anymore. Now, it was the couch onto which Martine tucked her feet up while she was watching a television show that taught her to bury a body with lime.

All at once I hated that couch, hated it with a sudden desperate venom. It had betrayed me by seeing my marriage disintegrate, by being here in this house. I wanted to watch it burn. I wanted to hose away the ashes of it with a pressure washer and watch them disappear into the earth.

"I'm surprised you're still awake," I said.

"It's only eight o'clock," Martine replied softly. She was cupping a glass of water in her hands, staring at the lipstick smudge on the rim of the glass. I wondered if she always put on makeup before bed, or if she'd done it because she had a guest. "I go to sleep at nine thirty. If I go now, I'll lie there awake until it's time."

"Oh," I said, awkward in the face of this quiet, soft woman who looked like I would have looked if my life had been entirely, catastrophically different from what it was. "I thought it was later."

I was uncomfortable, furious and sad and exhausted. Everything was too much. All of the things I felt seemed summarized by the lipstick on the rim of Martine's glass. She saw me staring at the smear, and she ran her thumb over it. It didn't solve the problem, though: now, there was lipstick on her thumb. She held that thumb carefully to keep lipstick from getting onto anything else.

I wanted more than anything to grab her never-broken wrist and wipe her unfamiliar hand on that blue couch. I wanted to ruin the upholstery. I wanted to make *her* ruin it.

"Why can't I ever fall asleep before nine thirty?" Martine asked the water glass.

I couldn't tell if she knew she'd spoken aloud until she looked up at me with wide, dazed eyes. "No matter how hard I try. I'm so tired all the time, with the baby and all. I can wake up any time in the night, but I can't take naps. I can't sleep. I can never sleep. Not until nine thirty, and not past six in the morning. Why?"

I drank my wine, winced at the sound of myself swallowing. "It's your programming, probably. He must have given you a non-circadian rhythm. It's—that's an early method, one we stopped using a couple of years ago."

"Can you fix it?" Martine whispered.

"I don't know," I answered.

"Why don't you know? You stopped using that method. You must know how to undo it." There was a note of desperation in her voice, high and wavering. Her grip on her cup of water was so tight that I heard the glass creak under her fingers.

"I don't have any remaining specimens from that generation." Martine's eyes tightened at the corners when I said the word *specimens*. "I'll look into it, though. I can look into it."

Martine set her water glass onto a coaster on the coffee table and stood. "I should make up the guest bedroom for you," she said smoothly. "You must be so tired, after the day you've had." Before I could say anything, she disappeared into the back of the house.

I drank my wine and waited. I ran my fingers over the piping on the edge of the arm of the couch. I dug my fingernails under the edge of that piping, squeezed until it hurt, didn't let go until I heard the soft *pop-pop-pop* of stitches giving way.

I pulled my hand away fast. I told myself that I was letting go to avoid doing more damage, but the truth is that I was satisfied by that tiny, invisible bit of harm I'd caused. A furious, animal part of me—a part I didn't want to think about or look at too closely—hoped that, in a few months, the piping would come free altogether. I hoped Martine would blame herself, never knowing that I'd been the one to pull the seam loose in the first place.

I wanted her to feel that bewilderment, the sudden fear that comes with something falling apart that had seemed so secure. I wanted her to wonder what else she'd neglected. I wanted her to wonder what else would fall away beneath her without warning.

It wasn't fair of me. Martine wasn't her own fault. She hadn't been the one to ruin my marriage. But I wanted her to hurt anyway.

Nathan was too dead to hurt anymore, and I wanted someone other than me to bear the weight of what had happened to my life.

I moved away from the arm of the couch, distancing myself

from the piping. I tried hard to occupy myself by setting my mind to the problem of reprogramming a clone—fixing the problem, instead of just disposing of the specimen and starting over. It had occurred to me before as an obvious next step in my research, and there was no reason not to pursue it, but I could never seem to focus on it as a problem that needed solving. Specimens were always disposable. Trying to hang on to them felt foolish, indulgent. I had never been able to think of a reason to bother.

But something low in my belly kept twisting at the way Martine had asked why she couldn't sleep. I imagined her lying there in the dark—newly pregnant, exhausted, knowing that she wouldn't get an extra minute of rest no matter how hard she tried. Knowing that, when the baby arrived, there would be no promise of respite.

No specimen was ever meant to live for as long as Martine had. No specimen was ever meant to endure this kind of responsibility. Clones were intended to be created for a purpose, and when that purpose was fulfilled, they were supposed to be finished.

The twist in my belly wasn't guilt. I don't regret that—why would it have been guilt? Martine's continued existence was wrong. It was an insult to the very science that had created her. It was a perversion of her own programming. And now, because of that—because of Nathan's decision to twist my work and make a woman who would live and live and live—I had a failure to contend with. A product was being used in a way it was never designed to be used, and that misuse was highlighting a weakness in my work. It couldn't stand.

It wasn't guilt. But it wasn't far removed from guilt, either.

I drained my wineglass and returned to the kitchen for the bottle. I listened hard, but I couldn't hear Martine. I wondered if Nathan had programmed her to work silently, to cry silently.

I wondered if he had programmed her to be able to cry at all.

CHAPTER
ELEVEN

I would have loved to experience some kind of relief after leaving Martine's house. But I went back to a place that was only barely mine. The town house fit me like a brand-new shoe, and it grated at me, knowing that Martine was ensconced in creaseless linens and fragrant soaps while I stumbled around in my nest of boxes and packing paper.

I suppose that kind of place is my natural habitat. The house I grew up in was only ever a house, not a home. It had looked older than it was, stonework on the outside with climbing ivy that my mother dutifully guided onto trellises, to prevent it from ruining the foundation. There were exposed beams on the inside, dark wood and white walls and more fireplaces than really made sense. The rooms were huge and drafty, the ceilings low, the doorways small. Every closet was lined with built-in shelves that were a little too shallow and a little too close together.

I remember that house as being huge and baffling, full of dark corners and hiding places. I suspect now that my memory is shaded by the kind of life I had there. It was a place that could have been charming, if only it had been entirely different.

———

My father's study was a mystery to me when I was a child. It was a whole room in that house that was dedicated only to his work. The rest of the house was connected—the living room and kitchen both led into the dining room via open arches, doorways with no doors in them, and the bedrooms were isolated upstairs,

ranged along a narrow hallway at the top of the stairs. But my
father's study was its own room, set back under the stairs with a
huge, heavy oak door.

When that door was closed, my mother and I were to stay
quiet, to avoid disturbing his work. When it was open, we stayed
quiet for altogether different reasons.

There were two chairs in the study—the one behind his desk,
where I was not permitted to tread, and the one in front of his
desk. That second chair existed for one purpose: our appointments. Once a week, and once a week only, I was invited to sit in
that chair and ask my father a question.

My mother told me later that these appointments began as a
result of my incessant childhood curiosity. I was relentless, she
said. I wanted to know why everything was the way it was, and
how it might be changed. By establishing a time during which
I was permitted to interrupt his work, my father kept me from
being too constant a nuisance. He corralled the disruption I represented, turned it into a discrete period of time during which I
was allowed to demand his attention.

That was my mother's story. My father said that the appointments began because he saw "great intellectual potential" in me.
He liked to maintain narratives like that, ones that portrayed him
as having keen insight.

My father also said that I was allowed to ask him any question,
any at all. This, of course, was a lie. I learned what kinds of questions were actually acceptable when I was six years old. It's an
appointment I will never forget.

He was telling me about the science behind magnets that day. I
sat across from him, my feet swinging off the edge of my chair. I
picked at my fingernails, one of the only things I could safely pick
at in his presence, one of the only fidgets he wouldn't notice so long
as I kept my hands in my lap. His explanations were concise and
direct, thorough, never condescending. He was a good teacher.

He had been speaking and drawing diagrams for close to thirty
minutes—I know, because he kept a thirty-minute hourglass on

his desk to ensure that each of my questions received an appropriate amount of answering, and the top half of the glass was nearly empty.

My father stopped at the end of a sentence about polarity, looked at me, and asked if I had any additional questions. He always asked this, and I was intended to respond that I did not, because the hourglass was nearly empty and there was not time for further discussion. But I hadn't yet come to understand that unspoken rule, and so, foolishly, I said that I did have another question.

I asked him why my mother had been in bed all day.

I wasn't trying to be impertinent—I hadn't understood my weekly meetings with my father to be limited to scholarly discussions. There were so many things I didn't understand yet. He said that I could ask him anything, and so I thought it was all right to ask about her.

His flat, gray eyes stared into mine. Anger flashed behind his veneer of calm like the scales of the fish that darted under the surface of the pond in my mother's garden.

He reached across the table and gripped my jaw in one hand. His fingers dug into the soft edges of my chin until they found the resistance of bone. In that moment, I became aware of the baby fat that was still on my face, and I felt a mortifying flush of relief at the way it still cushioned me.

"Try that again," he said, and the danger in his voice made my blood go still. I remember watching his face, trying to figure out where I'd gone wrong. Was it the way I'd asked the question? My tone of voice? Had I said a bad word?

I swallowed hard. My jaw ached in his grip. I tried again, my words flattened by immobility. "I'm sorry," I said, and at last, he let me go. I hesitated before deciding on how to proceed. *Try again,* he'd said, and so I knew that I must try again, and I must get it right this time. Trying again and failing was not an option. Heat began to flood the lower half of my face, and I knew that it would be red where his fingers had dug into my skin.

I tried again. "Could someone reverse the polarity of a magnet?"

When he favored me with a smile, my stomach sank with the weight of relief: I'd gotten it right. He turned the hourglass again, and spent another thirty minutes or so explaining various theories around polarity manipulation, the scale of experiments on the subject, concerns within the scientific community about the risk of increasing the scale of those experiments. I listened well enough to ask a few more questions—well enough that later, when he quizzed me, I would remember what I was supposed to. But fear hissed in the back of my mind. Fear of the grip he'd had on my jaw. Fear of the promises made by that barely restrained anger in his eyes.

When he sent me to bed, he grabbed my jaw again, gentler this time, though I still flinched. There was no anger in his touch this time. He looked into my eyes to make sure I was paying attention.

"Never apologize just because you think someone is mad at you," he said. "Never let anyone make you say that you're sorry just to appease them." His eyes darted between mine, back and forth, faster than I could follow. "No one respects a coward, Evelyn. Never apologize. Do you understand?"

I nodded, and he let me go. Even then, I could admit that I knew why my mother hadn't gotten out of bed. It wasn't really that I'd wanted an explanation for that. It was that I'd wanted an explanation as to why it couldn't go another way. Why did they fight, even when my mother bent to his every demand? Why was it inevitable that, after they fought, my mother had to be in a condition that rendered her unable to speak to me for a whole day?

That was the question I'd really wanted the answer to. That's what I'd wanted to learn. And after that conversation with my father, I'd learned that some questions simply weren't for asking.

Not every child learns that lesson. It's unspeakably galling, having to talk to people who never learned, who never felt the pain of a wrong answer, who never saw that fish-flash of rage in the eyes of the only adult who could tell them the truth.

In the months after I left Nathan, while I was staying in a temporary apartment, before I signed the lease on my bare-walled town house with its wall-to-wall carpet and cement-slab patio, I swam in that anger. I fielded countless questions from friends and colleagues and acquaintances, questions about what had happened and why things fell apart and who was to blame. Every time, I felt those same fish flashing behind my own eyes.

I couldn't tell my well-meaning friends and colleagues to *try again,* I couldn't grip their faces until their bones creaked, I couldn't make them understand that they shouldn't ask.

They weren't afraid of me.

They had no reason to be.

So I had to give polite, no-one's-fault answers that stuck in my throat like a sliver of bone. I'd tried so hard to structure my life in a way that would prevent me from ever having to swallow that kind of pain again, but I don't suppose Nathan considered that when he put me in a position to protect his reputation. Once he had Martine, I don't suppose he ever thought of me at all.

―――

In the week following Nathan's death, I left those bones to lodge in the flesh of Martine's throat. She was the one who had to answer questions about why Nathan hadn't returned his colleague's calls, hadn't attended their lectures. But no one ever taught Martine to be angry when people asked the wrong questions. She was young and soft and afraid. No one had ever shown her how to access contempt for them and their savage curiosity.

I will confess that I misunderstood Martine's fear, when she called me the evening after we put our husband in the ground.

A friend of his had called to confirm dinner plans, and she had to cancel on Nathan's behalf. "They thought I was his secretary," she said, her voice shaking. "They usually think that. I told them Nathan was unavailable. Was that the right way to do it?"

"Sure," I said, distracted. The HGH issue with specimen 4896-T was intensifying, and I was deeply embroiled in trying to find a solution I could explain to the director of the lab, next time he asked me why things took as long as they did, why they couldn't happen faster and cheaper. I remember thinking that I didn't have time to coddle her, that she should have known by now how to deflect curiosity.

She had, after all, remained hidden for a year and a half. Surely she could stay that way without my help.

"Does it always feel like this?" she asked. "I've never done it before."

"What, murder? I can't say as I've ever done it either, Martine." I was snappish, impatient. I didn't like the idea that Martine was asking me for advice about murder. I'd neutralized specimens before, but I'd never killed a *person*.

"Not murder," she hissed back. "Lying."

I froze.

She'd never told a lie before. She'd never had cause to. She'd stayed hidden, she'd allowed people to believe untruths, but she'd never actually spoken falsely.

When I was married to Nathan, our days together were pocked with small lies, the kinds of lies that made it possible for us to reach the end of the day intact. What must it have been like for her, I wondered, being unable to lie to him? Never knowing that it was an option? What measures had he used to teach her to think what he wanted her to think, so that she never had to mislead him about her opinions and ideas?

How many times had she learned to fear what would happen if she *tried again* and got it wrong?

She'd never lied before, to him or to anyone. I ached with impatience at the thought of the learning curve she'd need to scale in order to survive.

"It gets easier," I told her. "You'll get used to it."

———

Martine called me frequently in those first two weeks, telling me about people who were calling the house to ask about Nathan. Most of them thought they were talking to his secretary, and Martine didn't disabuse them of the assumption. It seemed to be the thing that kept her hidden: Nathan hadn't told anyone that she existed, and it didn't occur to them that he would have a secret wife who happened to keep his calendar for him.

She told all of them that he was sick. His teaching assistant, who had covered five days of classes when Nathan didn't show up to teach, and who wanted to know when to expect him back. His department chair, with whom he'd missed a lunch. A friend who waited at a golf course for an hour for a round that Nathan had scheduled. All of them heard the same story: Nathan was on a trip to the mountains, he would be gone for a while, he would call them as soon as he returned.

After the eighth phone call from Martine—nearly as panicked as the first phone call, and no less disruptive—I decided that enough was enough, and I returned to her home. I strode up the front walk with my coat unbuttoned and billowing, the wind biting at me, making me sharp and alert. Maybe that's a lie; maybe I would have been sharp and alert anyway, and I just liked the way the cold hurt the skin of my face and throat.

When Martine opened the door, I pushed my way inside. Her hair swung loose around her face; she twisted her fingers together in front of her, the knuckles overlapping in a way that was painful to watch. I tried not to look at her belly, but even so, I could see how much it had grown. She was more obviously pregnant than the last time I'd seen her. She was unavoidably, unquestionably pregnant. Somehow, that baby was still growing. That baby that shouldn't have existed *at all,* much less been *viable.*

She hadn't miscarried. She should have miscarried.

The baby should have been a tumor. It should have been a lie. It shouldn't have been growing. It shouldn't have been possible.

I forced myself to swallow the *how* and face the immediate problem. *How* was a question that could be answered later, I reminded myself; there were more pressing matters at hand.

"We need his schedule," I said. "You can't just keep telling people he's on a trip forever. You can't keep *calling me.*"

Martine bolted the door behind me, shaking her head. "I don't know where he keeps it."

"Where's his desk?" I asked, and she showed me to the little dining nook off the kitchen. There was Nathan's old rolltop, an antique we'd found together one weekend in the first year of our marriage. Back when we still went out adventuring on the weekends, when we still found things together, when we still got excited about furniture. I opened the left-side drawer and pulled out one of the black notebooks Nathan used to track his appointments. "Here." I handed it to her. "Go through there and find the appointments he's made. Find out what he's going to miss. Call people and tell them . . ."

"What?" Martine asked.

I stared at her blankly. I hadn't thought that far. Get the schedule, find the appointments, cancel the appointments.

But what excuse would cover the breadth of those cancellations? And what would we do later, when the expiration date on that excuse came and went? Each excuse would only last for so long. What then? Would we report him missing? Would someone else? And when the police came to investigate the missing Nathan—when they saw pregnant Martine—would they know what they were looking at?

She didn't even have an identity, as far as the law was concerned. She didn't exist. But given how easy she had been for me to find, it seemed obvious that even the most perfunctory police investigation into Nathan's disappearance would land them right where I was standing.

There was no keeping Martine hidden, if we didn't figure out how to prevent anyone from looking for Nathan. And there was no protecting my research—my legacy—if she was discovered.

"Shit," I whispered. "This isn't going to work."

"What isn't going to work? Why not?" Martine asked.

Reflexive fury swam under my skin at her questions. I breathed deep, forced it down. "We can't just cancel his plans. We need a longer-term solution." Martine stared at me, waiting for me to tell her what to do.

I closed my eyes, overcome by fury. I didn't begrudge her that instinctive submission, that obedience. She was waiting for instructions because she'd been programmed to be docile. But when I pushed down the flash of anger I felt at her questions, at her inability to come up with her own answers, something deeper had surfaced.

Fucking Nathan.

Martine couldn't do this on her own because of his cowardly programming. I couldn't abandon her or turn her in, because his baby, if discovered, would annihilate my career. All of this was his mess, and it was left to me to clean it up, and no matter what happened, I would bear the consequences.

It was just the same as it had always been. The years we worked in the lab together, before the pregnancy and the fight and the ring and his escape to stability—they'd been marked by similar disappointments. He'd always cut corners, always accepted easy answers. Our shared research was pocked with fights about his sloppy techniques, his inability to question his own results if he happened to like the answers he got. He called me a nag, accused me of micromanaging his data, but if I hadn't been there to check his numbers, he would have dragged me down with him.

Just like he was now. I hadn't been there to babysit his lab work when he made Martine, and now I was dealing with the results. More work for me, as always. Because of Nathan.

I allowed myself a few seconds of unadulterated rage. When I opened my eyes, Martine was still watching me, still waiting. I spoke to her with what felt like an absurd measure of patience.

"Martine. Did Nathan ever . . ." I stopped just short of the phrase *use you for.* "Did Nathan ever *ask you to help with* brainstorming?"

"All the time," she said easily. "I'm good at it."

Of course she was. Nathan couldn't handle a wife who was

smarter than him, but one who would help him whittle his own ideas into useful shapes? He would have needed that.

"Open a bottle of wine," I said. She started toward the kitchen immediately, and I felt a shameful flare of satisfaction at the speed of her obedience. "We've got some thinking to do."

―――――――

In the end, Martine turned out to be a valuable thought-partner. It is with great reluctance that I will credit Nathan that far: He crafted himself an excellent assistant. We talked through the angles of the problem at hand—talked for hours, drifting from the living room to the kitchen, Martine interrupting to point out holes in my logic or connections that were underpinning my ideas. She didn't voice her own opinion until dawn.

"We need Nathan," she said.

I lifted my head from my hands, felt the ghost of my lifeline imprinted on my brow. "We don't need him," I said. "We're smart enough to figure this out on our own."

Martine shook her head at me. She picked up my long-empty wineglass, took it to the sink, and started to wash it with a soapy sponge. She scrubbed the glass in a smooth, steady rhythm, her wrists rolling under the water. "No. We don't need him in order to find the solution to this. We need him *as* the solution."

I threw my hands up in a caricature of exasperation. This woman, this clone of mine, whose brain should have been shaped precisely like mine, who had all the same potential that I had at birth—I couldn't believe that she had come out of her tube this stupid. This useless. "Well, yes, Martine," I said, my tone keen-edged, "it would be very useful to have Nathan. It would, in fact, solve all of our problems. If only Nathan wasn't a *corpse,* we wouldn't be in this pickle."

Martine didn't flinch at the acid in my voice. She turned off the running water in the sink. She grabbed a dish towel and began to dry my glass, turning a slow half-circle toward me. "Yes," she said. "If only there was a way for us to obtain a living Nathan."

She held the glass up to the light for an inspection. I realize now that she was taking her time deliberately, waiting for me to understand. Waiting for me to catch up. At the time, I wanted to throttle her. As she rubbed a nonexistent smudge from the lip of the glass, her idea came into focus at last.

My initial response was one of horror and disbelief. "No."

"All right," Martine replied mildly, folding her dish towel with immense care.

"We can't," I said, my palms flat on the table.

She nodded, running a fingernail along the crease in the dish towel. "I understand."

"Under no circumstances—"

"Right."

"Martine, you have *no* conception of what would be involved in something like that."

Martine hung the dish towel on the handle of the oven, tugged at the edges of it until it was perfectly centered over the glass in the door. She didn't say anything for a few seconds. When she finally spoke, her voice was so soft that I almost instinctively asked her to repeat herself—but she was so clear, so careful, that I understood every word.

"You're right. I don't have any conception of what's involved. Perhaps you could explain it to me."

I stared at her, my head swimming. She stared back at me with a patience I'd never practiced. Her face was placid. She stood, cool as cream, looking like she could wait forever and never need to so much as sigh about it.

"Well," I said at last, buckling under her steady gaze, "I suppose the first thing is, we would need to dig up the body."

CHAPTER TWELVE

In interviews, I sometimes say that science was my first love. That is a friendly kind of lie. The truth is that I've never loved science. Loving science would be like loving my own fingernails, or my lungs, or my lymph. I've always had science, always lived it and leaned on it; I've never had reason to love it or hate it any more than a mushroom loves or hates the soil it grows in.

My first love was Nathan, and he made a fool of me long before he created Martine.

He was smart and funny and I loved the way he touched me, like his hands had questions and my skin could answer all of them at once. We met each other's friends, went to the beach, watched movies, spent hours reading together.

We talked about our work constantly, borrowing ideas from each other, slowly building a dream of changing the world together. I told him about my budding ambition to develop a system of hormonal conditioning, and his face lit up, and he said I was most beautiful when I was being unabashedly brilliant.

It didn't feel like flattery. It felt like love.

And it was easy, being in love with Nathan. It was easy being *around* him—he never made me feel afraid, never left me wondering whether I'd said something wrong. Even our fights were easy back then, a matter of unraveling miscommunications and reassuring each other of our good intentions.

It didn't occur to me at the time to be irritated by how quickly he folded when we had those easy fights. I thought he was being reasonable.

It didn't occur to me to suspect the way he talked about loving my mind.

I was young, and I was accustomed to a very different kind of man.

It didn't occur to me to watch for cowardice the same way I watched for anger.

―――――――

It should have been simple enough to clone Nathan. A matter of routine sequencing and reproduction, no different from any other subject. It should have been easy.

It was not easy.

Sampling wasn't an issue. Once we dug up the body, there was an abundance of tissue available to work with, and taking the sample was even easier than usual, since he was dead. There was no need to take care with the sample size or location, no need to be cautious or conservative.

It was the easiest sample I ever took, even though I took it while standing in a damp hole in Martine's backyard, choking on the awful sweet-rot smell of decay and turned earth. Two weeks in the ground had rendered Nathan soft, overripe. His skin hung loose and wet, drooping like worn-out nylons. I took a large sample, large enough that I felt confident about our ability to get a full sequence. Martine turned away when I took the sample, so she wasn't looking while I did it, but she flinched violently at the sound Nathan's flesh made when I cored his abdomen. She also refused to look at the cooler I used to transport the cylinder of tissue.

The sample was only about four inches in diameter, and I packed it tightly to keep it from bruising in transit. Martine handed me zip-top bags filled with cold water—better than ice for packing the delicate, decaying tissue, less likely to cause accidental damage—but she kept her eyes on the sink the entire time we were preparing the sample for transport. She wouldn't look at any of it, even though it was all her doing.

I suppose Nathan didn't program her to have a strong stomach.

Getting into the lab went just as smoothly as taking the sample did. We arrived in the middle of the night, when I anticipated the only other people on-site would be security staff, underpaid guards who would recognize my face and ignore my guest. All we had to do was get into the lab, prepare the equipment, sequence the sample. Dispose of the excess material. Leave the incubation accelerator to do its work overnight. I should have returned the next morning and found a toddler-sized lump of loose tissue floating in a sea of synthetic lymph and amnio.

It was a perfect plan, and it should have been easy to execute. Get the sample, process the sample, develop the specimen.

But it wasn't that simple. Of course it wasn't.

I pulled into my reserved parking space a few minutes after midnight. The empty parking lot felt liminal and vast, deshabille in its stark vacancy. Martine sat silently in the passenger seat, her hands in her lap. She stayed there as I got out of the car and popped the trunk. She didn't unbuckle her seat belt until I tapped on her window and raised the soft-sided cooler to eye level.

When I tapped on her window, she didn't startle. Her face didn't snap from blank distance into focus, the way it would have if she'd been far off somewhere, lost. She simply lowered one hand to her seat belt buckle, gently guided the band of the belt over her shoulder and out of the way.

I opened her door. She stepped out of the car with easy grace, smoothed her skirt, and looked at me with placid, patient eyes. Waiting to be told what to do, where to go. Waiting for permission.

I swallowed a gout of irrational fury at her. Martine couldn't help her programming; she'd been designed for this. She'd been made to wait for permission. It was there in every smooth hesitation. The way she watched for me to drink before taking a sip of her own drink, the way she stood in doorways until I made eye contact with her and nodded before she would enter a room. The way she sat in the passenger seat, belt buckled, until she knew for sure that I wanted her to get out of the car.

I remembered walking into the living room to find her sitting on the couch in her pajamas, listening for my footfalls.

I shook my head. It wasn't her fault that she was like this. It wasn't her fault that this was what Nathan had wanted. I couldn't hold it against her, no matter how frustrating it was. I couldn't hold it against her any more than I could resent a bulldog for breathing heavily.

She was made this way, and the only thing for me to do was deal with her until I could get her out of the way.

She followed me through the empty halls of the lab building, her kitten heels quiet on the industrial carpeting. I tried to see the building through her eyes, but it was too familiar to me. I couldn't distance myself from the way this place felt like mine.

Martine flinched at the *beep* that sounded when I swiped my card across the matte-black scanner outside the door to my lab. Normally I would have reflexively rolled my eyes at her twitchiness, but this time I had only barely managed to repress a flinch of my own. That *beep* seemed much too loud, much too sudden. I couldn't imagine how I'd managed to hear it every day for so many years without realizing how disruptive a sound it was. I had an impulse to ask the building manager to have it silenced, the same way I'd asked Seyed to felt the clipboards—but of course, the lab was soundproofed. That beep was only audible to people outside the airlock, and there was no way for me to explain why I would want to be able to enter my own lab unnoticed by other people in the building.

"It's okay," I murmured. "No one's here."

"You're sure?" she asked, her shoulders tight.

"I'm sure," I hissed. "There are no night shifts in this wing, and I'm the only one with after-hours access to my lab. We're alone."

"You're really sure?" she asked again as I opened the outer door of the airlock.

I fought the urge to grab her by the wrist and yank her in behind me. "I'm absolutely certain," I said, keeping my voice soft in the hope that my volume would convey some illusion of patience. "Please trust me."

She stepped into the airlock behind me. I warned her about the positive-pressure ventilation, the blast of air she should expect to encounter. I told her that it was to reduce the risk of particulates and contaminants that might enter the lab space. I explained the risk of spores and seeds. I was talking fast and low, delivering a continuous stream of information, more information than she could possibly want.

It was a nervous habit, teaching by reflex, one I'd picked up the instant I'd hired my first lab assistant after Nathan stopped working with me. I didn't have a partner to talk to, so I wound up talking to my assistant, walking her through my process whenever she was observing my work. Describing my actions and reasoning had come naturally to me, and I found myself falling easily into a rhythm of action and explanation.

My heartbeat slowed as I talked. The sense of fear that had crept into me in the hall ebbed. As long as I was teaching Martine about her environment, I was the one who knew what was going on. I was trustworthy. I was in control.

She stood patiently, listening to me talk, and waited as the cycle began. The air lifted tendrils of blond hair away from her face. She blinked rapidly several times, but didn't close her eyes. Her lips moved, but I couldn't hear her over the sound of the air cycle.

"What did you say?" I leaned close, a few strands of my own hair falling into my face.

"I said, are you absolutely *sure* that we are *completely* alone?"

I gritted my teeth. "Yes, Martine, for God's sake," I said, not bothering to temper my voice this time. The air cycle finished in the middle of my sentence, and the words "for God's sake" echoed in the airlock, unnaturally loud. Martine's brow furrowed for an instant, but she didn't say anything further. Her lips tightened. I wondered if this was what Martine looked like when she was angry.

I told myself that it didn't matter. Martine didn't have a right to be angry at me. I hadn't meant to shout, and even if I *had* meant to shout, this was her mess. It was her mess, and I was cleaning it up. What she was asking of me—the risk I was assuming on her behalf—was immense.

I had a right to shout.

And besides any of that, I'd told her so many times not to worry. I'd told her so many times that we were alone. I'd told her, and she just wasn't *listening*.

In that moment, I felt an animal kind of impatience, like there was a rope around my neck I'd have to chew through to get free. *I'll make her listen,* that impatience whispered, and I tried hard to ignore that whisper, even though it felt terribly, terribly right. I hoped she wouldn't ask again whether or not we were alone, because I didn't know how loud the whisper would grow if she persisted.

I tried to ignore it. I told myself that it didn't matter, and I opened the inner door of the airlock and stepped past Martine into the lab. I threw a hand out, reaching for the light switch by instinct.

Behind me, I heard Martine close the airlock door. The latch clicked gently in the same instant that the light switch did. The fluorescents flickered to life, illuminating my lab.

Tungsten lab tables. Tall, insulated tanks filled with amnio and specimens in various stages of development. The autopsy table, the gutters extra-deep to accommodate potential tissue liquefaction. My enormous fume hood. Whiteboards.

Cupboards, their doors hanging open, their contents disheveled. A box of scalpels on the floor, blades scattered across the linoleum alongside a few loose pipettes.

Bags of synthetic amnio, clutched in the arms of a short man in a black ski mask.

I let my hand fall away from the light switch and looked at the man holding my supplies. He stood, frozen, and stared back at me.

"I can explain," he said, three words he'd never said to me before. Not in all our years working together.

Behind me, Martine let out a soft *hmph*.

I understood right away, all at once.

She'd been trying to warn me. She'd been doing it in the best way she knew how—in a way that wouldn't cause a fight, that wouldn't force her to directly contradict me, that put the burden of annoyance squarely on her shoulders.

She'd tried to warn me, and I hadn't listened.

She was right.

We were not, in fact, alone.

CHAPTER
THIRTEEN

I can admit to having made mistakes in the course of my life, my career, my relationships. Do not mistake this for largesse on my part. I'm a scientist; examination of my own errors is part of my job. Without honest self-assessment, growth is impossible. If I can't rule human error out of my work, then my results simply cease to matter.

I try not to make mistakes. I try not to introduce new elements of human error into any environment in which I have a material investment in outcomes. Some might consider this isolating, but I'm not in the business of seeking out chaos simply to appease some arbitrary notion of social nourishment. I was fine as a child with few playground friends and a cold, authoritative father; I was fine when I was alone in a sprawling stone house with my mother and her clean hands; I was fine when I was the only teenager at my boarding school who didn't get invited home for holidays. And, as an adult with a longer list of successes than failures, I don't see a reason to force myself to rely on other people.

Every time I have tried to do it—every time I've tried to *need* someone—it's been a mistake. I tried to need Nathan, but I couldn't need him enough to satisfy his hunger to be necessary. Some inextractable part of him wanted to bear my weight, resented me for standing on my own. It's why he decided to create Martine, I think. She needed him, truly needed him, the way a dog needs someone to put food in his dish. She couldn't help needing him, because it was the whole function of their relationship: She made him feel essential in a way I never did.

But I learned early on that no one is necessary. After my father was gone, my mother didn't have to bear his weight anymore, and she could have taken mine. But she didn't. She left me to grow on my own, sent me away when she could, never tried to become the kind of mother she could have been in his absence. It was the best thing for me: I learned to breathe in a vacuum, to walk underwater, to be all alone in the world. Because of the solitude she gave me, I learned never to lean on anyone too hard, never to lean on anyone at all. Not even my husband.

But, as I said, I can admit to making mistakes. I learned my mother's lesson well, but I am not perfect. There was one exception to my rule.

Over the years of our working relationship, I began to lean on Seyed.

———

He wouldn't look me in the eyes.

He was wringing his ski mask in his hands, twisting it hard enough that I could hear the creak of the fabric against his palms. I wanted to tear it from his grip, wanted to throw it to the floor and force him to look at me. It didn't feel like he had a right to regret. I didn't want to give him the gift of guilt.

"Student loans," he said at last, his voice saturated with shame. "It's just so much, I didn't know how I'd ever pay it all off. And then someone approached me, they asked if I could sell them some supplies, and it . . . it seemed like a victimless crime."

"How long has this been going on?" I asked. "How long have you been using my funding to subsidize your side business?" He mumbled something in reply. I couldn't hear him. Rather than asking him to repeat himself, I waited. It was a trick I learned from my father, letting the silence thicken until it was suffocating. It worked as well on Seyed as it had worked on me as a child. After a few seconds, he swallowed hard and spoke again.

"About a year."

I swore, and he flinched. I thought of every time I'd had to fight for funding over the previous twelve months, every time I'd justified how expensive it was to operate my lab, every time I'd explained that marketability would have to wait another fiscal quarter. Every time I'd had to say that we weren't ready to go mainstream with a product, but that when we did, it would be worth the cost.

All that time, Seyed had been stealing from me. I fought down a flash of rage at the way he cringed, the way he was acting small and soft now that he'd been caught. Where was the confidence he'd needed to grift me for an entire *year*? I wanted to make him show it to me, wanted to force him to stand tall in his betrayal. Martine rested a hand on my arm. I looked at her, half to see what she wanted and half to get respite from the sight of Seyed cowering.

Her face radiated calm. She whispered for me to take a breath. Her mouth was curled up at the edges, the barest hint of a smile. She gave my arm a gentle squeeze.

It shook me, the expression on her face. The way she instinctively knew how to calm me down. She looked so much like my mother.

I wonder if, in that moment, I looked like my father.

I nodded at her, mirrored her smile, and turned back to Seyed. "Okay," I said. "This is unacceptable. But I can understand why you would decide to steal from me."

"I'm so sorry," he stammered. Martine gently squeezed my arm again.

"This is unacceptable," I repeated. I kept my voice level, but still, he flinched. "Who were you selling to?"

He hesitated. "They came to me," he said again. "Someone who was trying to reproduce your methods in a collectivized laboratory. They just needed to source some of the supplies we had extras of anyway, and—"

"Did we *have* extra?" I interrupted, sharp. "Or did you *order* extra?"

He twisted his ski mask again. "I'm sorry," he whispered.

I could hear Martine's breathing, slow and deep, and I realized that I was unconsciously synchronizing my own breathing to hers. Did Nathan program her to handle situations like this one, to soothe his anger that was so much like mine? Or did she learn how to do it over the year that she and Nathan had together?

Had he known that he needed someone who could calm him down, before the first time she did it? Or did he feel that cool hand on his arm, feel himself breathing slower, and recognize his own fury for what it was?

I could feel my own heartbeat pounding behind my eyes, but I breathed with Martine, and I was able to look at Seyed without succumbing to the overwhelming urge to slap him. He must have felt me looking at him, because he finally lifted his eyes to meet mine.

That's when he looked at Martine for the first time. He had noticed her before, but he had been so focused on me, so unwilling to look up at me, that he hadn't really seen her. Not yet.

He looked from her face to mine, then back again. He stared at her, his lips parted, darting glances at me. Comparing our features. Realizing.

Predictable and unstoppable as coastal erosion, his gaze dropped to her belly. I watched his expression shift from amazement to alarm to guarded neutrality. He managed to snap on a mask of professional calm—but not before his eyes met mine in an instant of stark horror.

"Who is this?" he asked.

"This," I answered through gritted teeth, "is Martine."

———

Seyed had lasted so much longer in my lab than I ever could have predicted. Longer than any of his predecessors had. To tell the truth, I hadn't expected him to stick around for more than a few months. My assistants rarely lingered longer than that.

My expectations for him were, of course, high. The position turned over rapidly enough that I'd stopped interviewing

candidates—I kept a pile of résumés on my desk and hired whoever was at the top of the pile when my assistants inevitably quit.
But Seyed was different. I hand-picked him, rescued him from
Nathan's dead-end postdoc program and brought him into the
bright and brilliant light of real research. I saw great intellectual
potential in him, and I decided that potential was worth nurturing.

When I told him to come work for me, I was taking a chance
on him. I had a fight with Nathan because of it, a ridiculous fight
about whether it had been right for me to "steal" Seyed from
him. I told him, of course, that you can't "steal" a person, short
of kidnapping them, which I hadn't even come close to. It was a
stupid, pointless fight, but still—it was a fight, and my marriage
never could afford more of those. I dealt with that so that Seyed
could have a chance at becoming the thing he was meant to be.

When I brought him into the lab, I expected him to be bright
but naïve, still damp-eared and wobbly-legged under his too-
crisp lab coat. I expected him to be just as flinching and nervous
and overeager as all the others. I expected him to tumble around
underfoot, getting in my way and wheedling me for mentorship.
Irritating me until he decided that he needed to find a different
lab, one that was less demanding.

But Seyed was nothing like what I expected. He showed up
ready to work, and he absorbed information seemingly by proximity. He listened when I explained things to him, even when
they were things he already knew, even when I was only explaining to fill the air with enough noise to cover my own doubt. He
asked the right questions. He disposed of his pipette tips properly.
He didn't have to be told to double-layer his gloves to keep fre-
quent changes easy, and he never left them around or, for God's
sake, tried to reuse them.

He didn't ever try to attend to my *feelings*.

He knew what was important, and he knew what wasn't.

Seyed's judgment was impeccable, and he always seemed to
make the same decisions that I would have, given the information
available. My fight with Nathan faded in the wake of all the other

fights we had, and I was left with nothing but a sense of deep satisfaction. I had been right about Seyed. I hadn't wasted my time on him, I thought at the time. He was exactly as proficient as I had hoped he would be, and getting better every day.

It made sense, then, that after he had been in my lab for six months—outlasting the previously held record for assistant longevity—I started to trust him with a brace of unsupervised tasks. He adjusted to the increased workload without hesitation. He seemed to flourish under the added responsibility. We fell into an easy rhythm.

I hadn't felt something so close to professional partnership since Nathan left the lab. I trusted Seyed. I learned how to lean on him. I let him become an integral part of my laboratory, which was always more of a home than home was.

He was the best assistant I ever had.

"She can't be pregnant," Seyed stammered, pointing at Martine, his eyes wide. "That's impossible. That's—"

"I know," I interrupted, not wanting to rehash the fight that had turned Martine into a murderer.

"Evelyn, what did you *do*?"

I realize now that I could have tried to lie to him. I could have told him that Martine was my twin sister. She was unconditioned, so we looked just different enough that maybe he would have bought it. Maybe he would have believed me, and things would have gone differently. I could have fired him on the spot and done the rest of my work alone, and then maybe I could have washed my hands of the whole thing once the work was complete.

But it didn't occur to me to lie to him. Even faced with immediate evidence of his deception, I still trusted him enough to tell him the truth. After all, on the scale of lies I had recently uncovered, stealing my lab equipment wasn't exactly dire.

And maybe I wasn't ready to lose the only person left in my life who I trusted. When I left Nathan, I decided not to forgive him. I chose to cut a deep crease into our relationship, a line that divided our life together into the time when I knew him and the time when I didn't. That choice scooped out the center of me.

I didn't have it in me to make that decision again, with Seyed. There are only so many excisions a body can handle. I wasn't ready to carry both of those betrayals as irreparable.

So instead of lying to him, I told him everything.

Martine cleaned up the spilled lab supplies without being asked, making more noise than she needed to. Giving us the space to talk without being heard. I told Seyed who Martine was, and *what* she was, and what she had done. I told him about Nathan the adulterer. I told him about Nathan the corpse.

I held his gaze the entire time, trying to read his reactions to what I was telling him. Trying to see if he understood the second chance I was giving him. He glanced between me and Martine several times, but he didn't say anything. He just listened.

When I finished talking, Seyed's eyes fell to the cooler in my hand. I hadn't set it down since we walked into the room. He stared at it, chewing his lip. I hadn't told him yet what was inside, but I could see that he knew.

There was one correct path he could take. There was one direction for him to go, only one, that was safe. Now that he knew everything, the risk involved if he decided to step wrong was much too high to be borne. I didn't know what I would do if he said anything outside of the very narrow field of good answers available to him.

I suppose I would have done whatever was necessary.

He nodded once, decisive.

"We'll need a tank," he said, then paused, thinking. "I think 4896-T is cashed. Her CPK is elevated. Myo, too. I was going to tell you in the morning."

Creatine phosphokinase and myoglobin, markers of muscle wasting—both of them waste products released into the blood, two of the louder swan songs of dying tissue. The compartment syndrome I'd feared had come to pass, cutting off blood flow to the subject's skeletal muscle, leaving those big slabs of tissue to waste. Atrophy. In a different specimen, one that would later be conditioned to muscle weakness or immobility, the subject might remain viable—but this one was supposed to come out of the tank active, ready to run. Ready to fight. She had to be able to demonstrate mobility. There was a choice to be made about what would happen to the specimen.

Even in the face of the bad news about 4896-T, I was awash with relief, because Seyed had given me the right answer. He was demonstrating that he still knew what was important and what wasn't.

The only thing that mattered was how we were going to move forward.

"Autopsy 4896-T and process the paperwork. Classify her as a standard growth-rate failure," I said. I looked to the dim rows of tanks, mentally scanning the backups we'd seeded when we created 4896-T. There were at least three fail-safes in the lab, static tissue groups waiting to compensate for the kind of unpredictable failure that 4896-T represented. "Activate 4896-V. I think that one will be close enough that we can play catch-up with it. Moderate the nutrient load this time, give the tissues a little less to work with."

Seyed was already tearing open the plastic wrapping on a folded lab coat. When he'd first arrived in my lab, he'd thought he would be wearing them all the time; now, he only wore them when he was working tableside, so I could afford for him to use a fresh one each time he needed the protection. The coat was spotless-white now, but by the end of the evening, it would need to go into the biohazard bin for disposal.

He pulled the lab coat on, started doing up buttons. The pocket bulged where he'd shoved his ski mask away. He paused on a button, looked up at me. "Do you want me to sterilize the tank first, or start the autopsy first?"

"Autopsy," I said. "I'll prep the tank." His brow furrowed for a second—I hadn't bothered with tank preparation in well over a year. I almost always left that kind of task to Seyed, trusting him to be as thorough as I would. Usually, our roles would have been reversed—Seyed dealing with the tank while I took care of the autopsy, ensuring that I had direct access to the data that would prevent repetitions of failure.

Then his brow cleared as he understood: the autopsy, this time, was a formality. We already knew what had gone wrong with 4896-T, and she was being discarded without any attempt at solving the issue. The tank preparation, on the other hand—that was too important to screw up. We only had one opportunity to make a new Nathan, to do it the right way, and I needed to know that it would go off without a hitch.

By making Seyed do the autopsy, I was sending him a message, and he had interpreted it flawlessly, just as he always did.

The message was this: I could move on from what he'd done. He had my forgiveness.

But he no longer had my trust.

CHAPTER
FOURTEEN

On the day I first saw Martine, Nathan told me he had to work late. I waited up for him at home, sitting at the dining-room table to avoid echoing my mother's couch-bound vigils. I sat there for hours, long after the wooden dining chair had numbed my thighs. I drank tea and read restaurant reviews, trying to find the most scathing ones to keep my anger alive. I didn't want to calm down, didn't want to lose my will to eviscerate Nathan the instant he walked through the door.

If I'm honest, I was a little excited. It was the first fight in a while where I was certain that I had the upper hand.

But he came home, and he dropped his jacket across the back of a chair, and the look on his face was so resigned that it took all the heat out of me.

"So," he said, "Martine tells me you came to the house today."

"I did," I said. "I met her this morning, but I've known for some time now."

I wanted him to try to defend himself. I wanted him to get angry, to blame me, to dig up all the old insults he had been slinging at me for years. I wanted him to tell me what was wrong with me so I could counter with this, his betrayal, an inescapable missile in my arsenal.

But he didn't even give me that. He just picked his jacket back up and smiled at me, a smile that wasn't bitter or triumphant or even regretful. It was the worst kind of smile I could possibly have imagined, and it hurt beyond any cruel words he could have mustered.

It was *polite.*

"I'll send a service to pack my things next week." He grabbed an apple from the bowl on the counter. "I won't need anything of mine before then. I've got what I need at home."

I was stunned into silence by this, until I realized that by "home," he meant the house he shared with Martine. By the time I found my words again, he had already walked out the door, loudly biting into the apple as he went.

A week later, he sent the service, as promised. I asked the head of the crew for a business card and, just a few months later, on the same day I received Nathan's notice of intent to file, I called the service again to set up my own move.

It was as easy as that. Nathan didn't fight. He didn't cry. He never even tried to stay. It was a matter of boxes and paperwork, and then it was finished.

We were finished.

———

There was so much to do, and so little time to do it in.

Nathan's tissue needed to be prepared, and then the tank needed to be prepared, and 4896-T needed to be neutralized and examined and disposed of. Normally, the entire process would take two days—one day for the old specimen, one day for the new.

For this work, we had a matter of hours, and no room for error.

It was two o'clock in the morning by the time we began working in earnest. Two thirty, really, because Seyed insisted I take Martine out of the lab while he drained and euthanized 4896-T. Sentimental of him, but I understood. Watching the neutralization of a specimen isn't easy, especially if they wake up.

Still, it felt like a waste of time. Martine could have turned her back, if she didn't want to watch.

By the time we returned to the lab, the failed specimen was on the autopsy table. Seyed had erected a cloth drape between the dissection setup and the rest of the lab. It was a screen we typically used to hide works-in-progress from view during rare visits from company executives who wanted to see where their money was going—they wanted to see our progress, but they were always squeamish about our process.

The drape seemed like overkill to me at first, but the moment Seyed made his first incision, I understood his reasoning. The sound of flesh parting echoed in the near-silent lab, and Martine flinched violently at the clang of Seyed dropping his scalpel onto a lab tray.

Perhaps turning her back wouldn't have been sufficient after all.

"Martine," I said, noticing the way her hands twitched nervously at her skirt, "would you like to help me get started?"

"All right," she whispered.

I could pretend that I let her help out of kindness, in order to distract her from the wet sounds that came from behind the screen. Or maybe I could pretend that I was exploiting her need to help—cruel and mercenary, taking advantage of her accommodating nature to make my work move along faster.

I could pretend either of those. I could even pretend that I knew which one it really was.

It doesn't matter. What matters is that Martine was the one who prepared the tissue sample for sequencing.

I loaned her a lab coat to protect her dress, anticipating that she would spill something on herself. I showed her how to double-layer her gloves so it would be easier to change them again and again, even if her palms started to sweat. I gave her careful, step-by-step instructions. I used a soft voice and small words.

When I thought she understood what I was asking her to do, I left her behind with a set of shears, a scalpel, and an emulsifier. I was already dreading the way I'd need to coddle her through the next few hours of work. I'd always resented having to cosset my assistants, but I was prepared to hold Martine's hand through the entire process.

Much to my surprise, Martine turned out not to need coddling at all. She was quick and efficient, and she asked for the right amount of guidance. I checked her work at every step of the process; every time, she'd done precisely what I'd asked.

We traded places at a few critical junctures—her taking over a menial part of the tank preparation while I handled a tricky bit of tissue separation or fluid sampling—but ultimately, it was her work.

I trusted her with a job that I should really have given to Seyed. He knew how to prepare samples, and he would have done it without any management from me. I could have let Martine deal with the tank preparation, and I could have done the autopsy, and Seyed could have prepared the tissue, and everything would probably have been fine. If I were going to do the experiment again, I'm sure that's how I would do it.

But it didn't occur to me at the time. Sample preparation is more concrete than tank preparation, smaller in scale. It's a more complex job, but it's simpler to explain, and the steps are easy to break down. And, all that justification aside—it felt better, somehow, giving Martine that job. Challenging her.

She sank into the task, enough that she didn't seem disturbed by the whine of Seyed's bonesaw. I occasionally caught her giving her work a satisfied smile.

For all that I'd feared she'd be incompetent, it was startlingly easy to guide her through the process. She was a natural. I hadn't expected to be proud of her, but there it was.

By dawn, we were ready.

Specimen 4896-T was bagged and ready for incineration. The yolk that would grow Nathan was prepared—machine-printed stem cells, a half-dozen growth factors, stabilizers, stripped-down free-floating cell frames, all suspended in a low volume of synthetic amnio. My hands shook with fatigue as I double-checked the levels on the emulsion. This was the compound that we were going to use to grow a new version of the man I'd married.

We didn't have extra growth materials to spare, not ones I could justify within my operating budget, especially now that I was going to have to reconcile my budget with Seyed's little side business. And we didn't have extra Nathan.

It needed to be perfect.

"Okay," I said. "I think we're ready."

There was nothing climactic about the work that followed. There was no charge in the air, no tension, no triumph. We were all exhausted. Seyed and I were trying to maintain our usual routine, while stepping around the betrayal that lingered between us. Martine stayed out of the way, watching quietly, her eyes lingering on the equipment.

Filling the tank went according to plan, exactly the way it always did. Seyed depressed the plunger that pushed Nathan's emulsion into the base of the tank. At the same time, I started the flow of substrate—a combination of synthetic amnio and perfluorocarbon. The two liquids entered the tank at the same rate, mixing together as they equalized. The process was exactly like tempering eggs; the amnio that was already in the tissue slurry made it easier to combine with the substrate. It kept the tissue from crystallizing too rapidly, from congealing into a sloppy archipelago of useless flesh.

Nothing went wrong. The tank filled steadily, blood-pink fluid rising to the top of the tempered glass. Bubbles moved slowly through the thick liquid, rising to break at the surface. By the time all of those bubbles were gone, the liquid would set like cooled gelatin.

On the day I realized that my husband had been having an affair, we had seeded specimen 5183-N. That night at the lab, I'd filled the tank myself, staying up late with work to avoid having to go home. I wasn't ready to confront Nathan, not until I had all the evidence to support my accusations. And I couldn't stomach the thought of sleeping beside him.

I'd stood in front of the tank for an hour that night, watching every bubble that drifted sluggishly skyward. Watching as the pink liquid in the tank smoothed itself out, clarified, and became a place where a person could grow. By the time those bubbles were gone, I knew that our marriage was a place where nothing could grow.

Not anymore. Not after what he'd done.

Martine stood beside me, now, staring up at the tank exactly the way I had stared up at it that night so many months before. She held the edges of her lab stool in a loose grip, drumming her fingertips under the lip of her seat. "It doesn't look like much."

"That's good," I replied, stripping my gloves so I could rub my eyes. "It's just broth right now. It'll take a few hours to thicken up." White spots danced in my field of vision. I pressed the heels of my hands to my eyes and tried to calculate how many hours it had been since the last time I'd had any sleep.

"Evelyn—" Seyed started to ask a question, but I cut him off.

"Take the rest of today off," I told him, intentionally brusque, leaving no room for argument. "Go home. Get some rest." I gave him a sharp look. "Make your delivery tonight, and make damn sure you tell them it's the last one. I'll see you back here tomorrow."

"Should someone stay here to keep an eye on . . . on him?" Martine gestured to the tank that would, within the next month, contain a replica of the man who had created her. The man who had gotten her pregnant. The man who had tried to kill her.

It struck me as fantastically funny, that she should think of keeping an eye on him. I swallowed a hysterical laugh.

"No," I said. "There's nothing for us to do right now, and even if there was, we wouldn't be able to do it with any kind of skill. Not right now. Honestly, Martine, look at you." I waved a hand at her vaguely, disdainfully, as though she were a mess—although in reality, it was difficult for me to discern any visible signs of fatigue on her. "You're exhausted. We all are. We'll go home, get some sleep." I nodded significantly to Seyed. "Wrap up loose ends."

Seyed handed Martine a pair of mirrored sunglasses. They were too big for her. "Wear those when you leave," he said, and Martine nodded, letting the sunglasses swallow half of her face. Beyond that, he didn't say anything. He wisely chose not to argue with my instructions.

This was not new: He usually did what I asked of him, usually acted without argument. But there was something different between us now. We'd had a respectful, easy partnership. Now, our interactions carried the flavor of *obedience*. It put the taste of ruin in my mouth.

So be it. He put himself into this position, and I wouldn't discourage him from being there. Maybe, I thought, someday—with a lot of time, and a lot of work—I could trust him again. We could work together again, the way it had been before.

We left, a sunglassed Martine walking a few paces behind me, just as the first of my colleagues began to arrive. None of them gave her a second glance. I greeted them without warmth, and they didn't think anything of it, because I always spoke to them that way. Cordial, but dismissive. Uninterested. As though I were on my way to something more important.

I didn't need them to think they mattered to me. I just needed them to stay out of my way. Martine kept the sunglasses on when we got to the car. She put on her seat belt, tipped her head back, and blew out a long stream of air. The sunlight caught some of the fine, tiny hairs that dusted her cheek. I couldn't help but stare at the places where her face was unwrinkled—the corner of her mouth, the plane of her cheek. Beneath those sunglasses, I knew that the corners of her eyes were smooth too. She had the beginning of a crease between her brows, though. I wondered what made her frown often enough to put that crease in place.

"Why are you helping me?" she asked, not looking at me, although I'm sure she felt me staring.

I didn't lie to her when I answered. I could have. It would have been easy enough to make myself seem kind. *Because it's the right thing to do,* or *because you need me,* or *of course I'm helping.* But after all we had already been through, I thought she deserved honesty.

"I'm helping you because I don't want to go down with you," I said. "If I don't help you, you'll be found, and my research will be compromised." I started the car, needlessly adjusted my rearview mirror. "There would be an ethical inquiry, an investigation into my methods. I would lose credibility. It would take me decades to recover from that. I can't afford it." I braked to let another car pass and took the opportunity to look at her. "This is risk mitigation. Damage control. I don't have a choice."

Martine nodded and pushed the sunglasses up onto the crown of her head. Her eyes drifted closed as she did it. After a couple of silent minutes of driving, she spoke, her eyes still shut. "I'm not sleeping," she said. "It's too early for that. My eyes are just a little tired, is all. Don't feel like you have to be quiet on my account."

I swallowed hard, because I *had* been staying quiet on her account. I had been trying to let her sleep, aware of how exhausted she must be. But, of course, it didn't matter how exhausted she was.

She couldn't fall asleep before nine thirty.

She had fourteen hours still to go. Fourteen hours of wakefulness, of waiting for sleep to come. I tried to imagine staying awake with her that whole time. A wave of nausea swept through me. In its wake, it left behind a primal urge to lie down someplace dark.

"Have sedatives ever worked for you?" I asked.

She gestured at her belly. "I've never tried. I was always either pregnant or trying to get pregnant. Nathan wouldn't let me take anything that might hurt our chances."

I thought of the Klonopin on my bedside table, tried to recall if it would be safe for Martine. Safe for the baby. I couldn't think fast enough, couldn't remember. I was too tired.

"It's okay," she said, her lips tightening into a perfunctory smile. I doubted that the smile extended to her eyes, but with the mirrored glasses in the way, I couldn't tell for sure. "I can still put my feet up and rest my eyes for a little while. Don't worry about me."

I drummed my fingers on the steering wheel. This fresh shame I felt was, I told myself, almost certainly a byproduct of my own fatigue. It wasn't as though I'd done anything *wrong*. Martine had known that she wouldn't be able to sleep until later, I reasoned, and she hadn't said anything. She hadn't asked to lie down during the window of time that would allow her to rest. That was her choice, not mine.

I couldn't be expected to manage her every need.

Still, my conscience twitched, a child plucking at a mother's shirtsleeve. It didn't matter how true it was that I wasn't in charge of Martine's decision; I couldn't convince myself that it was as simple as I wanted it to be.

Martine had been programmed to please. She had been programmed to obey. Nathan had used my technology to make her into the kind of person who would give up a night of sleep in order to help me with a tricky project, and I had known as much when I brought her to the lab. I'd forgotten about the limitation on her sleep cycle, but that wasn't an excuse—I'd used her, and she was suffering for it.

I sighed and let guilt and weariness crash through me, knocking my defenses flat. *Fine.* "Would you like to stay with me?" I asked, then quickly added a hopeful caveat. "If you'd prefer to be alone, obviously that's okay too, I just thought—"

"Please, yes," she said. Her voice was taut with exhaustion. "I would prefer not to be in that house at all today, much less by myself."

"My place is a mess," I warned her, turning onto my street. "I'm barely even unpacked."

"It's fine," she said with a faint note of irritation. It was the first time I could recall hearing her sound anything but placid. "I don't mind," she added, a bit more gently—but I clung to the contrast. She had sounded annoyed.

She had very nearly *argued.*

It was a relief, for reasons I couldn't quite get a grasp on. She wasn't completely pliant. There was something in there that felt familiar to me—a hint of the hornet Nathan had always accused me of being.

Maybe, I thought, Martine wasn't *entirely* different from me.

Maybe she wasn't entirely better.

CHAPTER
FIFTEEN

I woke up on my new couch in the middle of the night with no recollection of how I'd gotten there. The fabric still smelled like the showroom. I was under a fleece throw blanket, one I'd purchased the week before, when the prospect of unpacking enough boxes to find my blankets had nearly crushed me. I'd gone to the store in a kind of manic rage, indignant at the idea that I needed to open boxes to find the things that would comfort me. This was Nathan's fault, I'd thought savagely.

He *deserved* to be dead for the way I'd been unable to find a fitted sheet after an hour of searching.

The blanket I'd bought that day was soft and thick, and it imposed a kind of artificial coziness on the mostly bare living room. Even though I was the one who chose it, I resented it for being so comforting. It felt like a blatant manipulation, like an inadequate consolation. I hated it for being a thing I needed. I hated myself for clinging to it.

I gathered it around myself in the darkness of my living room as I tried to reconstruct how I'd gotten onto the couch. I remembered pulling onto my street. There was a vague fog in my mind where parking the car and entering my home should have been—and then a long gap of darkness, the thick dark velvet of deep sleep.

Wrapping the blanket around my shoulders, I padded into the hall on silent feet. The heater wasn't on. I suppressed a shiver as I tapped the button to activate the heat for the first time since I'd moved in. Something deep in the walls of the house clicked and hummed, and the smell of dust filled the air.

Martine hadn't thought to turn the heat on, though it was certainly cold enough for it. Was it that she hadn't been able to figure out the thermostat? Was she afraid I wouldn't want her to change the temperature? I thought back to the way she'd stood in the rain over Nathan's grave, the way it had taken her so much longer than me to start shivering. Maybe she just didn't notice the cold as much as I did.

I stood at the bottom of the stairs that led up to my bedroom and my office.

When I was four years old, my mother taught me how to use the stairs in our house if I needed to move around at night.

My father had been out at a dinner at the time, gone for hours, sure to come home smelling like juniper and cigarette smoke. My mother walked me up and down the stairs again and again, showing me how to roll each footstep through the balls of my feet. She pointed to the place where each step met the wall, taught me to set my feet there so as to avoid making the wood creak. She made me memorize the boards that groaned or clicked underfoot.

We practiced for what felt like hours, walking up and down the stairs again and again until I could do it as silently as she could.

Once she thought I was ready, she positioned me at the top of the staircase. Then, she waited at the bottom of the steps with her back turned and her hands over her eyes. I remember watching her fingertips tremble against the top of her hairline. "Walk past me without me noticing," she said. "Touch the front door without me hearing you."

I got it right on the first try. When my fingertips touched the white-painted wood of our front door, I shouted in triumph, and she scooped me up into a tight hug, laughing into my hair.

I said that I couldn't wait to show my father what I'd learned, but she shook her head. "We don't show him this trick," she said. "This one is just ours." Her eyes were so serious.

I remember nodding solemnly, satisfied that I had a conspiracy to share with her. Knowing already that I should only use my newfound stealth when my father wasn't looking.

I didn't know the *why* of any of it. I didn't understand, yet, what would have made my mother learn how to walk through our home without detection—but it was enough for me, at the time, to know that she and I had a secret.

I thought of her as I walked up the dark stairs of my little townhouse.

I walked on the balls of my feet, each step pressed to the place where the stair met the wall.

I didn't make a sound.

My bedroom door was open just a sliver. It swung into the room under my touch, the hinges quiet.

Martine was curled onto her left side, still fully dressed atop the covers. I was gripped by a surreal certainty that I was some- one else, a stranger in this room, watching myself sleep. Her body faced away from me, and it struck me that I now knew, for the first time, what my back looked like when I slept.

I studied the outline of it: the way Martine's shoulders and hips formed brackets at either end of her spine, the way her verte- brae stuck out at the base of her neck. Her hair was spread across my pillow, the blond bright in the vague wash of moonlight that grayed the room.

She looked so small. Her breath came slow and shallow. One of her hands, the left one, was curled tightly into a fist on the pil- low beside her face, the thumb tucked in under the fingers. Her other hand was draped across her navel.

It was a protective posture, guarded.

I had never watched a specimen sleep before. I had seen them unconscious, coiled fetal in their tanks, or splayed out on a table for examination. I had seen them sedated for conditioning. I had seen them dead, their chests thrust skyward by the foam block Seyed put between their shoulder blades to make them easier to dissect.

But I had never watched one sleep.

Did Martine lie down like that because of the way she was pro- grammed, or because of the way her body was shaped? Did she sleep on that side of the bed because Nathan preferred the other side, or was it the one she would have chosen for herself? Did she tuck her thumb in due to some trick of long-term conditioning, or because of a deep-seated instinct?

I wrapped my own fingers over my thumbs and squeezed gently, remembered my father telling me to keep my thumbs outside of my fists if I ever needed to punch someone. He told me to keep my thumbs out, so I wouldn't break them. I remembered the way he had folded my hands in his, the way he had crushed my fingers shut until I could feel the knuckle in my thumb straining. "See how much that hurts?" he'd said. "Now imagine if you were hitting something, how fast that same compression would happen. Your thumb would snap like a twig."

I'd nodded, biting my lip to keep from making a sound. If I did, I knew, he would squeeze just a little harder. Just for a second, to make sure I learned what he was trying to teach me.

If he hadn't taught me, would I have learned to sleep with my thumbs tucked in, like Martine?

I climbed into the bed with all of my clothes on, the fleecy blanket from the couch still wrapped around my shoulders. I turned my back to Martine so our spines faced each other. I tucked my legs up, let the soles of my feet brush against hers. She didn't stir.

As I listened to Martine's steady breathing, I let my right hand drift up to my pillow. It curled into a loose fist, close enough to my mouth that my breath warmed my wrist. I traced the contour of my index finger with the pad of my thumb as I waited for sleep, feeling the calluses that bordered each of my knuckles—tiny rough patches that I had earned over a lifetime of using that hand. They were mine.

I brushed my thumb across those calluses, feeling the places where I was my own, and I waited for sleep.

It was a long time coming.

———

The worst injury I ever received as a child was a broken wrist. My mother was the one who spotted the way I was hiding my arm, the way I was trying to do everything one-handed. She grabbed my arm from behind my back, her fingers wrapping around my wrist tight enough to make me want to cry out.

It was a narrow thing, my silence.

She made a small surprised sound, studied my face to read the pain. She held a finger to my lips and helped me ease my shoes on in silence so we could go to the hospital, the faraway one where my father didn't work.

She didn't ask me what happened.

I remember the doctor showing me the X-ray, pointing out the spiral fracture in my ulna. "Your bones are young, and this is a stable fracture," he said, "so you'll heal up fast. Did you fall off the monkey bars?"

I shook my head, and he repeated himself slowly. "You fell, didn't you? Off the monkey bars, right?" He was staring at me with urgent intensity, not blinking, and he only broke his gaze away from me when I nodded. "That's what I thought," he said, and that's when I first remember thinking that doctors and scientists must all know each other.

I'd stared at the fracture in fascination. There it was: evidence of the pain I'd been hiding for the better part of a day. My father rolled his eyes at the bright-blue cast, but that night in his study, he showed me a diagram of the human skeleton. I asked him what the doctor had meant about my bones being young, and in response, my father taught me about growth plates. I showed him the location of the fracture. He told me that I was lucky: in an adult, a spiral fracture might require surgery. He told me about the pins the surgeons might insert into the bones to try to fix them. He showed me a scar on his own leg, let me feel the bump on his ankle where a pin had been sized wrong.

When the cast came off, my arm was strange and damp and white, like the underbelly of one of the frogs I often found in my mother's garden. I touched it gently, feeling the ridges of my fingertips on the hypersensitive skin of my wrist. I knew that I was different than I had been six weeks before, that my body was changed forever, in ways that would be visible when I'd died and my flesh had sifted away from my bones. I knew that something inside me had been permanently altered.

I wondered at the power people had over each other, to make lasting changes like that.

I never got the chance to talk about it with my father. By the time my arm had returned to its normal color, he was gone.

CHAPTER
SIXTEEN

When I woke the next morning, I was alone again.

The other side of the bed—Martine's side, although I didn't want to think of it that way—was smoothed over, the pillow fluffed, the bed linens flat. I was still hunched up under the living-room blanket with my shoulders around my ears. I was just barely too cold to fall back asleep. The dusty smell of the heater had subsided, replaced by something kinder. Something sweeter. A faint note of vanilla, and the vague, humid scent of hot water.

I left the blanket in the bedroom, embarrassed to have been seen with it wrapped around my shoulders. I didn't like knowing that she'd seen me clinging to a blanket like a toddler. In fact, now that the crushing fatigue had subsided, I didn't like the idea that Martine was in my house at all. I tried to think of what else she might have seen in my home while I'd been sleeping.

When I got downstairs, I discovered things were even worse than I'd feared.

My entire living room was unpacked. My books were unboxed, nestled on my previously empty shelves. Lamps were assembled and lit. A tidy pile of folded throw blankets was on one end of the couch, and a candle I'd forgotten I owned was burning in the center of the coffee table—that must have been the vanilla scent I'd noticed. The room was warm and welcoming, arranged with more thought than I ever would have afforded it.

There wasn't a box in sight. It looked like a place where someone might actually *live*.

A clatter from the kitchen, a soft exclamation. I crossed the living room on quiet feet and stood in the door to the kitchen. Martine was standing on a chair, a dish towel over her shoulder, stacking a pile of plates in the cupboard. Her arm arched up toward a high shelf, the soft curve of her elbow belying the strength it surely required for her to lift that stack of dishes at such a precarious angle. Her hair was secured under a kerchief. It looked like the same one she'd used to tie her hair back when we buried Nathan, and I wondered if she kept it with her all the time, ready to unpack a house or organize a garage or bury a body.

"You didn't have to do all of this," I said. I didn't mean to be sharp but I didn't mean to be soft, either. I didn't keep my voice down, but she didn't startle, didn't react to my sudden presence. I thought of the way she always seemed to be listening, waiting. I realized that she'd almost certainly heard me—my uncautious footfalls creaking around upstairs, walking slowly through the living room, pausing in the doorway.

Martine had known I was there. And so she knew she was being watched. It didn't seem to bother her.

She was probably used to it.

"What else was I going to do?" she said, sliding a final plate onto the stack. She turned to me, wiping her brow with the back of one wrist. "I wake up at six o'clock, remember? I couldn't just sit there staring at the wall until you woke up too."

"You could have . . . I don't know. Read a book, or watched something on television, or . . . something." My voice was a little stiffer than I intended it to be, but I couldn't seem to make it gentle. "You didn't have to do all this work."

She shook her head. "There's no mending or anything for me to do." Seeing my face, she clarified. "If I want to watch television, I need to be working on something at the same time. I can't just sit. It makes me itch. And besides, once I opened a box of books, the shelf was right there. It was no trouble, really."

I felt a strange, sick kind of anger. *It was no trouble,* she said, about a task I'd been unable to bring myself to even begin. I couldn't tell if she was telling the truth about it being no trouble, or if she was trying to remind me that I'd been putting off something that should have been easy. I couldn't tell what she meant when she said that she couldn't just sit, either—was it that she got restless, or had Nathan programmed her to be physically incapable of resting? Was there any difference between the two? Was there any way for me to ask?

Did it matter?

A vision of my mother's disapproving face flashed through my mind. I could almost hear her voice: *Someone just did you a favor, Evelyn.*

"Thank you, Martine," I said, and I meant it, in spite of myself. "This was very helpful of you. I shouldn't have left so much for you to deal with."

"It's fine," she said. "Really. It's *what I'm for.*"

There it was again—a note of bitterness, a sharp edge. She climbed down from the kitchen chair and pushed it back under the tiny table in the dining nook before turning to me with a smile. "Besides, I'm all done. With the kitchen and the living room, at least. I can't speak for the rest of the house."

We stared at each other for a few seconds. I was bristling, but I didn't understand why. I felt as though I'd just been scolded, as though I'd lost some small battle. Something in the way she *couldn't speak for the rest of the house* felt like a threat. I was in a corner, and I didn't know how I'd gotten there.

Of course, I was being needlessly defensive.

It was one of the things Nathan had been right about during our fights, when he would tell me about the person he considered me to be—my need to control situations, the way I got irrationally angry when it felt like someone was implying that I didn't know what I was doing. "You can be a real bitch when you think you're not in charge," he'd muttered more than once, usually when I'd been trying to start a conversation about the household budget.

All right, if I'm honest: when I was trying to start a *fight* about the household budget. It was one of the tasks we divided over the course of our marriage: Nathan structured the budget and ran it, and I made sure that the bills got paid on time. It made sense at the time. It made good use of my ability to follow up on tasks, his passion for steady logistical planning.

It also meant that I didn't notice when money started disappearing to pay for Nathan's private lab space, the one I didn't know about. The one where he had been able to grow himself a new wife. When I did notice money missing—when I tried to confront him about it, tried to ask why our bank account balance seemed lower than it ought to be—he inevitably countered with a completely accurate assessment of the reason I was upset.

"You're just pissed because I'm not letting you supervise me," Nathan would say, and he would be right. I didn't like that he never told me the details of our finances. I didn't like having to trust his judgment.

The worst part of it is that I was right. I've always known that my need to control things to a minute level of detail is unhelpful, bordering on unhealthy. I try to keep it in check as much as I can. But then if I don't stay vigilant, my husband uses our money to grow a new wife, and my lab assistant uses my grant to support his side hustle, and I wonder why I bother trying.

There's no winning. Either I'm a bitch who needs to control everything, or I'm an easy mark.

Martine wasn't just a manifestation of my failure to create a foolproof cloning model. She wasn't just a symbol of my failure to hang on to a man who had been good when I met him. Before he married me.

She was also a consequence of my failure to keep a handle on things.

And now she was standing in my kitchen, and I didn't know where she'd put my cutlery, and she was hitting me hard with that cool, flat stare. Assessing me.

That was it, that was the thing I was bristling against. *How dare she,* I thought, and the thought was loud and sudden because Martine was daring to judge me, just because she had done something without being asked, something I hadn't even wanted her to do.

She had come into my life uninvited, and then she had come into my home and she had interfered with my belongings as though she had any right at all. *How* dare *she?*

I was filled with a strange, roiling fury. It swept through me, violent and threatening, rising. It was dark and cruel and familiar, and it nearly choked me to swallow it back, but I did. I decided to meet her on her level: kindness and manners. I decided that I would not be beaten at this game, not in my own home.

I smiled. "Really, thank you." My mother's voice came out of my mouth, smooth and low and only a little angry, in that way that it was always at least a little angry. "So kind of you. I never would have expected, certainly never would have asked."

"It's no trouble," she said again, her face placid.

"Would you like to wash up?" I asked. "I could loan you something of mine to wear, if you'd rather not wear something you slept in."

The effect of my words was as immediate as an injection delivered directly into spinal fluid. Martine visibly softened. She closed her eyes for a second, let her shoulders droop. She nodded. "I'd like that very much," she whispered.

Her voice broke halfway through the sentence, and I understood, and the bottom fell out of my belly and that dark roiling rage drained out, leaving me water-stained and empty, a monster with no middle to it.

Half-numb, I showed her to the shower and gave her a towel. Once I heard the water turn on, I let myself sink to the floor. I rested my head in my hands and stared at my knees, unblinking.

It had felt like a standoff, like a battle of wills. It had felt like she was trying to undermine me, trying to shrink me down by pointing out that I hadn't done a thing that came easily to her. It had felt like a brittle moment in which she was finally going to reveal her true quiet cruelty, because of course she must truly be quietly cruel, because she was made from the same stuff that I was made from.

I'd gotten it so wrong. That whole time, that sense of judgment and interference, that feeling I had like I could have closed my hands over her temples and pressed with all my strength until her skull gave in to the pressure of my rage—it was nothing. It was based on *nothing*.

Martine hadn't been playing some kind of passive-aggressive game with me. She hadn't been trying to saw away at the floor under my feet. She hadn't been setting a trap or baring her teeth.

She'd been waiting.

That's all it was. She'd been waiting for me to tell her to stop working. She'd been waiting for me to tell her that she was allowed to use my shower, that she could change out of the clothes she'd been wearing for days. I had fallen asleep the day before without offering her anything to wear, anywhere to wash. Had she eaten, while I'd slept dreamlessly on the couch all day? Had she had water? Or had she been waiting for permission then, too?

I closed my eyes and forced myself to breathe.

I wasn't prepared for this at all. I didn't know how to take care of her, how to understand her needs. I didn't even know how to find out what those needs were. I wasn't ready for this, and I shook with the knowledge that I couldn't do it right, that I would make mistakes layered on mistakes, that it would all go wrong because I didn't have any of the information I knew I needed to do it right.

I never wanted children, and I never wanted this.

But, I reminded myself, I hadn't been prepared for any of it—for the fact that my husband didn't love me, for the fact that Martine even existed. For the things she was capable of and the things she had already asked of me. Her care and feeding were hardly frightening by comparison.

The sound of running water stopped. I pushed myself to my feet and walked into the bedroom to get clothes for Martine. I rummaged through boxes until I found a dress I never wore, one that Nathan had bought for me as a gift, years before. I studied it with new understanding: the full line of the skirt, the scoop of the neckline, the fall of the sleeves.

When Nathan bought that dress for me, I remember being baffled. I couldn't imagine why he would think that I would ever wear such a thing, a dress that was so unlike any of my other clothes. I remember being faintly angry that he would give me such an unsuitable gift.

But, I realized, it hadn't really been for me.

So before I tapped on the bathroom door to hand the dress over, I knew that I would let Martine keep it.

It had been hers all along.

By the time Martine and I arrived at the lab, Seyed was already there, as usual. The shadows under his eyes were deep. His face had a hangdog quality to it, and I reflexively resented him for trying to work the exhaustion angle. I was tired too. That didn't change the fact that he had betrayed me.

Still. I couldn't help softening a little at the sight of him. I don't often feel pity, but that doesn't make me cruel. I'm not one to exploit vulnerability for the sake of punishment.

I'm not a monster.

"What do you have for me?" I asked as soon as we were through the airlock. He handed me a felt-backed clipboard without wasting time on a greeting.

"Numbers are good so far," he said. "I pushed the first dose of cortical primer twenty minutes ago."

I scanned the chart. Seyed had named this subject Nate-2. "Destroy anything with this labeling on it," I said, handing him back the chart. "This subject is named 4896-Zed. And push an HGH inhibitor, will you?" I looked at the temperature reading on the base of the new Nathan's tank. "It's a little warm in here."

Seyed nodded and got to work. I wasn't being any harsher on him than usual, but something of the old easy trust between us was still gone, the same way it had been the night before. There was no room for him to make mistakes like letting the temperature inside a specimen's tank drift too high. There was no space for banter. As always, I told him the work to be done, and he did it—but something was broken between us, and I couldn't imagine a way to get to a future where that wasn't broken. We would just have to keep hobbling forward, leaning our weight on that fracture.

I left Seyed behind, feeling uneasy. I joined Martine at the wobbly table in the far corner of our lab, where everything was labeled FOOD USE ONLY. Both of her hands were wrapped around a cup of peppermint tea. She was staring hard at the specimen tanks, her brow furrowed hard enough to deepen the nascent line on her forehead, the one I'd noticed before.

I wasn't prepared for her, and I didn't understand her needs, but this, I could read easily enough.

This, I could solve.

————

When I first proposed neurocognitive programming to Lorna van Struppe, she treated the conversation as a learning opportunity. I was her research assistant at the time, fresh and bright-eyed and ready to change the world. The ink on my doctoral thesis was still wet. I was a year away from meeting Nathan, still carrying water for Lorna as she explored enhanced embryonic development in reproductive cloning.

To her, my idea—shaping the mind of a clone as it formed—was an exercise. It was a critical thinking lesson. She had wanted me to figure out on my own why the thing I was talking about was impossible.

I'd raised it as a hypothetical, of course—a late-night what-if to kill time while the autosampler ran a routine. We ate pizza off of paper plates that bent under the weight of the grease in each slice, and we talked about why my idea would never work.

"First," Lorna said, "you'd need a full cognitive map of the mind you wanted to re-create."

"A full cognitive map of *anyone's* mind is almost impossible to create with any degree of accuracy," I said, taking the position she wanted me to take, opposing my own suggestion. Showing her that I understood the holes in the concept.

"Then you'd need to find a way to impose that cognitive map on a . . . what? A clean brain?" She said it without condescension, without malice, but the word "clean" had a weight to it that reflected the absurdity of the notion.

I'd pointed my pizza at her head. "Maybe we could come up with a mind-wipe ray. Zap, and your brain is clean as a whistle, and you can stamp someone else's brain on it. Easy-peasy."

She smiled. "There you go. Perfect. So you use the brain-zapper, and then you pop the new framework in there . . . how?"

"A computer chip?" I said, my mouth half-full. "Or . . . hormonal conditioning, maybe?"

"Oh, perfect, hormonal conditioning." She nodded overemphatically, her eyes crinkling. "Because we totally know which hormones correlate to which behaviors. We know that with absolute certainty. Not a bog of warring hypotheses at all."

"Right, it's easy," I'd said brightly. "And then you just have to lock in that framework to keep the clone from deviating too far during their first few weeks."

"Piece of cake." Lorna had laughed, and I'd laughed with her. I'd accepted that my idea was ridiculous, full of holes, impossible.

But later that night, I'd caught her watching me thoughtfully, and a few days later, she'd handed me a white paper on neonatal theories of cognitive development.

"Read this," she'd said, and I read it, and I began to understand.

━━━━━

"Are you ready to get to work?" I asked.

Martine blinked, looked at me. The words seemed to take a moment to process. "Sure," she said. "What do you need?"

"Well." I sat across the table from her and looked at her as though she were my equal. "We have a tricky job to do. What do you know about neurocognitive programming?"

Her face went very still. "I'm sorry," she said slowly. The edges of her voice were polished smooth. "I think I misheard you. Please, would you be so kind as to—"

"Yeah," I interrupted, impatient already with the way she couched her words in layers of apology, soaking up responsibility in advance, getting ahead of anger I hadn't even felt yet. "Programming. We have to program Nathan's brain. Do you know how that works?"

She took a sip of her tea and stared at a spot just over my shoulder. That line in her forehead grew just a little deeper. "No," she finally said. There were layers to that "no." A different person would have listened for whatever kind of pain was hidden there. A different person would have paid attention to them, would have asked her what was wrong.

We didn't have time for that, though. We didn't have time to waste on her emotions. Seyed had already started pushing the cortical primer that would help to define the structure of the new Nathan's brain as it formed. We needed to get to work.

"Normally," I said, "we would start this whole thing with neural mapping." I watched her for a sign of recognition, saw none. She stared at me, blank as a cell-frame, waiting. Always fucking *waiting.* "We take a picture of the brain we want to replicate," I tried, and she nodded once.

I mentally adjusted the way I was going to need to discuss this process with her. I simplified every explanation as much as I could. Since I'd first begun applying for corporate funding, I'd been forced to prepare consumer-friendly explanations of my process. We weren't there yet. We hadn't reached the point at which I needed to admit wealthy customers to my lab for invasive, inconvenient tours. But I'd spent so much time figuring out how to explain my work to someone who couldn't hope to understand it, and I dug deep into those explanations in order to talk to Martine. I spoke to her using every strategy I'd developed for the eventual day when I would start pitching the cloning process to a wider, stupider market.

It would have been easier, in many ways, to simply leave her in a corner, someplace she wouldn't get in the way.

But I had seen what happened when she destabilized, when

she thought too much about who she was and why she had been made. I had already buried that body and dug it back up again. The way she'd been watching the specimen tanks, leaving her in an out-of-the-way corner to think things over while I worked felt like more of a risk than I was willing to take.

Those were all the justifications I made to myself about why I was willing to spend the time it took to explain the cloning process to Martine.

But, of course, there are always other reasons.

I didn't want to work alone, just me and Seyed and the damaged thing between us. And maybe I didn't want to leave Martine alone, either. Everything was wrong, but keeping both of them close, broken as they were, seemed better than being without them. Some part of me hoped that between the two of them, I could salvage one entire ally. And besides all that, I really did need Martine's help. I needed more from her than I cared to admit.

I continued my explanation of neural mapping, trying to bring the entire concept down to a level Martine would understand. "We take a picture of how the brain works. How it makes choices, how it reacts to different stimuli. Then we make adjustments based on how we want the clone to be different."

"Right," she said, her jaw tight enough that I barely saw her lips move.

"That's what we use to make a subject's brain work like the original's brain, or differently from the original's brain," I continued. "It's complicated, the way we get the brain into shape—we have to deal with each section independently first, and then we deal with the way the sections interact with each other." In hindsight, Martine followed all of this fairly easily, but at the time, I felt certain that I was only bewildering her. I shook my head. "None of that is important. The thing that matters is that we make those adjustments up front, then program the clone's brain using the new map. That's how we make sure that, for instance, a clone of a politician will never try to pretend to *be* the politician, even though they look alike." I paused, trying to read her face. "Is this making any sense to you?"

She nodded again. "Sure," she said. "So, do you have a map for Nathan?"

I pulled my tablet out of my bag, pulled up a file, and showed it to her. "This is from five years ago. He helped me test a new scanner. It's the same scanner we use now, so we have all the data we would have otherwise, even if it's old." I tapped the screen, showing her an image of a thin slice of Nathan's brain. It was highlighted in colors that would mean nothing to her. "It's not ideal, but it's what I've got."

Martine studied the image. She touched a patch of bright green with the tip of her index finger. When she made contact with the screen, the image vanished, replaced by a long string of data I'd never bothered to analyze. "You said that 'we' had work, but it sounds to me like you're the one who has work. What am I here for?" She said it simply enough, but her eyes flicked to mine when she asked what she was there for, and I felt the weight of Nathan's death behind the question.

I set the tablet down. "We have a five-year-old scan of Nathan's brain to work with, right?" I asked. "Well, Seyed and I can run the analysis to help us get a handle on what traits we would have programmed into a clone of the person who Nathan was then. But . . . he's different now than he was when we ran that scan." I cleared my throat as Martine looked away. "He was different, I mean. In the moments before his death, he would have reacted differently to a lot of stimuli than he would have when I took that scan."

"I didn't know him five years ago," she whispered.

I clenched my fist in my lap, then stretched my fingers wide. I reminded myself to stay calm. I reminded myself to stay focused. "That's probably for the best," I said. My voice seemed to come from a far-off place. "You won't have as many biases as I will. You'll be able to give a more immediate analysis of his behaviors."

She looked at the brain scan with naked longing. I wondered, briefly, if I'd made a mistake. Martine breathed in through her nose slowly, visibly composing herself piece by piece—her forehead smoothing, her mouth softening, the desperation in her eyes ebbing away like sand through clenched fingers. "Right," she said once she appeared to be calm again. She pointed once more to that bright green section of brain. "What does this part mean?"

I pulled up the supplementary data, trying to remember the experimental systems we'd used for mapping back then. "That's his amygdala," I murmured. "Memory, emotion, attention—it's a good place to start. We usually program that one early." I found the section of the supplementary notes that corresponded to the slide she was looking at, and read the first bullet point aloud. "'Amygdala stimulus in response to memory related to image 785-W.' Hang on, all the images are here too." I opened the W folder, found the seven-hundreds subfolder, and there it was.

785.

Me.

"Oh," Martine said softly, tilting her head to try to see the picture the right way up. I wore a low-cut white dress, with a sapphire pendant resting halfway between the hollow of my throat and the nock of my breasts. My hand rested on a disembodied elbow, and I knew that Nathan's father was just out of the frame. In the photo, I was beaming, my eyes bright.

In the photo, I looked like I'd never been more sure of anything in my life.

I couldn't think of what to say. It all felt so unnecessary, so melodramatic. *There's no need to make it a production,* my father growled deep in the recesses of my mind. But there was no getting around the facts, regardless of how mawkish they felt.

"That slide," I said evenly, "is a snapshot of Nathan's amygdala responding to a photo of me walking down the aisle on our wedding day." I returned to the page of supplementary notes and pointed to his oxytocin levels, his endorphins. "These are elevated, which tells us that he feels—that he *felt* happy." I did not say that the levels reflected that Nathan still loved me at the time the scan was taken.

I let myself believe that Martine wouldn't be bright enough to put it together.

She pushed her chair back from the table without speaking. Her chair scraped against the tile, shrill and sudden, as she stood. She stalked across the lab and threw open the cupboard Seyed had been raiding when we caught him just a couple of days prior. I clenched my jaw, but I knew better than to try to predict what she was doing or why. She had proven that in the garden the night we buried Nathan.

She returned to the table with a fresh notebook in one hand and a box of ballpoint pens in the other. She opened the notebook, made a bullet point on the first page, and wrote "785-W: Amygdala" after it. She looked up at me with my mother's gray eyes and my father's hard, flat mouth.

"So," she said, her voice as clipped as mine usually was. "We'll need to change that in the next draft. How do we do it?"

—————

Five years before, when I had taken the test-map of Nathan's brain, he had still loved me. He had loved me enough to come into the lab on weekends for a month, while I perfected my method for running the scans. He had loved me enough, too, to come into the lab on weeknights, bringing food so we could share dinners without disrupting my eighteen-hour days. I was trying to solve what felt like a thousand problems at once, back then. I remember leaning across the table and kissing my husband, and thanking him for being one of the only things in my life that didn't need fixing.

Nathan loved me, I believed, and at the time, that was enough for me. I thought it was enough for him, too, back then.

But I couldn't figure out when that changed. Surely it was before the scrambled-egg morning. A decision like the one he made, to begin stealing my notes, to take my research and use it to end our marriage——that's not a decision that happens because some eggs are bad.

The way I see it, you mostly stop loving a person the same way you stop respecting them. It can happen all at once, if something enormous and terrible falls over the two of you. But for the most part, it happens by inches, in a thousand tiny moments of contempt that unravel the image you had of the person you thought you knew.

I've been over it so many times. Our life together, our marriage——I've spent more nights than I can count awake and wondering where all those tiny moments were. When was the first moment that Nathan looked at me with disdain? How many times was he resenting me without me realizing it? Where did all that indifference live?

I can find a lot of the moments, but they don't seem to be enough. They come together like the skin of a person, but without bones or muscles or a central nervous system to hold the thing upright. I'll never know what I missed.

I'll never understand enough to be satisfied.

All told, it took Martine and me two weeks to complete our initial review of Nathan's cognitive mapping.

Here are some things that I was wrong about:

- Green beans. Nathan didn't like them. He never had. I had never read that part of his initial scan closely, didn't check his food preferences against what I'd thought was true. Why would I? He'd been telling me he liked green beans for years, lying for some reason that was forever opaque to me. Martine knew he hated them. She said that he thought they tasted like sulfur.
- Dogs. Sometime in the five years since the scan, Nathan had become slightly afraid of them. Not a phobia, but an aversion, a tension. Martine said he was bitten by a dog shortly before I first knocked on her door. I couldn't remember a dog bite. I couldn't even remember an injury.
- The sapphire. I never suspected that he would notice the fact that I didn't wear it. It lived in a fire safe in the bottom of my closet, when we were married and after, and I always thought it had evaporated from his awareness the same way it had mine. But that wasn't the case—apparently, it hurt his feelings. He was disappointed that I didn't like it more, embarrassed by my disregard. The word Martine used was "crestfallen." Even after all that time, he had been upset enough about it to tell Martine how he felt.

• Me. Of course. How he felt about me. How much he respected me. How much he wanted me. How much he loved me.

Martine was wrong about nothing.

Nathan, it seemed, told her everything. Even things that hadn't been his to tell.

Things about my childhood. Things about our sex life. Martine knew it all.

I told myself that it didn't make sense for me to be angry about it—what possible reason would he have had to lie to her about any of it, to conceal any of it from her? It's not as though he needed to worry about breaking my confidence, not when he was already breaching my trust in such an irrevocable way. It's not as though he needed to worry about Martine telling me what she knew—or, for that matter, telling anyone what she knew. She was isolated, and I was ignorant.

I'm sure Nathan didn't think he was doing anything wrong.

Normally, I wouldn't have done such a thorough assessment. The duplicative clones I developed were never intended to function as completely convincing stand-ins for the people they resembled—that was a cornerstone of the ethical justification for the research. Every time I applied for more funding, every time I appeared in front of a review board, every time anyone asked how my work was in any way prudent, I had to be able to prove that I wasn't making *people;* I was making tools.

It's why Martine was so underdeveloped, so dependent. Nathan had clearly gotten access to one of my own early neural frames, but he couldn't replicate my entire mind, my every thought process. He couldn't make her a whole person, with self-direction and a fully developed sense of agency.

No one could.

That is the part I decided not to reveal to Martine. I discussed it with the only person I could: Seyed.

I didn't trust him again, not yet—but I could feel the trust returning, seeping into me like meltwater into a basement, and every day I leaned on him again just a little more. It felt good, having another person to share this enormous secret with.

It was nice, is all. Confiding in Seyed about the risks we were taking. It was a comfort. Seyed and I sat up at my kitchen table most nights over increasing volumes of whiskey and wine after Martine had gone to sleep, talking about the risks we were taking and the impossibility of the work we had taken on. We drank too much and didn't eat enough, because our bellies were too full of the magnitude of our project to digest anything else.

In a way, I suppose we were trying to heal the thing that had become broken between us, because we needed to be whole in order to carry our shared burden.

This is the thing we had to carry: Even if we succeeded at the impossible thing, we would never be able to tell anyone. We couldn't publish. We couldn't even whisper. We would just have to sit on our achievement, letting the world remain ignorant of the possibilities we'd uncovered.

The possibilities we'd *created*.

"This is going to be groundbreaking," I often said, a phrase that was becoming a trigger for the whole familiar litany. "We're making a man. Not a subject, not a tool—a *person*. We're making a whole *person,* and we never even get to brag about it."

Seyed's answer shifted depending on how much he'd had to drink. On the nights when he was most sober, he disagreed with me. We weren't making a person, he would insist. We were making a clone. A more complex clone, but still.

But during the course of our project, few of Seyed's nights were sober. He was under a great deal of strain, I could under-stand that. There were several days when he had to manage the lab almost entirely on his own while I worked with Martine, and he was taking on a larger portion of specimen conditioning than usual. On those nights, when he drank enough to make his eyes glassy and his hands clumsy, his arguments vanished.

"We've always been making people," he would slur, staring into his glass as though it could look back at him. "This whole time, that's what we've been doing. It's just different for you this time, because it's a person you *knew*. But it's not different for me, not really. It's always been like this."

But as Martine and I worked through the five-year-old catalogue of Nathan's neural processes, I began to believe more and more that Seyed was wrong. I began to understand that I wasn't going to be making a person I knew.

I began to see that I hadn't known Nathan at all.

————

The morning I had my scrambled-egg epiphany, Nathan was already running late. He was anxious to get to work. He had spent the months prior embroiled in a pitched battle with another faculty member over . . . something. If I'd been a more attentive wife—if I'd been Martine—I would have known what the conflict was about, would have remembered why he was so upset. But Nathan's problem was some heated, petty conflict in which I had never been able to feign interest, even when pretending to listen would have prevented an argument.

The problem was that if I'd cared—if I'd paid attention—Nathan would have wanted me to fix the problem for him. Oh, sure, he would have framed it as a discussion, as a back-and-forth about what I would do in his shoes, as brainstorming solutions together.

But in the end, I would inevitably find myself in charge of solving his problem, holding his hand as he figured out how to deal with problems he had almost always caused himself. Over the years of our marriage, I learned that it was better to ignore him when he started dropping heavy hints about his worries at work.

It was the only way he would ever learn how to handle things on his own.

I was doing it for the sake of his growth, really.

It didn't matter. What mattered was that on the morning I had my breakthrough, Nathan was looking for a fight. He was too much of a coward to have the fight he needed to have with whoever was causing his problems at work, so he decided to take it out on me. He was looking to be angry about something.

When he walked into that smoky kitchen, he found his outlet.

The eggs and the pan went into the trash, which I suppose was fair; both were ruined. He made an incisive comment about my cooking—something about wondering how someone who claimed to value competence could be so inept at a basic skill. That was less fair.

I tried to explain that I'd spaced out because I'd had a huge breakthrough. I didn't apologize, but I offered to make him something new to eat, if he would just wait a few minutes. But of course, he wasn't interested in what I had to say. He was interested in being angry at me. He was interested in causing a scene.

He had stormed out of the house, slamming the door so hard behind him that the coffee mugs rattled against each other in the cupboard.

But when Nathan got home that evening, he apologized for his temper. He kissed me and handed over a bag of takeout. He made a joke about not wanting to make me cook. He apologized for not listening to me, the kind of apology that made me think he really understood what he'd done. Nathan said he should have been more invested in my work and my process.

He asked me to explain my breakthrough.

I was still brittle from the way he'd acted that morning. I wanted to make him apologize more, wanted to make him feel guilty. He'd hurt me, and I wanted to hurt him back, so I struck at the vulnerable underbelly of his apology. I asked him if he was even slightly interested in me. I asked if he actually wanted to know about my work at all.

"Of course I want to know," he said, his voice tender. "I'm sorry if I made it seem like I don't care. I do. I care so much about your work. Will you tell me? This is about the clone project, right?"

It was a stupid question, and I remember chewing on it. I could have bitten into it hard; all of my projects were "the clone project," and his question was so vague that I could have accused him of having no idea what I was working on. But I decided that he was doing his best, even if his best wasn't very good. I decided to let it pass.

I sat down at the kitchen table with him, and we ate Chinese food out of boxes, passing a carton of rice back and forth between us. I told him about my breakthrough. I was recalcitrant at first, petty, making him beg me for information, making him apologize again and again—but he asked questions, smart ones that proved he was listening, and I started to get excited.

I told him about the work I'd been doing, the ideas I had, the direction I knew I could take my research if I could just get the funding and supplies I needed.

We talked for hours. When we finished eating he pulled me up from the dining-room table by both hands. He tugged me into the bedroom, leaving the half-eaten boxes of food on the table, and he pressed me down into the mattress in our little bed and he kissed my temples and told me that I was brilliant.

The next morning when I woke up, I was alone in our bed. I remember smiling into my pillow, thinking that we'd done right by each other. Thinking that we'd fought and made up and now things were better than they'd been before. I felt like we'd cracked the code, we'd figured out the secret to being married. I felt like we were going to make it.

I wrapped myself up in my bathrobe and padded out of our bedroom feeling victorious. Maybe that's why I didn't think too much about it when I found him standing over my desk in our shared home office. He was examining a few pages of notes I'd left on my blotter, his brow furrowed. I stood in the doorway for a moment, watching him look at my papers. When I asked him what he was doing, he said, "Nothing," and then he kissed me and went to get dressed for work, and I didn't ask any other questions.

I didn't think about it again until years later, when I finally found out what he'd been doing. What he'd done.

I didn't consider why Nathan might be so interested in my work, in my research, in my notes. I thought that was how love worked. People who love each other, I thought, would naturally be interested in each other, interested in what they were doing.

I assumed that I could trust his intentions.

It didn't occur to me that he was trying to mine information out of me. It didn't occur to me that he was trying to use my own research to replace me. I felt grateful for his interest, for the way we were talking again.

I thought we were coming out of a little rough patch, one caused by work stress and weariness, so I told him everything about my work. It became a thing we bonded over, me sharing with him over dinner and coffee and drinks and pillow talk.

Every advance I made.

Every roadblock I overcame.

Every victory, all the way up until I harvested my first viable adult specimen a year later. Right up until I discovered Martine, two years after that.

Of course I had told him everything.

I didn't think I had any reason not to.

———

While Martine and I combed through Nathan's scans, Seyed primed the suspension every day, laying groundwork for the mapping we'd do later. Lorna had been right to laugh at the idea of turning an existing brain into a fresh start. It was far more realistic to simply make one from scratch.

The specimen was still a loose slush, a slowly thickening slurry of dividing cells that wouldn't consolidate without direct stimulus. The tank contained a thing that looked like a jellyfish with four thick tentacles that would eventually become limbs, and dark patches where smooth muscle and neurological tissues were starting to gel. Gradually, patiently, with the right balance of neurons exposed and developing, Seyed gave it shape.

I kept catching Martine staring at the translucent mass that we were going to turn into a man. I walked into the lab one morning after a coffee run to find her standing in front of the tank, her fingers pressed to the glass, watching it as though she could urge it to grow.

"Don't touch that," I said, setting her tea down on the FOOD USE ONLY table.

"Why?" she asked, turning to look at me without taking her hand away from the tank.

A thousand answers occurred to me, none of them true. I could have fed her a lie about her body temperature disrupting the interior climate of the tank, or I could have told her that the glass was fragile, or that her skin oils were corrosive. The lies were too obvious, though—she would have seen right through me.

Getting caught in a lie is so much worse than saying nothing.

But I couldn't give her the real answer, either. The real answer was so true as to be cruel, and I was trying so hard not to be cruel to Martine. *Don't touch that, because you don't belong here.*

I deflected instead. "We have work to do. Come on."

She pursed her lips at me and stood there for several seconds before turning her back on the tank and joining me at our table. It was something she'd begun doing—taking time before following instructions. Putting space between my request and her response.

It was uniquely infuriating to me.

She wasn't supposed to be able to fight her programming like that. She wasn't supposed to *change*. Neurocognitive programming was intended to be static, immovable, and the fact that Martine was starting to shift hers felt like a direct insult to the integrity of my work.

So I did my best to ignore her moods—moods she shouldn't have been able to have, although I could chalk that up to Nathan's incompetent, lazy execution of my early protocols. I did my best to treat her as I would have treated any research assistant, to speak to her the same way I spoke to Seyed. The same way I spoke to anyone who was in my laboratory, participating in my research, using materials acquired with *my* funding.

But even then, she visibly chafed. She made faces at things I said, rolled her eyes when I was snappish, and even when she wasn't being petulant, she hesitated for several seconds before obeying my directives. Every single time, Martine hesitated.

I suppose it would have been virtuous of me to celebrate her developing independence. But the truth is, she was more useful to me when she was obedient. As much contempt as I felt for the way Nathan had programmed her, it was so much simpler not having to worry about her feelings.

I could understand why he would want her pliant, even if I couldn't respect his cowardice in *needing* her that way.

I didn't need her to be perfectly obedient. I could handle her as she was. But I liked her better when she did as she was told.

That didn't mean that I was the same as Nathan had been. He'd created Martine to be this way; I was merely taking advantage of a thing that was already there. I didn't forge the tool. I just wanted to use it effectively. That didn't make me a monster. It wasn't wrong of me, wishing she would behave as she'd been designed to.

Besides, even if it did make me a monster, there wasn't time to think of it that way. I was far too busy for navel-gazing.

There were more important things at hand.

CHAPTER
NINETEEN

Martine and I were not, strictly speaking, living together during this time. She had her place. I had mine.

But neither of us had a home.

Martine had spent her short life trying hard to make her house into a home, but she had been trying to make it into a home for Nathan, not one for herself. She spent a few nights there, but more often than not, I drove her directly from the lab to my town house.

We didn't discuss it. We just slept back-to-back in my bed, curled away from each other. As the nights got colder, I began to sleep under the covers, but Martine never did—she stayed on top of them, perfectly still. She woke before me each morning, and by the time I got downstairs each day, she was already dressed.

I didn't unpack a single box after she arrived. I did tell her that she didn't have to unpack for me, but I didn't tell her very many times. I didn't fight her on it.

She did that work for me, and I let her.

A month into Nathan's neurocognitive programming—six weeks after we filled a sterilized tank with the treatment that would become specimen 4896-Zed—I came downstairs in the morning and found Martine in the kitchen, washing her underwear in the sink.

"What are you doing?" I asked. "I have a washing machine."

"I don't want them to stain," she muttered, scrubbing the fabric against itself with strong, sure fingers.

"Did something happen?" I asked, and she shook her head.

"Just a little blood."

"How much?"

She turned the underwear inside out to show me. They were made of lace, the same color as the skin of her arms, and the fabric of the cloth crotch insert was stained the deep rust of saturation.

"I think that's more than you're supposed to bleed when you're pregnant, Martine," I said, trying to sound calm. I looked at her belly, which became more obvious every day. I didn't know anything about obstetrics, not beyond the basics, which were functionally useless to me. I didn't know if she was supposed to look the way she did then, or if something was wrong. Her belly was locked up tight, and there was something in it that I didn't understand on every possible level.

I hadn't been able to let go of that—the shouldn't-be-possible of her pregnancy. It was another subject of my late-night conversations with Seyed, trying to figure out the unthinkable *how* of her baby. It was like a blister, and every time she rested her hand on her abdomen, something in my brain stung, because I still didn't have answers.

Regardless of all that: if something was wrong with her impossible baby, I couldn't help her with it. "We should probably call your obstetrician." She looked at me blankly. "Your doctor?"

She shook her head again, turned her attention back to lathering dish soap on the surface of the fabric. "I don't have one of those," she said. "I'm sure it's fine, though."

I reached past her and gently turned off the water. I took her hands in mine and eased the underwear out of her grip. "It's not normal to bleed a lot when you're pregnant," I said, gentling my voice as best I knew how. "And I don't know how much is okay when you're this far along. Did you ever go to a class or anything?"

She shook her head, and I felt a far-off pang of culpability. I had never asked. I hadn't asked if she had appointments to get to, if there were books she should be reading. I had been thinking of the baby as her responsibility, as her problem. It never occurred to me to ask about it, because in spite of myself—in spite of all evidence to the contrary—some part of me kept thinking of Martine as though she were an actual adult. As though she were more than two and a half years old.

She didn't even know that she should be worried about the blood. Nathan had never told her, had never offered her the tools to learn. She didn't have a cell phone or a computer. I wasn't even sure if she knew about the internet. She had trusted that he would tell her what she needed to know, and he had failed her.

And now, so had I.

"Okay," I said, pushing the guilt aside for later. "How are you feeling *now*?"

"Fine," she said. "A little bit of cramping, maybe."

I was still holding her underwear. I looked down at it again, let my mind click into the clinical perspective that would let me dodge the strange, invasive intimacy of looking at someone else's underthings. The bubbles of soap foam had already subsided, and it was immediately apparent that most of the crotch of the garment had soaked through with blood. I tried to calculate how many cc's of blood she'd lost, but I didn't have experience with the relative absorbency of lace. "Are you still bleeding?"

"A little," she said. She answered without hesitation, without embarrassment. She didn't seem troubled by my questioning. The first few weeks of her life had almost certainly been defined by questions like this, Nathan trying to figure out if he'd gotten it right. Her eyes slid away from mine. "I took a pad from under the bathroom sink. I hope that's all right. I didn't—"

I cut her off. "Of course that's fine. Anything you need here is yours, let's just make that a rule, and if you're ever not *sure*, you can ask."

I wasn't being kind to her. It was just simpler this way, not having to worry that she was suffering because she was afraid to take something of mine. That's all.

I took Martine to a clinic downtown, the kind of place where

I would have expected to see protestors holding picket signs and screaming about murder. As though they knew anything about murder. There were none, but Martine still looked nervously at the camera next to the buzzer at the outer door.

"Is this another lab?" she whispered. I shook my head and told the person on the other end of the camera that we were there for a walk-in appointment. We entered the clinic through a set of nesting doors. It did feel a lot like the airlock at the lab, once I thought about it—except that my airlock wasn't bulletproof.

"This is a doctor's office," I said. "They'll be able to make sure the baby's okay."

It was perfect. The woman at the front desk assured me, without being asked, of the confidentiality of our visit. I reflexively told her that I was Martine's sister, realizing even as I said it that she hadn't asked. We'd brought cash; I had coached Martine on my salient medical history in the car. I didn't need to tell the woman taking our fake names anything at all. She was going to make a point of not remembering me. She looked between us briefly, her face unreadable, and gave me paperwork to fill out.

I stayed with Martine during her appointment. I held her hand during the ultrasound. When the doctor said that she wanted to perform a manual examination, Martine placed her feet into the stirrups at the foot of the bed without flinching. Her eyes unfocused, and her grip on my fingers went loose.

She'd told me that she'd never visited a doctor's office before, but she seemed to know how this kind of exam would go. I hated Nathan more in that moment than I had hated him in any other moment since the day I'd met him.

After the exam was complete, the doctor asked me to step out of the room.

"Please don't go," Martine whispered.

"I'm sorry," the doctor said, looking at me as though she meant it. "Martine and I have to do this part alone."

It was only five minutes or so before the doctor walked out.

She smiled at me as she passed, the smile of someone who had seen a hundred of me before and would see a hundred more of me before her next day off. It was a comforting feeling, one I would later reflect was almost certainly intentional. It was her job to make me feel as though I'd been seen, but wouldn't necessarily be remembered. She was giving me the gift of as much anonymity as I wanted.

Martine came out of the exam room a few minutes later, fully dressed. The hair at her temples was damp, smoothed down, and I pictured her standing at the sink with water on her fingertips, arranging herself before leaving the room. She told me that the doctor had promised results within a couple of days, and that she was supposed to rest in the meantime.

I waited until we were in the car to ask how she was doing.

"I'm fine," she said.

I turned out of the parking lot, more carefully than usual. I kept my eyes forward, not looking at Martine. "What did she do while I was gone?"

Martine's voice was taut. "Just asked me questions. She wanted to know if I was safe. Asked if I was being forced to do anything I didn't want to do."

"How did you answer?" I asked, tracing the stitching on the top of the steering wheel with my fingertips.

"Yes and no," she said brusquely. "Respectively."

I don't know why I couldn't seem to believe her. It felt too simple. I was sure that she was holding something back. "Are you sure?" I asked.

"Yes."

"You're sure you want the baby?"

She sighed. "Yes, Evelyn." She sounded irritated, and something in me flared hopeful and defensive at the same time. "I want the baby."

I chewed on the inside of my cheek. Ultimately, I said the thing that I couldn't imagine *not* saying. "Why?"

Martine erupted with fury the like of which I'd never seen

from her before. She whipped off her sunglasses—the oversized mirror shades Seyed had loaned her after our first visit to the lab—and threw them against the passenger-side dashboard. "Because I want it, okay? I want something that's mine. I'm sorry if that's stupid or simple or obvious or whatever you think I am, but I just want to be allowed to *want* something!"

She crossed her arms for a few seconds before folding awkwardly forward to pick up the sunglasses from the place where they'd landed, half-folded over the gearshift.

"Okay," I said, slowly, softly. It took no effort at all to recall the way I'd spoken to Nathan during our fights, when his volume rose, when he began to throw things. I made myself into the most reasonable person in the world, someone who would never engage in anything resembling provocation. "I understand. I didn't mean to imply—"

"Oh, of course you didn't mean to *imply*," she snapped. Her voice held only the barest hint of venom. Her heart wasn't in this fight, I suddenly realized—it was something that she was trying on. That was why she had thrown her sunglasses. She was imitating the anger she'd seen before, seeing if it fit the way she was feeling. "You didn't mean to imply what you really think. You would never want me to know *that*."

I couldn't decide if the right thing to do would be to throw her over, forcing her to admit that she didn't want the conflict, or if I should give her the chance to stretch her legs. "What is it that I really think?" I asked, keeping my voice reasonable.

"You think I'm . . ." She paused, her face turned to the window. Her voice dropped low again, soft, almost ashamed. "You think I shouldn't. Want this baby, I mean." I didn't answer her, didn't know how to. She wasn't wrong. It felt more complicated than that, but she'd summarized things accurately enough. I didn't think she should want the baby.

And was it more complicated than that, really? I told myself that it was a question of choice, of agency. A clone getting pregnant wasn't just wrong because it felt strange. It was wrong because, no matter how much Martine developed her own personality and desires, she didn't have a right to them. She was a made thing. She was a tool, and tools don't have the right to decide how they're used.

Nathan shaped Martine's brain to make her think that she wanted a child, and then he used her accordingly. Legally, she couldn't advocate against being used to incubate a child, regardless of what she thought she wanted—and she couldn't advocate *for* it, either. Because of that simple fact, there was no ethical excuse for what Nathan had done. There was no way to square that circle and make it okay, even if Martine said she was happy with the life he'd given her.

I didn't think she should want the baby. I didn't think she should be *able* to want the baby.

"This should never have been an option for you," I said at last. "Nathan made you into someone who wouldn't say no to him, and he took advantage of you."

"Is that what you think?" she asked, the pitch of her voice rising. "You think he took advantage of me? I *want* this, Evelyn. I've always wanted this. I've never been as happy as I was the day Nathan let me hear my baby's heartbeat. I know you can't understand that."

I shook my head at her, braked a little harder than necessary. "You only felt happy that day because you were programmed to feel happy. You only want this because Nathan designed you to want it. I know *you* can't understand *that,* because it's part of the base we use to build a clone's brain. You're designed to not resent the way you're made. It's wrong that Nathan used you the way he did, but—"

Martine unbuckled her seat belt and told me to stop the car.

"What?" I glanced between her and the fast-moving traffic. "No, Martine, we'll be home in a few minutes. Put your seat belt back on."

"No," she said, her voice shaky. "Let me out. Pull the car over and let me *out*." In the same moment that she reached for the door handle, I activated the child-safety locks. She yanked at the handle over and over, making frantic animal sounds as she did.

"Put your fucking seat belt back on," I said. My voice came out quiet and dangerous. Out of the corner of my eye, I saw her go still. She buckled her seat belt again slowly, quietly, and stared at the dashboard for the rest of the ride home.

When we got to my house, I unlocked the door. She stayed where she was, her hands in her lap, until I told her that it was time to get out of the car.

"You don't understand," she whispered, still in the passenger seat. "This baby made it worth everything Nathan put me through. It's—I could survive him, because I knew I had this." She touched the rise of her belly with featherlight fingers. "I can get through all of it," she whispered.

We sat in the car in silence, Martine staring down at her lap, me struggling to figure out a way to talk to her. Trying to decide if I was supposed to argue or apologize. When it felt like the oxygen in the car was depleting faster than I could bear, I opened my door. By the time I was on my own doorstep, Martine was behind me.

She spent the rest of the afternoon in the bedroom, folding laundry and putting it away. I checked on her twice—once to see where she had been, and once to tell her that the clinic had called.

"They said nothing seems wrong," I said. "They said you should probably take it easy, and to come back in if there's more bleeding. For now, though, everything seems fine."

"I'm so glad," Martine said, smiling at me as she slowly folded a shirt. Her hands moved smooth, rhythmically. She ran her palms across each fold, leaving a tidy crease.

When she had finished, she put the shirt onto a pile that seemed much too tall to have been that week's laundry. Then, she reached into my dresser and pulled out a shirt I hadn't worn in weeks. She shook it out, laid it flat, and began folding it again.

"I'm so glad," she repeated, and she kept smiling, as she looked right through me.

CHAPTER
TWENTY

I stopped talking to my mother when I was thirteen. That was the year she sent me away to school, a good school that she paid for with the yields of my father's life insurance. In the state of Georgia, it only took four years to declare a death in absentia, and the moment his insurance policy accepted the death certificate, she started calling schools for me.

It wasn't that she wanted to get rid of me. I knew it at the time, and I never bothered to perform petulance at being sent away. We had been too close together for too long, and the four years between my father's disappearance and my first year of eligibility at boarding school had been especially difficult. While he was present, we had been forced into a default state of camaraderie, helping to shield each other from the worst of him. But then he was gone, and we began to see each other up close for the first time.

I resented the way she still fluttered and trembled, even after everything we'd been through together. I suspect that she resented my aptitude for my father's work in spite of her determination to encourage me in those directions.

It was for the best, us being apart.

I didn't stop speaking to her out of a sense of animosity. I didn't stop speaking to her at all—we just stopped *talking*. Our conversations were logistical, formal.

Would I be coming home for the summer? No.

Could she send money so I could buy food for a holiday party in the dormitory?

Of course; would I like a little extra for gifts for my friends? No need.

I still called her once every year, on the anniversary of my father's disappearance, in September. She wore a blue dress to my wedding and cried a little during the ceremony. She sent flowers after I told her about the divorce.

We were cordial.

But the last time I talked to her—really talked to her—had been a few years after my father's disappearance. A few weeks before she handed me a stack of boarding school brochures to choose from. We'd been discussing my future, and I'd told her that I wanted to be a research biologist.

"Like your father?" she'd said, exactly the thing I'd been hoping she wouldn't bring up.

"I'm not like him," I'd answered, and she'd nodded. She gave me a long, bright look, and I'd tried hard not to feel afraid. "I mean it," I'd added. She said that she knew, that of course I wasn't like him. I remember going to my bedroom and quietly, quietly locking the door.

I stopped talking to my mother too much that day, because if I *was* anything like my father, I knew that I could never let her see it. I packed my things a month later, and I went away to school. I didn't return to my mother's house again until long after she'd moved away to remarry a man I'd never met. She left every piece of furniture in the house, everything precisely as it had been when I was a child, covered in heavy white drapes to keep the dust from settling over it.

After that fight with Martine, I wished that I could still talk to my mother. I wished that I could have asked her why she decided to have me at all. It sounds maudlin—*did you ever wish I hadn't been born*—but really, I couldn't believe I'd never asked her in the first place.

The question seems so obvious now. Had she truly wanted a baby? Or was it that my father had wanted a baby, and she had wanted to keep the peace with him? Or had she been convinced her entire life, by her friends and by her parents and by their parents, that she *did* want me?

Had she ever looked at a positive pregnancy test the way I once had, with grim resignation? Had she ever run a hand across her belly in the possessive way Martine did, with unerring confidence in the rightness of her decision?

I wished I could ask her whether I, like Martine's baby, had made the things my mother endured feel worth the trouble.

I wished I could ask if I'd made them worse.

———

I couldn't sleep that night. Every time I closed my eyes, I saw the door to the doctor's office at the clinic—the way the doctor had looked at me when she opened it, her smile tight and vague. I knew that no one would sequence Martine's blood, and even if they did, they wouldn't recognize the signature marking her as a clone. I knew that I wasn't at any real risk of discovery. Still, Martine and the doctor had been in there alone. I hadn't been there to answer prying questions or help her lie about her medical history. I hadn't been there to make sure that our secrets remained secret.

And that was only going to continue. I didn't want to spend my life supervising Martine in order to keep myself safe. I didn't want to have to maintain the latticework of lies for her. But I didn't see another possible future, either.

I got out of bed and crept down the stairs for a cup of tea. I sat at the tiny table in my dining nook, the one on which I'd signed my divorce papers such a short time before. I wrapped my hands around my mug and tried to imagine how Nathan had done all of this for so long. How had he hidden it all from me? How had he hidden Martine, an entire person for whom he was entirely responsible?

The truth, I knew, was that I just hadn't been looking. I resented the moments when I had to pay attention to him at all. That had always been true of our relationship; some of our worst fights came about as a result of me resenting him for being needy. There was a helplessness in him that I responded to by pulling away and ignoring him on instinct. It bred my contempt, and I never fought that contempt back, not once. It always felt justified.

Because of that, I had never paid enough attention to recognize when he was hiding something. Hell, I never paid enough attention to recognize when he had been bitten by a dog. I had no idea whether Nathan had been a good liar or a terrible one—I doubt I ever would have spotted a tell on his face, even if he had one.

Maybe that's what he wanted from Martine. Maybe it was more than obedience, more than a willingness to give him a baby. Maybe he wanted someone who would pay attention to him.

But no, it had to have been something more than that. He had wanted someone who would pay attention to *only* him. Someone whose goals and hopes and fears and desires would be solely influenced by his needs, by his whims.

It was why he'd tried to murder Martine for asking whether her own desires mattered to him. Before that moment, she had been an unblinking gaze directed at Nathan. In the instant when she had asked permission to consider herself instead, she had failed him. She had failed him in the exact same way that I had been failing him all along.

Martine found me there in the kitchen, watching my tea grow cold.

"What are you doing up?" I asked, trying to remember the details of her sleep-function programming. I couldn't recall the mechanism we'd used in the iteration of programming that I suspected Nathan had stolen. It all felt so far away in that moment.

"I woke up to use the bathroom and saw that you were out of bed," she said. Her voice still had the rough edges of sleep in it. "Are you okay?"

I refilled the kettle and considered the question. "No," I said. "I'm not okay. But I'm okay." Martine sat in the chair I hadn't been occupying and watched as I pulled down a mug for her. It only occurred to me to ask her the same question after the silence between us had stretched long enough for the kettle to boil. "Are you okay?"

"No." She said it slowly at first, as though she were trying it out. She repeated it again, this time with more conviction. "No, I'm really not."

I gave her a cup of the mint tea she'd been drinking in the mornings. I sat down across from her and looked at her. The line in the center of her forehead was a little deeper. Her face looked softer than it had when we'd first met. This, I thought, is what I would look like *if*.

I cleared my throat and decided to try to be the kind of person who knew how to say the right things.

"Do you want to talk about it?" I asked.

"I'm scared," she said. "That appointment today was scary, and I don't know if I can do this, which is a scary thing to think about."

It was the first time I'd heard her express doubt, and she'd done it so immediately, so openly. She hadn't tried to hide it at all.

My instinct was, of course, to ask her if she still wanted the baby—but I remembered her outburst in the car earlier, her vehemence. Her hurt. Her anger. I sipped my nearly cold tea and waited, hoping she'd continue on her own, but she simply mirrored me, drinking her own tea. "What's scary about it?" I finally asked.

"I'm alone," she said. "I was never supposed to have to do this on my own. Nathan was supposed to be with me the whole time." She set her tea down and sat back in her chair, ran her hands over her belly. She wasn't looking at me. "I don't know how to do anything, you know? And I have no idea what I'm missing. I didn't know that the bleeding could be a bad sign. I didn't know that there were books I was supposed to be reading, or classes I could attend. What am I going to do when the baby comes? How am I going to take care of it, without him there to tell me how?"

I shook my head. "You shouldn't have to," I said. "This isn't fair to you."

"No," she agreed. "It's not."

I stood up then, walked through the kitchen and into the living room. I returned holding an old biology textbook. I'd used it as a yearbook at the end of my first year at the boarding school my mother sent me to when I was thirteen. The insides of the covers were thick with signatures, and more than a few of the illustrations had been defaced. I handed it to Martine.

"This might help," I said. Seeing the look on her face, I hesitated. "Can you read?"

"Of course I can read," she murmured, opening the book to the first page of text. It showed a long double helix of DNA, each nucleotide color-coded. "That was one of the first things Nathan taught me. Why will this help?"

"Well, you don't know anything about your body, really," I said. She frowned at me, but I continued. "I mean, you don't know how it works, or why it does things. Right?"

"Right," she said. "So you think I should learn about it?"

I nodded. "I think it might make you feel better about, you know. What's changing." I tried very hard not to look at her belly. "And if there's anything you don't understand, you can ask me. Or Seyed." I hoped, on a deep level, that she would ask Seyed. "And tomorrow I'll see if I can find something for you to read about pregnancy. And childbirth."

She smiled at me. It was a warm smile, a real one. It didn't look like it was calculated to make me feel welcome or calm. She thanked me, and even as she was saying it, her eyes slipped away from mine and fell back to that strand of DNA. She took a sip of her tea and began to read.

After a moment, she stood up and walked out of the room. She returned with the same legal pad she'd been using in the lab to record Nathan's traits for programming. She flipped to a fresh page and wrote down a word. She wrote in tidy, even cursive. When I asked what she was doing, she answered without looking up again.

"I'm writing down words I don't know," she said. "So I can ask about them all at once, instead of one at a time."

I swallowed a smile of my own. "Can I show you something?"

She looked up at me with her eyebrows raised. Standing next to her, I flipped to the back of the book. I showed her the glossary, the index, the appendices. "A lot of the things you have questions about will be here," I said.

She beamed. She looked up the word she hadn't understood—macromolecule. Her lips moved a little as she read the definition. She turned back to the first page of the textbook and, tracing the lines with her index finger, reread the paragraph with the word in it. "Oh," she murmured.

She turned the page, and I realized that, to her, I had disappeared. She had been starved for the information that was suddenly at her fingertips, the information that my bookshelves were filled with. The information that, ultimately, had created her.

I padded back up the stairs and went to bed, and sleep came more easily than I could have hoped. When I woke a few hours later, Martine was still at that little table. She was reading about the human skeleton. The legal pad was covered in her neat, careful cursive.

She was still smiling, and she was still reading, and she was so absorbed that she didn't even hear me leave the house. I eased the front door shut behind me, locked it, and got into my car to head to town. There was still one brick-and-mortar bookstore downtown, I was certain of it. They would have the things Martine needed. The things that would help her understand how to have the baby, how to give birth to it and raise it and survive on her own.

For the first time, I was certain that she could do it all.

CHAPTER
TWENTY-ONE

After two and a half months of development, specimen 4896-Zed was ready for conditioning.

The clone's progress could not have gone more smoothly. His growth timeline was perfect: forty-five days of neural priming while his tissues developed, thirty days of programming. We pushed hormones, stimulants, suppressants, and steroids to shape the personality of the man he would become. We built him core-to-surface, structuring his adrenal responses to help with the more complex modeling that would need to follow.

I wished I could have shown him to the lab director as proof of concept. *This works, and I did it so cheaply that you didn't even notice it. Now leave me the fuck alone and let me work in peace.*

Specimens were always sedated throughout the active process of conditioning—and during a specimen's first week out of the tank, we kept them completely unconscious. It was simpler that way. We didn't need to explain why we were doing the work that we were doing. We could shape them efficiently, without hesitation, without apology.

But specimen 4896-Zed was still unfinished—and it was our job to finish him.

We drained his tank on a Wednesday.

———

The first time I ever broke someone else's bone, it was an accident. I was playing a game of tag and ran hard into one of my classmates. He landed wrong, and he broke his thumb. He didn't cry at first, just stared at the wrong new angle of his thumb in bewilderment. It wasn't until a teacher came running that he realized something was wrong. It wasn't until that moment that he started to wail, the way children do when they see that an adult is afraid for them.

The second time I broke someone else's bone, it was on purpose.

It was a failed specimen, one of the first. She had grown too quickly for her own blood supply to sustain. Her fingers and toes were black, rotting, and I knew that the rest would quickly follow. I drained her tank, pushed a bolus of secobarbital, and waited for her to die.

It was cowardly of me, wanting to practice on a dead clone rather than a live one. I can admit now that I was afraid—I didn't know if the pain of the fracture might cause even a sedated specimen to wake up, to flinch, to shout. To cry. I didn't know how much force might be required for me to do the thing right, and I didn't know how well she would metabolize a sedative, and I was afraid.

Once she was dead, I broke her wrist. I gripped it tight and twisted it hard and fast, and I felt the snap of bone reverberating through my fists. It was so much easier than I had expected—so much easier than I had feared—that I let out a giddy little laugh.

Later, of course, I would realize that the specimen's bones had been brittle. They had grown faster than they should have, and part of her nutrient balance had been miscalculated such that her long bones were particularly weak.

The next time I needed to break a specimen's wrist, I struggled. More difficult bones—the humerus, the femur, the skull—required my patience and my sweat and, more often than not, Seyed's help. Still, every time I felt a bone break under my care, I felt the same flash of euphoria.

Every time, I had to suppress that same laugh. *I did it, I broke it, and it will never be unbroken again.*

———

Nathan didn't have an appendix. One of his molars was missing, knocked out in a middle school brawl. He had a scar on his bottom lip from where he'd bitten through it as a toddler. His collarbones were uneven. His arms were freckled.

When he died, Nathan had a road-rash scar on his right knee from a cycling accident. He had calluses on his index fingers, and a scar on his arm from a dog bite I'd never heard about. He had a mole on the back of his neck, a new one. He had a burn on his left hand that Martine had, at the time, suspected would leave a scar.

When we pulled specimen 4896-Zed from his tank, he did not look like Nathan. He was smooth and white and soft and strange, as though he had just been removed from a full-body cast. If he went out into the world unfinished, he would move wrong.

I never sent a subject into the world unfinished. Damaging a fresh specimen, weathering it just the right way to make it mirror the person it was supposed to emulate—that was the final layer of polish.

4896-Zed would not be awake for that polishing process. After that first week, as the conditioning tapered down, we would begin to ease him into consciousness, encouraging him to use his limbs and experience the pain of healing that would inform his mannerisms. 4896-Zed would need to slightly favor his right knee, to fidget with the scar on his lip. He would need to be awake for a fortnight, so that he could practice being Nathan.

All of it came with a risk of discovery. But I didn't have any visits from the lab director or from potential investors on the schedule, and they didn't make unscheduled visits. Those were too unpredictable for them; there was no way to anticipate what might be on display.

There's a lot in the process that investors don't like to see. There's a lot that lab directors don't like to see either. The night before we began to condition 4896-Zed—Zed, as we had begun calling him—Seyed argued with me vehemently about whether to let Martine participate in the work. "She shouldn't see this," he said. "She shouldn't know what we do here."

"She already knows," I replied, pushing Seyed's water glass toward him to remind him to hydrate.

He had been showing up at the lab hungover with increasing frequency since the night we'd seeded Nathan's clone. I hadn't called him out on it, but I couldn't afford for him to be slow on the first day of conditioning. He took my hint, drained his water glass, and continued his argument.

"She might know intellectually, but seeing it is something different." He shook his head. "Martine is too sapient for this. She'll know that this is how *she* was made. It's fucked up, Evelyn."

"This isn't how she was made," I said. "Nathan didn't condition her. He left her . . . fresh. Look—if she asks, I'll be honest with her about it. Okay?" I waited for Seyed to stop frowning at me. "I promise," I added, trying not to roll my eyes at him.

"If she's not okay, you'll let her stop?"

"If she's not okay, I'll let her stop," I said.

I was, of course, lying. He wasn't my friend. I didn't owe him any guarantees, and I was well within my rights to make him an empty promise in order to shut him up about Martine and her *experience*. The thought of excusing Martine from any part of the conditioning process stirred a cold, cruel rage deep in my marrow. If I'm honest, I should admit: I was fully prepared to hold her by the back of the neck and make her watch as specimen 4896-Zed bled into the gutters of the autopsy table.

I let that bitter fury carry me through the next morning's preparations. I watched Martine's face closely as we drained Zed's tank, as Seyed helped me shift him onto the autopsy table. I watched her for any sign of hesitation or weakness. I didn't realize that I was doing it at the time, of course—but I was doing it, all the same. I was looking for a flaw, for something that would prove how different we really were.

I couldn't admit to myself yet that my antipathy toward Martine was ever-so-slightly waning. She had been studying hard, tearing through my old textbooks, asking me if I had more. Over the prior weeks, we had spent the morning drives to the lab discussing new things she'd read about. She had cornered Seyed over lunches, peppering him with questions about tissue structure and human development and synaptic decay. She had begun to speak more directly, more honestly. She hadn't entirely stopped waiting for permission, but she was less hesitant, less passive. It was abrasive at times, made her less easy to direct—but I was starting to respect her a little.

Perhaps that's why I watched her so closely. Perhaps I was cautious of that respect.

When I handed Martine a sanding block and told her to debride Zed's knee, my dwindling contempt raised its nose to the wind, scenting for blood. She asked me what "debride" meant.

"Technically," I answered, "it means the removal of dead tissue. Infected skin, scabs, that sort of thing." I gestured to the perfect, unblemished knurl of Zed's knee. "In this case, it means you're going to re-create the injury that led to Nathan's scar. Sand his skin away, like the asphalt did when he fell." I outlined the area with a ballpoint pen, in case she couldn't remember the exact location. "Take everything within that oval down to dermis, then a little beyond. It should bleed."

Martine studied the rough oval I'd drawn on Zed's kneecap, then looked at his face. I waited for her to falter.

"How deep is he under?" she asked, her voice muffled by her surgical mask. The mean cruel core of me crowed in triumph: she was scared to hurt him, I was right, she was weak, weak, *weak*. But then she turned to me and continued before I could answer: "Should we strap him down, in case he fights?"

I hadn't expected that from her. I hadn't expected that at *all*.

"He's out," I said. "He's deep enough under that we'll be able to yank his tooth this afternoon without trouble. I wouldn't worry."

"Good," she replied, and then she descended on his knee. She held the skin taut with one gloved hand, and she swung the sanding block in great circles, scraping away healthy skin with every downstroke. "I figure," she said, her eyes intent on her work, "the road only scraped him in one direction, so I shouldn't go back and forth. Unless you disagree?"

I shook my head, then realized——she wasn't looking at me.

She had asked my opinion, but she wasn't watching me with fearful eyes to make sure that I approved of her choice. She hadn't stopped her work to see if I was going to object. She wasn't thinking of me at all.

"Yes, that sounds good," I said. I watched her for a few more seconds, but it was obvious that my supervision wasn't required. I turned away from her, walked to the autoclave to check that the dental instruments were ready for the afternoon's work. When I looked over my shoulder, she was still bent over Zed's knee, humming to herself as she swept away layer after layer of his skin.

After I had performed Zed's tooth extraction, I asked Seyed to deal with the cleanup. I told him that I wanted to make sure Martine was feeling all right about the work she'd done that day. He would need to rinse Zed's body of blood and saliva, would need to dry him and transfer him to a recovery bed for the night. He would need to wash down the autopsy table and dispose of the biowaste and autoclave the instruments. It was a two-person job, but Seyed didn't so much as hesitate before agreeing to handle it.

"She's probably wrecked," he said, watching as Martine lathered her forearms with antimicrobial soap.

"Probably," I murmured. I was watching her too. The firm, unhesitant motion of her hands. The angle of her neck over the sink, as she watched the soap run down the drain. The slight, satisfied lift at the corners of her mouth. "Don't worry," I added. "I'll check in on her."

But that night, when I asked Martine how she was doing, she smiled at me. She was absently rubbing the underside of her belly, pressing on a place where I suppose the baby was pressing back. Spirals of steam rose from her peppermint tea between us.

"I'm wonderful," she said. "Just wonderful. How are you doing?"

"Are you sure?" I asked, squinting at her. "Because conditioning can be difficult to watch. Or to participate in."

She shook her head and reached for her tea, lifted it to her lips to blow across the surface of it. Her lips nearly touched the edge of the mug. "I don't mind," she said. "It's nice to be able to set Nathan right."

"Zed, you mean?"

"Yes, of course," she said. "Although I think we should start calling him Nathan soon." She sipped her tea with her eyes closed. "So we get used to it, for when he wakes up. We want him to respond to the right name, don't we?"

"Soon," I said. "But not yet. Not until the conditioning is done. What did you mean, 'set him right'?"

"We're putting him back the way he's supposed to be," she said. "We're making him into the man we loved." The heel of her hand palpated her belly again, a long, firm press.

"Did you love him?" I asked. She nodded, her eyes still closed.

"Very much," she whispered. "Did you?"

I hesitated, stared into my cooling tea. It was hard, after the year it had been, to remember the way I had loved Nathan when things had been good. Or when things had been bad, but still worth fighting for. It was hard to remember what that had felt like. "I think so," I said. "Yes, for a long time. I loved him, when I loved him."

"What about when he died? Did you still love him then?"

I looked up from my tea and found her staring at me, her gaze intent. "I don't think I did," I said after a moment. "I think that, by then, I hated him."

She nodded. "Yes," she said. "Me too. I hated him too."

"At the end?" I asked.

"Every second." She shook her head. Her eyes shone with tears. Belatedly, I recognized the restrained fury hidden in the set of her mouth. "I hated him every single second."

TWENTY-TWO

Martine took to the work of conditioning Zed with startling enthusiasm. She never flinched. Not when we pulled out his appendix, not when we took a brûlée torch to his hand, not when we broke his collarbone. She never hesitated, never looked away.

There was one last piece of work, the most delicate procedure—the thing that would, if all went according to plan, turn him from Zed to Nathan. The scar on his eyelid. I had saved it for last because it would heal the fastest, and because it was small enough that if we ran out of time, it wouldn't be a deal-breaker. It was a tiny scar, one he couldn't recall the origin of—a little puckering at the corner of his left eye, mostly covered by lashes, but white enough to show up in photographs. I was doing the close-up work, cutting a deep valley into the flesh next to his eye. Martine held his eyelids open wide with one gloved hand.

He stared up at us, unseeing, his brain still wrapped tight in the heavy blanket of sedation.

"Hemostats," I said, holding a hand out behind me. Seyed dropped the tool into my palm. I gripped the wedge of skin I'd cut loose and tugged at it.

"Will he remember any of this?" Martine asked. She was so close to my face that she whispered. Her breath was warm on my temple.

"No," I said. "He won't remember anything before waking up in the hospital suite."

"So he won't know that we made him?"

I shook my head. "We programmed him to respond to any

stimuli as though he has organically formed memories. His brain
will fill them in, for the most part. He'll think that he's Nathan.
He'll think he remembers the things that Nathan is supposed
to remember. We'll tell him that he got hit by a car, before we
drop him at the hospital, so if he has any neurological weirdness,
they'll think it's a concussion. Easy."

Martine was quiet.

There was a tension there, thick and snarling. It made the room
feel humid. It plucked at the place just behind my navel, the place
where old fear lived. Heavy-falling footsteps and the sound of a
key in the front door and my mother looking over her terror-
straight shoulder at me, seeing me peeking around a doorframe,
shaking her head so I'd know to creep away to bed.

I breathed in slowly through my nose, out through my mouth.
I tugged on the strip of flesh again, and it pulled loose with
a sound like tearing silk. I dropped the hemostats onto Zed's
chest and replaced them with a fresh set, these ones gripping a
compress.

Blood climbed up into the white fibers of the gauze.

"Is something wrong, Martine?" Seyed said it so casually.

"No," she said, the lie obvious. I switched the saturated compress for a fresh one.

"It seems like something's wrong," I murmured. "You can let
his eye close now."

Martine sighed, lifted her hand away from Zed's face. I risked
a glance over at her. She was pushing her palms into the small of
her back, stretching, making her belly surge toward me. "I didn't
know," she said. "That's all."

"Didn't know what?" I asked. I risked removing the gauze from
the wound I'd made, but blood welled up fast, and I pressed a
fresh compress to it fast.

"I didn't know that I was a clone. Not for the first few months,"
she said. "Nathan told me that—that we were married, and that
I'd been in an accident. He told me that I might not remember
things." She paused. "I believed him."

"Good," I said. "That means it works. I wasn't sure if it would, to be honest."

After a moment, Martine excused herself, said she needed to use the lavatory. I watched Zed's blood slowly wick up into the compress I held, and I listened to the sound of Martine removing her gloves, washing her hands, walking out through the airlock.

Seyed took her place beside me at the table. "Nice one," he muttered.

"What?" I asked. "Was I supposed to tell her how sorry I am that Nathan lied to her? I don't see why that should rank, compared to everything else he did."

"Yeah," he said. "I think that's exactly what you were supposed to do."

The bleeding had slowed enough for me to remove the compress. Seyed handed me a syringe filled with liquid adhesive. Carefully, carefully, I began to fill the little valley next to Zed's eye.

"Why are you so invested in her well-being?" I asked. "She's a specimen. It's not like she's *me*." *Steady hands. That's the way.*

Seyed didn't say anything. I finished applying the adhesive. It would need three minutes to cloud over and get tacky, four minutes to fully set; then I could put a bandage over it, and we would be finished. I hit *start* on a timer that would click every minute, reminding me to check. "Hey, answer me," I said, straightening up and pulling my surgical mask down around my neck.

I looked at Seyed for the first time that day—maybe, I realized, for the first time in a while. I'd been around him, but we had been orbiting each other loosely during the conditioning process. He had been handling the things that I couldn't. We'd been acting as a relay team more than we'd been acting as partners.

I'd been giving most of my attention to Martine.

Seyed didn't look well. He'd grown a patchy reef of stubble across his cheeks and neck. He was bloated, and his lips were badly chapped—bitten, maybe, or just neglected. His eyes were hollow. He looked permanently hungover.

I cleared my throat loudly, and he jumped—but still wouldn't look at me.

The timer clicked. I glanced down at the adhesive. A couple of pink threads of blood had wound their way up into it, but it was still largely clear. When I looked back at Seyed, his eyes were squeezed shut.

"There's something I have to tell you."

"Okay," I said. "Are you still stealing from me? Because—"

"No," he said. "No, I'm not. I mean, I stopped after you found out. It's not that."

"Get on with it, then," I said.

His breathing was loud enough that I could hear it over the monitors in the room. "It's about Martine," he said. "You asked why I'm so invested in her."

I swore. "Don't tell me you have feelings for her, Seyed, that's such a *massive* ethics violation—and also, God, it would be *weird*, you can't just—" The timer clicked again. I checked the adhesive, which was starting to cloud over.

"Let me say it, please," Seyed said. "I have to say it."

I waited, but he didn't speak. The silence stretched between us, interminable, as he gathered his courage. I wanted to shake him. I wanted to slap him. *Out with it.*

I wish I could say that I already knew.

"I helped."

That's all it took. Two words, and I saw it all. Still, I waited, as though there were any explanation he was going to give me other than the one I knew was coming.

I wanted to give him a chance to lie.

I would have accepted the lie.

I would have known he was lying to me, and I still would have pretended not to know, because then he could have stayed. He could have kept my forgiveness. We could have pretended that nothing had happened, nothing beyond the stealing, and that was small, really. Compared to anything else, the stealing had been nothing.

But of course, Seyed didn't want to lie. The not-telling had been corroding the meat of him already, and I hadn't noticed.

I never notice. Not when it matters.

"I helped Nathan make——" he said. "I didn't know at first. I didn't know that she was what he needed the supplies for. He just asked me to take some things, things you wouldn't even miss, for his own research. And I owed him," he added, his eyes pleading with me to understand. "He's the one who introduced me to you, he got me this job, in a way. I just wanted to pay him back." He licked his lips, swallowed hard. "But then he had a hard time with some of the sequencing, and then he had an emergency with the protein chains and he called me, and it's——I owe him so much, you know?——and I knew how to help, and he offered me so much money, all under the table, and." He stopped himself midsentence, took a shaky breath.

The timer clicked.

The adhesive was cloudy. I touched my glove to it to check the set. It was tacky.

Almost there.

"You made her," I said. "You made Martine?"

Seyed shook his head fast. "No, I just——I helped Nathan out with his project. I assisted. That's all."

The absurd thing I thought first was, *Seyed's seen Martine naked.* Then, less absurd: *Seyed's seen Martine's sequencing.*

"So you knew?" I said, and my voice came out quieter than I wanted it to. It came out soft and dangerous, like it had when I was trying to make Martine put her seat belt back on, but I wasn't doing it on purpose this time. "When we sequenced that hair, and I saw the marker on it. You knew that was Martine's hair?"

"I suspected," he said. "I mean, I was pretty sure. But I didn't think he was . . . doing anything. With the project, I mean. I thought it was just labwork, seeing if he could pull it off. I always thought he failed."

He let out a deep sigh, one that was tinted with relief. He was relieved to have told me. He'd transmuted his guilt into my anger, and now I was the one who had to carry it, and he had the audacity to be relieved.

"Did you help with her programming?" I asked. I wanted him to say yes, wanted to give the rage that was winding tighter and tighter in my throat something to strike at.

He shook his head. "No," he said, "that was all handled before the protein-chain thing. I didn't even know it was going to be *you* until—the sequencing was all methodology, and—"

"God," I said, "of course he needed your help with the sequencing. I *knew* he couldn't have done it on his own."

Seyed laughed, a short breath, and I looked up at him sharply.

He wasn't allowed to laugh. We weren't comrades in understanding Nathan's incompetence. We weren't on the same side of things, not anymore.

He'd had his chance to stay in my good graces. He'd had his chance to lie.

The inner door to the lab opened. Martine walked in, stopped after a few steps, looked between us.

The timer clicked.

The adhesive was set.

"Martine, please come help me bandage this wound," I said. She walked over slowly, not looking at Seyed. Her eyes were locked on me.

She didn't ask what was wrong. She didn't ask anything. She helped me tape a patch of gauze over the adhesive. She stayed silent. She stayed calm.

She moved when I asked her to, but otherwise, she was very, very still.

My brain spun. Had Seyed helped bring Martine out of sedation? Had she recognized him? I remembered the horror on his face when he'd realized who she was—had that been real? He must have thought that he was caught, must have thought that I knew. I remembered the way his face went gray at the sight of her belly.

The anger in my throat coiled tighter, tighter, tighter.

Once the gauze was in place, I stripped my gloves off. "Seyed," I said, "please clean this up."

"I'm so sorry," he breathed. "I'm so sorry, I didn't know—I never would have—I didn't realize what he was doing, I didn't know that she could get—that he would—have a baby, I didn't—"

"Thank you," I said. Soft, clipped. The way my mother had always thanked any nurse who lingered too long over either of us. It was the opposite of an invitation. The conversation was over.

The drive home that night was quiet.

Martine kept her hands in her lap, her eyes downcast. When I parked in front of my house, she didn't get out of the car. I didn't either. After a minute, she whispered an apology.

"What are you sorry for?" I asked.

"Whatever I did," she said.

I was about to tell her that she hadn't done anything at all. Then I hesitated, because maybe she had. "Did you know Seyed? Before the night we went to the lab?"

She shook her head. "No," she said. "That was the first time I met him." She didn't ask why I'd asked the question. Her eyes were still on her hands. She was sitting so, so still, and I could read my mother's prey-animal fear in the angle of her shoulders, and abruptly, the coiled-up thing in my throat unraveled.

The next few minutes are divided into vivid snapshots in my memory. Martine's hand on my shoulder, heavy enough that she must have been pressing hard. The sound of the passenger door closing. The smell of her hair as she reached across me to un-buckle my seat belt. Stumbling a little next to her as she helped me through my own front door. Wine splashing into a cup in front of me, red as the blood that had welled up next to Nathan's eye.

I was not crying. I would not cry.

After she coaxed me into the first sip of wine, though, I told her. I told her everything that Seyed had told me, and all of the pieces that it had snapped into place. I told her about how Seyed had given Nathan access to my supplies, had helped Nathan understand my research, had made it possible for Nathan to betray me. Had made it possible for Nathan to create her—a better version of me.

She topped up my wine, laid her palms flat on the table. "So when you asked if I knew Seyed, you were asking if I knew that he was . . . in on it." I nodded. "I didn't know," she said simply.

It was as though some piece of scaffolding had been taken out from under me. My anger at Nathan's deception, at Seyed's betrayal—it all felt so brittle. It fell away, just for a moment, and then I was able to think back to the time before I had found out what Seyed had done.

Martine had been out of the room.

Because I had hurt her.

"What I said before," I started. "I should have been more sensitive to what you were dealing with. The whole process is . . ." I swallowed hard, took a sip of wine to move the words in my throat. "It can be difficult. I can't imagine what it was like to realize that Nathan lied to you the same way we're going to—the way we're going to lie to Zed."

She nodded. "It was upsetting," she said. "But I understand."

"Do you?" I asked.

"Maybe not," she said. "Maybe I'm just programmed to think I understand. Maybe it's a reflex. Maybe I can see both sides of things because it's the best way to make sure I never get angry. But even if that's true, I still understand. I can see why it's necessary."

I reached for her hand. She let me take it, and I looked at her, and she nodded.

"I know," she said. "You don't have to say it."

I should have said it anyway. But, like a coward, I accepted the pardon with gratitude. I held Martine's hand as I finished my wine, and she poured me more, and I did not apologize.

CHAPTER
TWENTY-THREE

The last time I saw my father alive, we were in his study.

I was due to have my wrist cast removed the next day. I was asking him to explain body fluids to me. I was confused by the different systems. I didn't understand the difference between lymph and plasma, couldn't sort out why they needed to be separate. We talked for an hour, and when the hour was up, he reached as always across the desk to shake my hand.

I aimed the webbing between my thumb and forefinger at his, just like he'd taught me. I gripped his palm, firm but not tight, and I pumped his arm twice. *Three times,* he'd told me, *makes you look nervous.* He gave me an approving nod—I'd gotten it right—and then he let me leave.

Our meeting was over.

I was nine years old.

I didn't miss him, precisely, once he was gone. I thought about his disappearance often—the circumstances that surrounded it, the things that were not to be discussed—but that was hardly the same as missing him. The place in our lives where my father had been was raw and strange. It was like the crater left behind by a pulled tooth, one that had been abscessed and throbbing for years. That emptiness was something to notice, something to run my tongue across constantly, bothering the wound until the gap in my gum closed. It was the taste of blood, clean and sharp and somehow comforting.

But the hole where my father had been healed over with surprising speed, and my mother and I fell into an uneasy routine.

There were things we didn't talk about, not ever, and there was part of the garden I didn't help her with anymore. We never bothered to clean out his study—just closed the door and pretended that the house was one room smaller than it had always been. After a few years, I went away to boarding school, and the silence around his absence became even easier to maintain. It was all simple enough.

I didn't miss my father until I found myself at his alma mater, attending classes that he had taken decades before. Even then, walking halls that he'd walked, I suppose that it wasn't *him* that I missed. Whenever I found myself struggling with a professor's lecturing style, or with a tricky bit of theory, or with a complex lab, I longed for my weekly hour in his study. I would sit in my dormitory with some seemingly unsolvable problem before me, and I would think wistfully of those easy answers. I would remember my feet kicking at the legs of the armchair that was mine to sit in, the big carriage clock behind his desk ticking away, the low rumble of his voice explaining things until I understood them.

And whenever I finished untangling my problems on my own—whenever I sorted out the professor's shorthand, or found the root of the theory, or completed a titration successfully—I missed that handshake. I missed the grown-up feeling of having successfully completed a maneuver that existed solely to prove that both parties knew what they were doing.

I missed knowing without a doubt that I had done the thing right.

―――

Seyed wasn't at the lab when we arrived the next morning. I was relieved that he wasn't there for me to deal with. It was time to wake the subject.

I rummaged through a drawer, pulled out an old stack of résumés, and flipped through it. After a moment, I dropped it into the recycling bin. The résumés I had were too old to be of any value. I would need to ask Human Resources to siphon me some fresh ones.

Martine and I got set up, prepared ourselves to talk to Zed. Not Zed, rather—he was Nathan, now. Martine and I had agreed to start calling him that to each other as well as to his face, so we wouldn't slip up and confuse him.

Nathan.

He was laid out in his recovery bed with an IV in one arm, the long snake of a catheter winding out from under his bedsheets. His vitals beeped along merrily on a monitor at his bedside, their steady rhythm a constant reminder that things were going just fine. His wounds were nearly healed already, a benefit of how new he was. His tissues were childlike, pliant, malleable. That healing factor wouldn't last, of course, but it was useful in these early stages, when he needed to mend quickly enough to scar.

He looked almost exactly like the man I remembered. His thick brown hair was already growing out of the short cut that Seyed had given him on his first day out of the tank. His eyelashes fell across his cheeks, light but startlingly long. His mouth hung the slightest bit open. His lips—thin, wide, perpetually curled up at the corners—still shone with the layer of lanolin that Seyed would have smeared across them the night before, to keep them from drying and chapping and cracking.

Martine and I stared at him for a long time. There was nothing to be said, no reason to say it. I knew what she was thinking, and I'm sure she knew what I was thinking too.

This was Nathan.

I would be lying if I pretended that I was never tempted to change him. I had complete control over the person he was going to become. And I could have built this Nathan differently, could have tried to turn him into someone I could spend a life with. Someone who had a little more courage, who paid more attention to detail. Someone who could keep up with me, who wasn't threatened when he couldn't.

I could have made him into someone who still loved me, who

loved me again. And then, when he was finished, I could have made a public display of taking him back, repairing our marriage, reconciling. I could have given myself a brilliant, docile, grateful man who no one would question my relationship to.

But that person I would have made—he wouldn't have been *Nathan*. Anyone who met him would have known that something was wrong. It was always in his essential nature to fall just short of what I needed him to be. I could finally see that. He was never going to be good enough; the original Nathan was born to be a disappointment to me at every turn, all the way down to his marrow.

I couldn't extract that from him. Not without making him someone entirely new. Someone I could never have fallen in love with in the first place.

So I didn't.

This man Martine and I were looking at, this senseless clone waiting to be woken up by the two women who defined him— this was the closest thing we could get to the real Nathan. This was the man we had known, the man we had loved, the man we had hated. The man we had buried. We reconstructed the frame of him, and we built a ghost in the shape of our memories, and then we shoved the two together. We fixed the frame and the ghost to each other by etching the sigils and scars of his life into his skin. We had made this man, together.

We had made him. And now, he was ready.

I pulled the curtain around his bed shut, so that when he opened his eyes, he wouldn't be able to see the lab. Martine stood over my shoulder, white lab coat stretched over her belly, mouth and nose and hair hidden behind a surgical mask and cap. I draped a stethoscope around my neck, lifted a surgical mask over my own face.

We were in disguise, dressed as a believable lie, one he would have no reason to inspect too closely. Two doctors, protected from pathogens, professional, distant. Nothing to recognize. Nothing to remember.

We were ready.

I took him off the sedative that had kept him below the surface of twilight sleep for the previous week. We had pushed him deeper under for more disruptive procedures, let him drift closer to the surface of wakefulness in between. Now, without any sedative to drag him down into the dark, Nathan woke up quickly.

His mind was flexible, malleable, ready to accept fresh stimulus. His eyes fluttered open, and for a few minutes, he had the same vague stare as a newborn. The room wasn't a room to him yet—it was shapes and colors, contrast and motion. His brain was digesting an overwhelming amount of input, forming patterns, attaching the patterns to vague memories that might make the patterns recognizable. For all our care to stay covered up, there was no real risk of him connecting our faces with the patterns he might have affiliated with us; his brain would see "mask" and "stethoscope" and attach those things to "doctor" long before it would attach my eyes to the complicated memory that was "Evelyn."

We waited. Once he started blinking the hard, stuttering blinks of a freshly emerged swimmer, I said his name.

"Nathan?"

His face swung toward me, and, with what looked like great effort, he focused on me. His eyes found my mask, my stethoscope. *There you go. Doctor.* I lowered my mask, trusted that I would be anchored in his mind as Doctor, and that his brain would take that as settled. That it would focus on processing all the other input around and behind me. That he would be too overwhelmed to recategorize me.

I smiled at him. "It's good to see you awake, Nathan," I said. I would need to repeat his name a few times, make sure it stuck in his mind as his own. His consciousness was still a little plastic, just soft enough that I could leave a fingerprint in it as it cooled. This moment mustn't go to waste. "How do you feel?"

"Uh," he said. "I, uh. What—?"

"I'm afraid you were in an accident, Nathan," I said. "You were in an accident on your way home from your vacation in the mountains. You got home from your trip, and there was an accident, Nathan." I nodded, kept smiling. His head bobbed a little, mirroring mine, following me. *Good.* "Some things might be a bit fuzzy. Nathan, do you feel all right?"

"Uh, a little sore," he said. His first sentence. The cadence was almost right. "Feels like I got hit by a bus. Is there, could I have a glass of water? Please?"

Martine's arm appeared in my peripheral vision, long and slender, and white as the flesh of a pear. She held a half-empty glass of water in her unshaking hand. When Nathan went to take it, she held on to it for a few seconds, until his grip was sure.

"Nathan, you're in the hospital," I said. "But you're all right, Nathan. Just a slight concussion and some contusions."

"I don't remember the accident," he said, his voice breathy from gulping at the water. Martine took the glass back. I heard her duck out through the curtain to get more, but I didn't take my eyes off Nathan's. He was still looking at me with open concern, with childlike trust.

"No, Nathan?" I said softly. "You don't remember the car swerving into the crosswalk and hitting you, after you got back from your vacation in the mountains? You don't remember the headlights in the rain, Nathan? You don't remember how your head hit the pavement and the car drove away just as you lost consciousness? Nathan, wasn't it a red car with a dent in the hood? Wasn't a white kid driving, Nathan? Wasn't a white kid with dark hair driving the car, the one that hit you after your trip to the mountains?"

"I'm not sure," he said, but he said it slowly, and yes, there it was: a fingerprint in the warm plastic of his memory. "That's . . . that sounds right. But everything is a bit fuzzy."

A bit fuzzy. He was mirroring my language now. That was good—it would be useful over the next week, getting him to start using the little turns of phrase that had pocked the original Nathan's speech. We would keep him lightly sedated, just a *bit fuzzy,* for that interval. We would keep him impressionable.

"That's okay, Nathan," I said. "I'm sure it will come back to you."

Martine reentered the room. Her eyes were glassy, but not red. She knew how to cry without getting caught. The motion of her entrance caught Nathan's eye, but he looked back to me almost immediately.

"I'm sure it will come back to me," he said. Then, blinking, looking hard at my face: "Has anyone called my wife? Does she know where I am?"

CHAPTER
TWENTY-FOUR

Martine and I stood in the airlock that separated my lab from the rest of the building, letting the cycle run again and again. Every time the cycle ended, I hit the button on the wall that would make it start again. We stood uncomfortably close to each other, so close that we had to move our hands carefully to avoid hitting each other. We let the noise of the air cycle and the thick seal surrounding the inner door muffle our words so that Nathan wouldn't be able to hear us.

"How did we overlook this?" I hissed. "Fuck."

It was a massive problem, an oversight of catastrophic proportions. We had programmed this new Nathan to be as much like the old Nathan as possible. A little gentler, maybe, a little more suggestible, but not by much—not so much that anyone would notice a big, sudden change. We had put so much work into making sure that he was the person we'd known, the person who was petty and brittle and focused and charming and bold and impatient and selfish and curious and quietly cruel.

I had been so focused on getting the job done, on getting it done right.

I hadn't thought nearly enough about what would come after.

"It's fine," Martine said. "I can handle it."

I shook my head hard, hit the cycle button again. "No," I said, "there has to be another way."

"He knows that he has a wife," she said.

"He could have meant either of us," I said. "He might still think of me as his wife. I could——" But I cut myself off midsentence, because I couldn't.

I knew my husband well enough, I thought. I knew that he hated all three of his suits. I knew that he had a good relationship with his father, and that he was smart enough to know never to ask about mine. I knew that he was stubborn when he was sick. I knew that he was gentle with children and animals, awkward around teenagers. I knew that the phrase "go big or go home" made him irrationally angry, and that any mention of his inability to grow facial hair would send him into a spiral of insecurity.

On our wedding day, I knew that he loved me, and I knew that I loved him, and I thought that no matter what else happened, we would be the one certain thing in each other's lives.

"It's fine," Martine said again, her eyes sliding away from mine. "Send him home with me. We'll just . . ." She hesitated. "We'll pick back up where we left off."

A tidal wave of horror rose up in me, overwhelming, too much all at once, flooding into all the places where *it's fine* wanted to live.

It was sudden, the way I knew how I felt about Martine.

With most people, I knew how I felt about them within minutes of meeting them; I categorized them as useful, annoying, charming, friendly. With most people, I found a place where they fit and I put them there, and that was how I felt about them until they gave me a good reason to change my mind. They rarely did. But Martine——I had spent so much time trying to sort out the answer to the question of Martine. I'd spent months being irritated at her, resenting her limitations, admiring her growth, fearing her, learning to like her, struggling not to hate her. I had spent so much time unsettled by her, by the way I couldn't figure out where she fit in my life and in my world.

But there in that airlock, all at once, I knew how I felt about her. It was, all of it, the exact same way I felt about myself.

All the same frustrations, all the same moments of affection.

Everything I felt toward Martine, I felt toward myself, too.

Of course, then, I wanted to find some way to protect her. And of course I resented her for it.

I couldn't send her back to the life she'd been living. I couldn't put her back into that house where she was constantly waiting for permission, where she was quiet and careful and uncurious. I couldn't do that to her.

But I couldn't take Nathan home, either. I couldn't undo the last year. The way we had programmed him, he didn't love me anymore. I'd gotten a little drunk with Seyed the night we implanted those emotional memories into Nathan's brain. It had been surprisingly awful. I had refused to talk about it, had doubled down the next day on making sure that the new Nathan would know that he didn't love me.

Not anymore.

His betrayal, our broken marriage—it was part of the geography of who he was. It was part of him. He didn't recognize me in the context of the lab, not so fresh out of sedation, but he would recognize me soon enough, and he would see me as a woman he had stopped loving years ago.

I couldn't make Martine take him. I couldn't take him. But one of us had to take him.

I hit the button again, and the airlock cycle clicked back to life.

"He'll hurt you," I said.

"He won't," Martine replied. Her shoulders were set in a brave square. She looked me in the eye, right directly in the eye because we were the exact same height and her eyes could immediately find mine without searching. "We programmed him to be difficult, but not to be violent. He was never violent."

I crossed my arms. "You know what I mean. He'll hurt you the way he hurt you before."

"I can handle it," she said, and I was taken aback by the stubborn note in her voice. It was as strange as listening to a recording of myself for the first time. *Is that how I sound?* "I handled it before you came along, and I can handle it now."

"No," I said, "no, you don't have to—"

"I do, actually," she interrupted. "I do have to. Because Nathan made me for this. It's what I'm for, remember?"

I flinched at the echo of my own cruel words from the tea shop, from that fight that felt like it had taken place in another reality. Martine rested her hands on her belly, which was enormous already, bigger than anyone could possibly overlook.

"I have to do this, Evelyn. I have an imperative. It's who I was made to be."

We argued for what seemed like ages, me hitting the airlock button once every couple of minutes, Martine digging her heels in with astonishing dedication. I tried a dozen different tactics, but in the end, it was an empty, hopeless argument, and she called me on it.

"You don't have a solution." She said it with flat finality. "You don't have a solution because there isn't one. You keep trying to convince me that I'm wrong, but you know we don't have anywhere to go from there if I am, so why are we doing this? So you can make yourself feel better about it?"

"No," I said, and I meant it. "I want to figure out something—there has to be a better way, a way to protect you."

Martine shook her head, her eyes smiling, her mouth flat. "I always knew it would be like this," she said. "I assumed you'd thought it through."

It hit me hard, just the way it had hit me hard every other time I'd let her down, failed in my unexpected role of caregiver to this person I'd never wanted. Even as I felt myself collapsing around the pit of guilt at the core of me, part of me raced to justify the way things were going to be. *Really,* that part whispered, *she's right. She's made for this. It will be just like it was going to be before. You don't have to solve it.*

"He's going to wake up soon," she continued. "We have to go back in there. I'll change into a dress, tell him I'm visiting. I can act like you called me."

"But you can't lie," I said. "I mean, you sort of can, but you're

terrible at it." I felt slow and stupid, like I was a step behind somehow and I didn't know how I'd gotten there.

"I can lie to him," she said. "If it makes him happy. It's always
been easy for me. I suppose it's part of my programming." Her
smile was cold. "I can lie if it means I can tell Nathan what he
wants to hear."

She walked out of the airlock mid-cycle.

A red light flashed above the door to the lab. It kept flashing
until I hit the button again, restarting the cycle, reassuring the
system that I was going to stay put until the vents had finished
cleaning the outside world off of me.

By the time I got inside, Martine had already changed into her
regular clothes. She was wearing a soft pink cardigan I hadn't seen
before, one that seemed perfect for the woman I'd met at that tea
shop. Pearl earrings, a full skirt with a waistband that stretched
high over her belly. Her dishwater eyes that were my dishwater
eyes shone with bright anticipation, and she'd pushed a headband
into her flat, colorless hair, the hair that was just like mine, only
longer. She looked the part. She *was* the part.

She was made for this, and looking at her now was a stark
reminder of how different she was from me, and the awful truth
that every difference was on purpose. There were no coinciden-
tal differences between us. Anything I admired about her was,
by necessity, something I found lacking in myself. I had to hate
her just a little if I was going to survive any of this, because if I
truly believed she was better than me, it meant that the original
Nathan had been right to make her.

If Martine was better than me, the original Nathan had been
right to stop loving me.

I closed the airlock door behind me, coming fully into the lab
just in time to see her duck behind the curtain that separated
his bed from the lab where he was made. "Oh, Nathan, there
you are!" Her voice drifted across the lab, bright and sweet and
relieved. "I was so worried. Nathan, I came as soon as I heard."

"Martine," he said, his voice slow and slurring. There was a beep—her dialing down the sedative drip, letting him begin to come back to himself. "Thank God you're here. I was in an accident."

"What happened, Nathan?" Her voice again, high and soft. "Oh, your poor face. Thank goodness you're all right."

I stood just inside the lab and listened to them talk. Martine put on an incredible performance: the worried wife, who hadn't heard from her husband in a few days. She kept saying his name, kept reminding him about how he'd been in the mountains for a few months on a solo trip, a last long trip away from home before the baby came. She layered her fingerprint on top of mine and pressed down until the ridges and whorls were deep enough to stay.

I looked over my lab—tungsten tables, tall tempered-glass tanks, massive fume hood, autopsy table, cabinets. All of it was scarred by this. Martine and Seyed and Nathan. All of them had carved their initials into my lab. This place would never be mine again, because some part of it would always, always be theirs.

Ours.

I had never wanted anything to be *ours*. At least, not with Martine or Seyed. And not with this version of Nathan. Not with the version of him that was relieved to see Martine. Not with the version of him that liked her better.

"Who's your doctor?" Martine asked in a carrying voice.

"I don't know." Nathan's answer came soft. He sounded embarrassed. "I didn't get her name. She looked like—"

"It's okay," Martine said quickly. "I'll find her. I'll find out when you can come home."

She kissed him. It didn't sound passionate, but it didn't sound removed, either. When she came out from behind the curtain, she looked around the lab, and in the seconds it took her eyes to find me, I saw it.

She was happy.

She was relieved that he was back. She hadn't been acting, hadn't been injecting false affection into her voice. She was glad to see this man again, the man who had kept her trapped under a bell jar of domesticity, the man who had wanted her to look only at him.

She was glad to see him again.

"Okay," I whispered once she had crossed the lab to me. I put my lips next to her ear, barely breathed the words so that only she would hear them. My heart pounded in my throat, and I tried hard to control my breath so that she would hear my words and not my panic. "Okay. I get it."

"It's so good to have him back," she murmured, her chin bumping my shoulder. "I know you think it's stupid, but I missed him, I missed him so much, and—"

"Listen." I cut her off because I couldn't bear the idea of hearing more. "Listen, I get it. I understand. But he tried to hurt you before, and he might try to do it again."

"He wouldn't, I know it," she said, and the bright hope in her voice struck me hard in the ribs.

"I won't send you home with him without protection," I said. The idea took shape faster than blinking, forming in my mind as though I'd set an electric current into the amnio of my mind. "But there's a solution. A killswitch. It's easy. I do it all the time. The people who . . ." I hesitated, then realized I was hesitating because what I was going to tell Martine might hurt her. It felt like weakness, that consideration. "The people who use clones want a way to get rid of them without getting messy."

Martine pulled her head back just enough that she could look at me. Her gaze darted between my eyes.

From behind the curtain, Nathan called her name. Martine and I turned to look in the same moment, our eyes on the cloth that separated us from the man we had made.

"Just a minute, love," Martine said. "I'll be right there." Then she looked at me, her chin set firm, and nodded. "A killswitch," she said softly, so softly it was like a sigh. "Whatever that is—you'll tell me later, yes? For now, let's get it over with." She smiled, her eyes slipping back to the curtain. "Let's finish this."

CHAPTER
TWENTY-FIVE

The day my cast was removed was also the last day I would see my father. My mother brought me home from the doctor and sent me upstairs to wash the sour cast-bound smell from my arm. I stayed in my bedroom for the afternoon, reading on my bed with my feet kicked up behind me as the square patch of sun that shone through my window parallaxed across the floor.

I used to spend whole days like that, tucked away in my bedroom, creeping downstairs for food every few hours or whenever I heard the dull thud of the study door closing. Some days, my mother would leave snacks and water on a tray outside my bedroom door.

She was always better at the stairs than I was—I never heard her come or go. I just opened the door to see a stack of cookies or a wax paper–wrapped sandwich tucked close against the doorframe, where someone who wasn't looking wouldn't spot it right away.

Not that day, though. Not the day my father went missing.

That afternoon, I had heard the dull thud of the study door, and it sounded to me like an opportunity. I eased the door to my room open, turning the knob all the way so the latch wouldn't make a sound. I crept out into the hall on sock feet and padded down the stairs as silently as I knew how. The bottom floor of the house was mostly dark, with the curtains drawn, lit only by the flickering glow of a dying fire in the living-room hearth.

When I was halfway between my bedroom door and the front door, I became aware of a strange, rhythmic sound. A sawing, ragged noise, like when the vacuum cleaner got stuck on something.

By the time I was at the foot of the stairs, the noise had resolved itself into two separate sounds.

I could recognize both as labored breathing—one strand of steady, panting gasps, met by a counterpoint harmony of uneven wheezes, wet and gnarled, choking.

Halting.

Slowing.

I wanted to run, but I didn't. I knew better than to run in the house.

I walked softly, instead, and I poked my head around the corner of a hallway wall, leaning just far enough that I could see the back of the living-room couch. That couch was between me and the sounds. I could see my mother from the waist up. She was wearing a dress with a Peter Pan collar, buttoned to the throat. The collar was white and starched and flecked with something dark, a shadow that also crept across the sliver of her face that I could see from my odd angle. She stood, breathing heavily, looking down at something on the floor, the firelight gleaming off of her hair.

The congested inhalations that formed the topnote of the melody I'd heard from the stairs—those were coming from something I couldn't see, something on the floor at her feet.

A shadow stretched underneath the couch, huge and distorted in the firelight.

My mother turned her head just a little, that familiar, warning arc to her neck. Just enough to let me know that she'd heard me, but not so far that she could see me. Just enough to let me know that I should sneak back to my bed. This, I understood, was not the time for me to be downstairs.

The next morning, she sat at the foot of my bed, the mattress dipping just below the place where my feet ended. I pretended to have been sleeping. I pushed myself up onto my elbows and rubbed my eyes. I nodded silently as she told me that she didn't know where my father was, that he hadn't come home the night before. Her eyes bored into mine as she spoke. She wasn't blinking.

There was a right answer. I knew there was.

I did my best to find it, and present it to her, the way I knew she wanted me to.

"All right," I said, taking care to not clench fistfuls of my bedsheets. It seemed very important, in that moment, to keep my hands still and relaxed. "Should we call the police?" At the sight of her face, I quickly added, "To tell them that he didn't come home?"

She blinked then, and her face relaxed into a smile. She patted my foot under the covers. Her hands were soft, scrubbed, but one of her fingernails had a deep split in it, and the damp scent of the garden clung to her. "That's a very good idea," she said. "Yes. We'll tell the police that your father didn't come home, and that we're worried."

She looked at me for a long moment, not saying the thing that she was thinking. I looked back at her, not saying the thing that I was thinking. She reached forward and tucked a lock of my hair behind my ear, loam-smell drifting off her in eddies.

"Get dressed, now, so you're presentable when they arrive."

When the police got to our house, my mother fluttered her clean hands at them, fidgeted, apologized over and over and over for the inconvenience. They told her that she was worrying too much—that my father had probably stayed at his office overnight, would be home any minute. They traded he's-having-an-affair glances, so obvious that even I could read the subtext. I stood beside my mother with my hands in my pockets, and when one of the officers squatted down to look me in the eyes, I let myself look scared.

He told me not to worry. He told me that my old man would be home any minute now.

My mother's hand rested on my shoulder, light as a fallen leaf, and she told the officers that she would call them again if my father wasn't home soon.

"He'll call," she said, putting a brave tremble into her voice. "He'll want me to know where he is. I'm sure I'll hear from him any minute."

———

Nathan spent another week in recovery.

He imprinted on his own name, his age, the facts of his life. He clung to whichever memories we reminded him were important. Martine and I helped him to identify the patterns that he could hang a consciousness on: here's how to talk, here's what to look for. He learned to see what we told him to see, and he was too busy learning that to pay too-close attention to the rest of it.

I occasionally caught Martine in contemplative moments, and it wasn't hard to discern what she was chewing on. The thing we were doing to this new Nathan was precisely what the original Nathan had done to her, once, in a time she didn't remember. A time she had forgotten by design. He had told her that her name was Martine, and that she was his wife, and that she loved him.

She had believed him.

The line between her brows grew a little deeper. It wasn't my concern—Martine was who she was, what she had been made to be, and I couldn't make myself responsible for her feelings about it. I never asked her about those moments of reflection. I demanded her participation in the final stages of Nathan's programming.

She never faltered. Just as she had never hesitated during Nathan's conditioning, she never once buckled under the strain of his final proofing. I told myself that was a sign that she was okay with everything. I decided not to pry up the edges of it.

I didn't need to know.

And so, during the new Nathan's final week in the lab, I didn't ask.

The morning they left the lab holds a surreal clarity in my memory.

It was early when we walked out of the airlock, still half-dark.

The air outside the laboratory building was cool but edging away from crisp; the year was lunging toward spring.

We had called the taxi from the phone in the laboratory instead of using an app. It was Martine's suggestion, doing this thing the old-fashioned way so that there wouldn't be a digital trail connecting her to the lab. I summoned the car while running my fingertips over the old takeout record, the running tally: S, E, S, E, S, S, S, E, E, S, E.

Martine's name and phone number were still written there too, in Seyed's precise lettering.

We walked Nathan out to the parking lot together. He was sedated to the point of stumbling so he wouldn't be able to retain a memory of where he'd been. Martine had dressed him in clothes that belonged to the original Nathan, a sweater and slacks and shoes that had gone unoccupied for nearly five months. It seemed strange that they should fit him so perfectly, a coincidence to remark upon, except that, of course, it was no coincidence at all.

It was craft.

Nathan leaned his weight on Martine as he stepped out of the laboratory for the first time in his life. The eyes that belonged to this version of Nathan had never seen anything beyond the curtain that surrounded his bed. He was sedated enough, of course, that he was hardly seeing anything even then—the world would be a blur, vague and huge, for the first few weeks of his new life. Soft enough for his brain to gum on. Shapes and noises and patterns, gentle and digestible.

The halls of the building were as dark and liminal as they had been the night I first brought Martine to the lab. The taxi was waiting already by the time we got out to the parking lot. It was a white taxi with green doors, and the windows were smudged from the inside, where some other passenger had pressed their hand or rested their head against the glass. The driver didn't look up from his phone when we opened the back door.

Martine helped Nathan into the car, her hand on his elbow. She climbed into the backseat after him. She was seven and a half months pregnant then, huge already. Carrying high, or so she told me. She struggled a little with the seat belt, maneuvering her belly with care. Beside her, Nathan's head lolled against his window, leaving new smudges on the glass, overwriting whatever had been there before him.

I closed the door after Martine once she was settled. I watched closely to make sure that she was tucked all the way into the car, that she wouldn't get caught by the closing door. She turned her attention to getting Nathan buckled in. She was still hunched over him when the taxi began to pull away, too occupied to look back at me. I watched them drive off into the morning. The tail-lights and turn signal of the taxi were strangely anticlimactic, too practical for the gravity of the moment.

I stood in the parking lot with my hands wrapped around my elbows. I couldn't make myself move for a long time after they left. It felt important that I stay, just in case. It felt important that I wait to be certain.

It was done.

They were gone.

TWENTY-SIX

I had four months of peace.

Peace, or something like it.

Martine and I met up a few more times over the course of Nathan's first month at home, checking in, making sure that things were going according to plan. She came to my house each time. It was a place where there was no risk of anyone seeing us together, asking awkward questions that would get her found out. Each time, when she walked in, I had a sense that she was checking on things, making sure that the house was the same place she'd occupied for the months of the new Nathan's development. Seeing that the space she had carved out for herself was still vacant.

We drank tea, and she updated me on his progress. He was brilliant, she said. He told his friends and colleagues everything he was supposed to, everything we'd stamped into him during that ductile period just after we woke him up for the first time. He had told people all about his research trip in the mountains. Some time at a cabin, a retreat to get his head on right about the divorce. An accident just when he was coming home. A head injury, a concussion, nothing serious but enough that he was a little off. His memory was fuzzy about a lot of things. Yes, he could still work. No, there was no need to check in on him.

"They all buy it," she said on her last visit. "Without hesitation. They believe him so much more easily than I thought they would. None of them seem to think he's acting strange." She drummed her fingernails against the side of her teacup. "I guess he was never really close enough with anyone that they would notice the little differences."

"No," I said. "I suppose he wasn't."

It was true. I couldn't think of anyone Nathan had been close with, not truly close. He'd had colleagues, old college friends, distant family, people he occasionally spent time with—but none of them had been interleaved with our life. None of them had followed up with me after I left him. I remembered, in the weeks after I moved out of our house, how my triumph had been punctuated by guilt, knowing that there was no one who I could be certain he would lean on. I'd been too angry with him to let that guilt change my own trajectory, but still—it had been there. The knowledge that I'd left him alone.

Well. Alone except for Martine.

I wondered, then, sitting across from Martine, if I was any different. It seemed that no one was noticing the differences in the new Nathan. No one had detected the ways we'd softened him just a little, the tiny details we'd shifted or overlooked or even gotten entirely wrong. I wondered if I was close enough with anyone that they would have seen the same differences in me. If I had been replaced with a reasonable facsimile of the person I'd been, would anyone notice?

Martine, I thought. Martine would notice. She was close enough to me, had spent enough time with me, had seen me in a raw enough state—she knew the marrow of me. If someone took me away and replaced me with a thing that moved like me and talked like me and had my memories, Martine would be able to spot the stitches that held it together.

In those strange months of solitude—those four months of peace—I often wondered whether Nathan would have seen it. The original Nathan, the one that I had divorced, and the one that Martine had killed. Would he have noticed if I went away and came back just a little wrong? Or had he only been able to see the parts of me that he wanted to fix?

Had we ever seen each other clearly enough for that?

———

After the first month, Martine and I shared a last cup of tea at my house, and then she left with a promise to call me if anything went wrong.

She eased herself up out of her chair, bracing her hands on her back in a parody of pregnancy. She was just a week from her due date by then. Our farewell that day felt strangely professional, transactional: we'd done what we set out to do, and our business was concluded.

I wondered if I should hug her goodbye.

I didn't.

———

I hired a new lab assistant.

Seyed had sent me a formal letter of resignation, citing a desire to live in closer proximity to his family, thanking me for the years of mentorship and growth he'd received in my employ. We had a tacit understanding, one we'd never discussed explicitly, but one that was necessary for both of our survival: he wouldn't tell anyone about Nathan and Martine, and I would accept his resignation without reporting the thefts, and provide a letter of reference should the need arise.

I sent him a brief message acknowledging the letter, so he'd know I understood. Our ties were severed. He didn't reply to it, but the word "read" appeared beneath it less than a minute after I hit send. It was enough. We were square.

HR processed his resignation as soon as I gave them notice. There was a fresh pile of résumés waiting for me the next morning.

My new lab assistant, Seyed's replacement, lasted for about a month. The one after that hung on a little longer, six weeks. I suspect she was hoping to get fired so that she could collect severance, but in the end, she broke before I did. She rotated out of my lab, and I was reviewing the next résumé in the pile before the airlock finished cycling behind her.

In my weaker moments, I missed Seyed. Not just the way we'd worked together, the easy rhythm, the implicit trust I had in his competence. I missed *him*. Seyed had been the kind of person who I thought might have been able to see the differences in me, if I went away and came back. I had plenty of colleagues, plenty of peers, but almost no *friends*. I had colleagues. I had Lorna, vaguely, in the periphery of my life. But Seyed—he had been something like a friend.

The pain of what Seyed had done—his betrayal of me, my work, my marriage—it never really calcified into anger, the way it had with Nathan. I waited for the resentment to come, to sweep away the confused ache of his deceptions. I waited to feel glad that he was gone, waited for the moment when I would be able to tint all my memories of him with bitterness. I longed for that release.

It didn't come. I couldn't make myself overwrite the way it had felt to be understood by him—the way it had felt to trust him. I kept my new assistants at a polite distance. I told them that they could call me Dr. Caldwell, and if they slipped up and called me Evelyn, I didn't acknowledge that they'd spoken at all. I kept things courteous with my other colleagues. I swallowed my occasional flashes of anger at the fact that none of them, not one, had noticed the strain I'd been under for the three months it took to make the new Nathan.

None of them had noticed the months that preceded the entire crisis, either. The awful weeks between realizing that something was wrong, finding out about his affair, seeing Martine, confronting him, moving out, filing for divorce. The sleepless nights and the fury and the sadness and the strange fog of everything suddenly being all wrong.

None of my colleagues had known about all that turmoil. No one except Seyed.

My anger at my colleagues was, of course, profoundly unfair. If anyone had noticed that something was wrong with me, I would have resented them; if they had commented on my state,

I would have been livid, embarrassed, outraged at them for prying, indignant at any implication of trespass into my personal
life. I was overwhelmed by the way my life fell into disparate
pieces to be examined and recategorized—but I never would
have confessed to that. I would never have admitted to struggling
under the weight of the project Martine and Seyed and I had tangled ourselves up in.

It was unfair. It was unreasonable. Still, part of me was furious
that my colleagues, who I hardly knew, had never cottoned on to
the fact that something was *wrong*.

None of them had noticed me changing.

I found myself watching them more closely. Strangers, too—at
the store, on the street. I watched the way they looked at each
other, the way they avoided looking. The way people carefully
dodged each other's attention, half lifting their hands to politely
acknowledge and preserve the space between them.

I wondered how many of them had people in their lives who
would notice. If they went missing and came back different; if
they lost night after night of sleep to endless fights; if their eyes
were raw from crying alone in the empty rooms of an unfamiliar
home. If they were distracted by the all-encompassing fear of
Getting Caught, or aglow with triumph at having accomplished
something so secret that they'd never be able to tell anyone what
they'd pulled off.

If they were trapped in a home with a monster who'd made
them to suit his awful, practical, deeply limited specifications.

Anyone who noticed would care. But who would notice? Who
would pay close enough attention?

For the first time in my life, I had no distractions at all. There
was nothing to pull my attention away from my work—and yet,
obscenely, my work suffered. I stopped pushing myself. Still, the
only person who seemed to notice my failure to innovate was my
lab director, who pointed out that I hadn't given him my expenditures report when I said I would. I moved that meeting back,

back, back, and his requests for data grew more and more impatient. My funding for the next year wasn't guaranteed, and I couldn't even apply for it until I sat down with the lab director to hammer out the details.

But I couldn't bring myself to do it. I moved through my days with the knowledge, concrete and immovable, that there was not a single person in my life who knew me. No one knew the person I'd been before. No one knew the person I was, after. No one would have been able to spot the unsubtle wounds inflicted by the interval between my moment of glory at the Neufmann Banquet, when I received the greatest honor of my career, and my moment of glory at the flank of a green-and-white taxicab in the wee hours of an April morning, when I let my greatest accomplishment out into the world.

When the new Nathan went home with Martine, I became an alone-thing, more alone than I had ever been before. More alone, even, than I had been that first night in a town house full of packed boxes.

From that moment, I was the only one who knew what I truly was. I was the only one who knew what I had done.

To be alone with that knowledge was the most dreadful thing I had ever felt. It was a vast, deep, terrible kind of understanding. I knew, finally, how my mother had felt in the minutes before she had heard my sock feet padding down the stairs in the night. I knew that I had done what I had to do, and I knew that I could never tell a soul. I knew that there was a part of me that would never be not-alone again.

My mother had spent the duration of her marriage to my father whittling pieces of herself away, leaving void space for him to whiff through when he swung his fury at her. Once he was gone, she grew to fill those spaces again—to take up the amount of room she should always have been allotted. I had wondered for so long why she stopped there, why she didn't spread like a climbing vine, devouring the void he left behind. I spent my adolescence nurturing a quiet disdain for the way she failed to become a monster in his absence.

Nathan had, of course, fed that disdain. He had recognized a vulnerability in it, a weakness in the way I loathed the parts of me that mirrored my mother. The fear, the fluttering, the impulse to hide and apologize and placate. I was horrified by her willingness to accept her circumstances, by her failure to imagine that her reach could extend beyond her grasp. I tried to root out any part of me that might accept less than what I was capable of, and I dug deep, and still Nathan never let me feel like I'd dug deep enough.

Something felt different in Martine's absence. I was alone the way my mother had been alone. She'd had me around the same way I had my new lab assistants around—I was present, and I needed to be managed, but I wasn't with her, not really. That night, when she stood breathless in the living room, she carved out a hole in the world. She and the thing she had done were all that would fit there. She climbed inside of that space in the fabric of reality, and from then on, she was alone with what she had done.

That was the kind of solitude I came to understand. It took up space, the space I'd always sneered at my mother for failing to claim as her own. It was in the room with me, always, that lonely knowledge of all the things I could never tell anyone about. It curled up next to me in my bed at night, the soles of its feet pressed against my calves, and breathed my air. It looped its arm through mine and walked beside me.

I could never tell a soul about what had changed me, and if I never told anyone, then no one would ever know. No one would guess, just from looking at me, even if they came to know the person I was in the aftermath of making a new Nathan. No one would look at the seams that held me together and guess that they were scars.

Of course my mother decided to stop growing. Of course she decided that it was enough to simply be the person who she was without fear.

I still scolded myself at the moments when I resembled her. When I caught myself at the threshold of an apology, or when I twisted a napkin between my fingers, or when I realized my eyes were darting around a room, looking to see where everyone was. Every time I wanted to shrink myself down, I revisited the bitterness of her fluttering at the police, telling them how thankful she was for their kind words.

I still thought of her as a coward.

But I stopped fighting the knowledge that I could be the same kind of coward she had been.

There was a comfort there, in being hidden. I'd always known it. Being so alone was, in a way, safe. I wrapped myself up in it, burrowed down into the cool quiet decay of my secret.

Of course my mother had decided to stay where she was. Of course she had expanded only to fit the boundaries of her container. The appeal was deep and irresistible. It was the childhood sense of victory that came with fitting into an impossibly small space, tucking myself away into the dark. *They'll never find me here.*

By accepting the isolation that came along with my secret, I could rest assured that no matter what, I would always be at least a little hidden. No one would ever know me, not fully, because no one would ever know what had happened.

There was a piece of me now that no one would ever be able to reach.

My life developed a steady rhythm. I worked at a mechanical pace, delivering progress in my research and avoiding conversations about the future of my lab. I ran through laboratory assistants at a reliable clip. I ate salads for dinner, prepackaged pasta. I drank wine. I walked around in my new neighborhood every few nights, aimless, trying to keep myself from becoming a recluse. I took out my recycling once a week.

I settled into the new way things were. I was doing well enough. Not flourishing, maybe, but there was nothing *wrong*.

For those four months, I had peace.

And then, in September, Martine called.

———

Their house looked the same as it had when the original Nathan was still alive.

There were small changes—Martine had planted bright chrysanthemums along the path that led to the house, and a wreath of red and orange leaves hung from the front door. But it still looked like the home that Nathan had wanted for his new life. A place for Martine to work hard at keeping nice. A place to raise a baby. The porch swing and the picture window were still there, just the same as they'd been on that crisp, surreal night when I walked across the lawn practicing the speech I would make to Martine about boundaries.

Nothing about the house looked different. Nothing about the house betrayed the blood that had spilled inside it.

On the night Nathan died, Martine had opened the door before I could land a single knock. Not this time, though. This time, I pounded away at the door, watching the leaves on the wreath shake.

It took her long enough to answer that I grew uneasy.

She'd sounded frantic on the phone, more panicked than I'd ever heard her. *Please, you have to come to the house, something's happened, I can't talk about it on the phone, please, you have to come now.*

I spent the drive to her house quietly praying that she hadn't killed him again, deciding that I couldn't save her a second time. But when she didn't answer the door, I started to worry. Maybe she'd called for some worse reason, maybe she *couldn't* answer the door, and what if we'd programmed the new Nathan wrong? What if we hadn't softened him? What if we'd made him brittle, mutable, dangerous? What if we'd poured the foundation of him wrong, and he'd turned out even worse than the original?

Maybe that's why, when Martine finally did answer the door, the thing I registered was relief. I sank with it, the weight of

knowing that she was all right. It was a strange way to feel after
so long.

She looked past me as though there might be someone with
me. "You're alone?" she asked.

"Of course," I said. I looked at her, then, not just at the fact of
her whole and present, but at the details of her.

She was different. Of course she was different. Not pregnant
anymore, for one thing. Slim, slimmer than me, her features
winnowed down to sharp planes that I didn't recognize from my
own face. Her eyes weren't quite sunken, but there was fatigue
etched into her, the deep kind of fatigue that I suppose must come
with a new baby.

She had cut her hair short. It looked good on her, modern and
fresh, young. I would never have thought to cut my hair that way,
and I immediately filed the cut into a resentful category of things
I could never try because Martine had tried it first.

She was covered in soil. It was smudged across her face,
worked into the creases of her clothes, under her fingernails.
Eddies of loam-smell. I breathed it in and tried not to remember
what that smell had meant to me the other times I'd been surrounded by it.

"Come inside," she said. "Please. You have to hurry."

There was a trail of earth in the entryway to the house. Muddy
footprints led to the backyard. She'd been pacing, waiting for
me. "What's the rush?" I asked her.

"The baby's asleep," she said, and I couldn't tell if she was
answering me or just talking. Her words came too fast for her
to order them properly. "Nathan's at work. He has drinks after
with—with someone, with his supervisor or something, I don't
remember, it's—what time is it?"

"One-something," I said. "What's going on?"

"We have a few hours," she said. "Good, okay, we have a few—
you have to come, it's—please, I can't tell you, I have to show
you, you have to see."

I followed her through the house, stepping around her muddy footprints on the tile. She walked in front of me, clenching and unclenching her fists over and over again. Dirt clung to the fine hairs that dusted the nape of her neck.

I watched her, the familiar way she moved through the world, and I bit back irritation at myself for having missed her.

Then we walked into the backyard, and I forgot everything I had been thinking. My resentment, and my relief, and my longing—I lost track of all of it.

I lost track of everything that wasn't the bodies.

CHAPTER
TWENTY-SEVEN

There were twelve of them.

I had never studied specimen decay before that day. I could consider that a lapse in the scope of my research, but really, it just wasn't ever necessary. Whenever a specimen failed during the development or conditioning process, we autopsied it and then cremated the cadaver immediately. There are no burials for bio-waste. Specimens who were used outside of the lab, made to spec and then discarded after their usefulness expired, were likewise cremated; it was in the disposal clause of every contract, so that there wouldn't be human remains floating around in the earth with the DNA of living people in their tissues.

Before that afternoon in Martine's backyard, I had never seen what the tissues of a clone looked like after any amount of subter-ranean decomposition.

Most of them were still partially buried. Hands and faces and soft white calves sticking up out of the soil, each one less un-earthed than the last. A shovel was next to the farthest-flung body, the blade sunk deep into the soft soil of Martine's mostly demolished rose bed. The yard was a horror of holes, but the rose bed was the best-tilled section. There, in the wreckage where the flowers had been, were a dozen corpses uprooted in what I could easily read as an increasing frenzy.

The cadaver that was closest to the house, the fully uncov-ered one, was hardly touched by decay. Her head was pillowed by a torn-open plastic bag, one that looked to have been wrapped tightly around her face until just before my arrival. Knowing what I do now, I can guess why she was in such good condition: an intersection of the way clone tissues develop in stasis, soil pH, and the lime in the garden shed. So many boxes of lime—he must have bought them wholesale at the outset of his project, must have been planning for at least a few burials right from the beginning.

Nathan was never one to check his assumptions during research. He was always just lazy enough, and just smug enough, to assume he had things right.

But it turns out that the wrong kind of lime, applied in just the wrong way, will act as a preservative. And clone tissues are different, that's always been true. They may look the same, but they behave differently. They're brand-new, and they don't know how to decay, not the same way human tissues do.

Still. That specimen, the first one, had been in the ground for at least two years. She was only a dozen yards from the house, a face and a body and a pit of churned earth.

I did the math, later, after we dug through Nathan's study, after we pieced together the truth. She had to have been buried for at least two years, at least that long, because Martine was nearly two years old by then, and there had been no overlap between their lives. They'd never met. Underground for two years, and still the specimen was fresh enough that I could immediately recognize her.

She looked exactly like Martine.

She looked exactly like me.

I walked outside and down the porch stairs, past Martine, who stood on the back porch with her arms folded tight to her chest. Everything was too loud, too heavy. Each of my steps felt individually significant.

Martine was watching my back and I could feel it, could feel her watching me, could feel the hum of the air between us. I found myself looking toward the sky to see if there were any planes passing overhead. It felt impossible that we were alone in that yard, that no one else could see all of this death. It was too big for the two of us alone to witness.

But there was no one else. It was us, and it was them.

"What happened?" I asked. It came out as a whisper, impossibly quiet, but Martine still heard. She still answered.

"I was gardening," she said. Her voice was very nearly steady. "I was going to put in a couple of saplings." I turned back to look at her, and yes, there were two saplings. Apple trees, they looked like. Right next to her. Still in pots, too skinny to hold themselves upright, so they were each tied to a thick stake. Had they been there before? I tried to remember seeing them, walking past them, but there were a dozen bodies in the yard and those little trees could have appeared by magic for all I knew. She could have pulled them out of her pockets while my back was turned. "I started to dig and I . . . I found her," she continued. "She had that bag on her face. I ripped it open to see who she was, and that's when I saw the other one. The next one."

I reached the first body, the one that was almost entirely unearthed. She was on her side, not curled up as closely as a sleeping Martine might have been. Her face was turned toward the sky. Her mouth was open. Her teeth were dark with soil—it must have landed there while Martine was digging up the other bodies, after she'd torn open that plastic bag to see whose body she'd found.

I could see without having to look closely that her mouth was full of earth. I didn't want to know that, but it was the kind of thing that makes itself immediately apparent. The hang of her jaw, and the rich thick darkness behind her teeth—I knew without thinking, and that's not the kind of knowledge one can just let go of. I looked at her mouth and the smell of turned earth was so rich in the yard that I choked on the taste of it.

One of her arms was behind her, flung back as if in a stretch. Her hand almost touched the outstretched fingers of the next corpse.

I could see it in my mind clearer than anything—Martine

finding the first body, digging her up, brushing dirt away from her face. Uncovering that second set of fingers, lifting her shovel again, and then again, and then again, angry and afraid, how many are there? I could picture her hoeing this awful row with increasing speed, harvesting the nightmare of it. These dozen lifeless faces hidden beneath her roses, some of them half-rotted, some of them choked with soil, all of them identical to hers. This strange family she'd never met.

Her secret lifeless sisters.

I made my way from the first corpse to the last. Martine had barely uncovered this last one, the furthest from the house; it was just a loose mound of earth next to a spill of white-blond hair and a chin. If not for the other bodies, I would have mistaken it for a protrusion of roots next to a paving stone. I would have walked right past her.

I crouched down and brushed at the half-turned earth. It looked as though it had hardly taken any digging at all to get to her. Something in me bucked at the improbability of it, demanded that I acknowledge it as a hoax. She was right *there,* superficial enough that someone could have *tripped* over her. How long had she been so close to the surface of the soil? How could she have been so shallowly tucked into the earth, but still hidden?

"I had to stop there," Martine said from her place next to the house. "I called you after I found that last one. I couldn't . . . I couldn't keep going."

I swept my hand across the dirt one last time, uncovered the awful meat of the clone's face. She was much further gone than the first body, most of her flesh missing. She was harder to recognize as a human thing.

Eddies of loam-smell drifted up around me as I shifted the soil. I swallowed hard.

Focus, Evelyn. Focus. That's the way.

"She's wrong," I muttered to myself, and then I said it again to Martine, louder. "She's all wrong. Here, come see."

Martine had changed since we met, but not so much that she

didn't come to me when I called her. She didn't hesitate, didn't object. I listened to her approach, her footsteps light through the freshly ruined section of her garden, and then she was there next to me, ready to look at what I wanted her to see.

Should I say that it occurred to me that she might not want to see? Should I pretend that it was a consideration? I wanted her to look with me, wanted her to understand what I understood. I didn't want to be the only one who knew what Nathan had done. I could keep my own secrets, but I didn't want to keep his. Not this one.

"Look," I said, and I used my middle finger to trace the air just above the spiral of the rotted specimen's exposed jawbone. It twisted like the central spire of a shell, dozens of teeth forming a long ridged spine along the outer contour of the helix.

"What," Martine said, and then she didn't say anything else. She reached out her own hand, touched the bare white bone with her fingertips where the flesh had sloughed away.

"She's wrong," I said. "She came out wrong. She's a failed attempt." I looked along the row of partially exposed bodies, and as they came into focus, my loose understanding of the situation took solid form in my mind. I straightened up and walked along the row, looking closer this time, stopping in a few places to expose the specimens more thoroughly.

Each of them was, in some way, wrong. The ones furthest from the house were worse, more obvious blunders. One had a chest that was caved-in; I recognized the shape from my own early failures, a problem with the development of cartilage and collagen. Another looked hollow, deflated: her bones had never set. I used my hands to scoop soil away from the legs of a third, and I saw the purple weblike mottling of too-tight fascia. A growth-rate failure. I went on down the row, finding all of Nathan's hidden mistakes.

Only the last body, the fully unearthed one, looked like a true success. Something, I knew, had been unsatisfactory to Nathan— something about her hadn't turned out the way he wanted it to.

It could have been anything. Her voice, her programming, her imprinting. Her fertility.

Nathan hadn't liked the way she turned out, so he had killed her, buried her with the others, and started over again.

I counted the bodies out by letter. There were a dozen of them. A through L.

"Martine," I whispered. "You were his thirteenth try."

A swell of noise rose from inside the house. Martine looked away from me, up at a half-open window, toward the rising wail.

The baby was awake.

―――――

We should have examined Nathan's personal files before we attempted to program him.

I can take responsibility for that error. With the clarity of hindsight, I can see how I rushed things. Digging Nathan up and taking a core sample and rushing off to the lab to get started on his replacement—it was all too fast, too sloppy, predicated on the assumption that I knew enough to proceed, when really, the very fact of Martine's existence should have demonstrated to me that I didn't have the contours of Nathan's interiority fully mapped.

I didn't know all of his secrets. Neither did Martine.

Taken together, our view of the man Nathan had been was a more comprehensive picture than either of us could see individually—but we had missed so much. This huge window of time and energy and focus in which he had been hiding an ambition, a secret, a *project*.

We hadn't known, and we hadn't thought to look. It was an unforgivable oversight driven by desperation, and reinforced by our own hubris. We knew that we didn't know everything about Nathan, but we imagined that we knew him well enough.

We were wrong.

Before the pregnancy, Martine told me as she led me into the house, the nursery served as Nathan's home office. It had always been a temporary accommodation, she said, looking over her shoulder at me, her pace quickening as the baby's cry grew frantic. "I've been getting that room ready my whole life."

It was the one room I hadn't seen, the night I helped Martine bury Nathan's own, freshly dead body. It had made sense for me to see the rest of the house, with all that had to be done, but there had been no reason for her to show me the nursery, and it hadn't occurred to me to ask. If I'd thought about it at all, of course, I would have known that there was a nursery in the house—but I had figured that the picture I had of Martine's home was thorough enough. It was sufficient.

I thought I'd seen enough to understand.

But there it was, on the other side of a white door: the nursery. The room that represented the things Nathan wanted, the things Martine wanted, the life they had worked to build together. The walls were washed green with white wainscoting, a hand-painted trim of dark boughs flecked with tiny purple flowers. Two layers of curtains hung across a small, high-set window—one layer thick, the other sheer, both closed tight to keep the room dark. A mobile hung above the crib, bumblebees and felt flowers. The carpet was thick, and there was a rocking chair in one corner, and I could see Martine's hand in all of it, every color, every corner, every detail.

"This is lovely," I said, and I meant it. I truly did.

"His desk is still in the dining nook," she answered, "but some of his files are in the closet." I slid the closet door open, and there they were: a half closet's worth of banker's boxes, stacked up underneath a double row of hung onesies on impossibly small hangers. I searched the boxes as Martine changed the baby. She murmured as she did it, small sweet noises that didn't quiet the baby, but that seemed to shift the tenor of her cries to something less emergent.

"What's her name?" I asked, opening the first box, flipping through tax returns.

"Violet," Martine said. "After Nathan's grandmother." On the changing table, Violet wailed, her limbs flailing in the same jerky motions as a freshly dry specimen.

I found the records I wanted in the third box I investigated. I opened it just as the crying stopped. I looked over my shoulder, the lid of the box in my hand, just in time to see Martine settle back in the rocking chair with the baby at her nipple. I felt a strange flush of embarrassment, not at the sight of her breast, but at the contentment on her face.

That wasn't meant for my eyes.

It wasn't meant for anyone's eyes. It was a moment in which, I realized, she wasn't calibrating her expression to any purpose. She wasn't trying to make anyone else feel happy, or important, or safe, or guilty. She'd been created and molded to think constantly of what her face and voice and body might incite in others. She'd been made to manage the emotions of people around her. She'd been made to be careful.

But in that moment, her contentment belonged to her, and to her alone. She had made something, and she owned it entirely, and no one could take it from her.

It wasn't a feeling I would ever have. The idea of holding an infant to my breast made me feel faintly ill, the same way I felt whenever conditioning a specimen required the removal of a fingernail. But I could never begrudge her the privacy of it—the ownership of that moment. And I couldn't shake the feeling that I was intruding upon it, just by existing.

I wasn't supposed to be here.

I confirmed that feeling as fact when I opened the box labeled HEALTH INSURANCE and found a stack of yellow notebooks inside. Thirteen of them, the same kind of notebooks we had used as graduate students. They were labeled in Nathan's spiky, uneven hand, thick black marker in the center of each yellow cover.

Agatha. Bethany. Corinne. Dinah. Edith. Faith. Genevieve. Helen. Ingrid. Jacqueline. Katrina. Laila.

Martine.

They were filled with notes on Nathan's progress, his methods. Each of the first dozen ended with a full-page black X, a marker of the day he'd given up on the specimens. The dates began to overlap—he was preparing new attempts before the old ones had failed, refining his methods.

Martine's notebook ended with a reflection, a page-long journal-style entry. It was dated only a couple of weeks before I had confronted him with proof of his infidelity.

The entry described his certainty that he had finally succeeded. He was relieved. He was elated. He could finally have the life he wanted.

The only thing left to decide, he said, was what to do about me.

I stared at the words with a strange sense of distance. *The only thing left to decide is what to do about Evelyn.* Having seen what he did about the first dozen iterations of Martine, I had a feeling that I knew what his approach to dealing with me was going to be.

"What is it?" Martine whispered.

I looked up and realized that I'd been sitting on the floor, reading silently, surrounded by notebooks, for much more time than I'd noticed. Martine was still in the chair, cradling Violet in her arms, rocking at a steady rhythm. I couldn't tell if the baby was asleep or just quiet.

I kept my voice low and steady. I showed Martine the covers, the names, the dates. I didn't share the details of each failure with her, but I gave her the broad strokes of my understanding: Nathan had rushed, extrapolated, experimented, and failed over and over again. Every time one of his attempts to clone me—to improve me—failed, he killed the clone, buried it, and started over again. All told, it seemed to have taken him barely eighteen months to successfully reproduce my results. At least, that was what he'd recorded. Three years in all between his first failure and his final one.

I couldn't read Martine's face when I told her that she was his success. That she was the pinnacle of his accomplishments. "You were a real triumph," I said, and she looked away, her lips white.

"He was going to kill you," she murmured. In her arms, Violet made a soft, high noise.

"Yes," I said. "I think so."

"He was going to kill you," she said. "So that he could be with me. And then he was going to kill me, because he thought he had failed again. That was his solution to both of us."

I put the lid back on the box. "Yes," I said. "Yes, that about sums it up. He would have killed both of us, and buried us in the garden, just like he did with all of the . . . women." I swallowed hard around that word.

They weren't women. They weren't *people*. They weren't *me*.

They were specimens, subjects, bodies, corpses, cadavers, failures, data points. They were biowaste.

But to Nathan, they had been women.

He hadn't created them with a single function in mind. They weren't there to absorb bullets, grow organs, host experimental therapies. They were supposed to be wives. He had created them to live alongside him. Incomplete lives, maybe, but he probably hadn't seen it that way. He'd bought a house, and clothes, and rose bushes for the garden. He'd been trying to make a home and a life with each one of the clones he built, just like he'd tried to make a home and a life with me.

There wasn't a notebook with my name on it. But the reality was that Nathan hadn't thought of me as a different kind of thing than the specimens he buried in his backyard. To him, we were all iterations of the same experiment. We were all vehicles to carry his dreams.

There hadn't been twelve attempts prior to Martine. There had been thirteen.

I was his first failure.

TWENTY-EIGHT

The baby needed so much more from Martine than I could have anticipated. I trailed around the house with the two of them as Martine and I talked about the truth of the man she'd lived with for nearly her entire life. Martine strapped Violet into some complicated tangle of fabric, one that let her wear the baby like a shirt. She said something to me about the necessity of skin-to-skin contact in development, the importance of early bonding.

I like to think that my study of infant development was comprehensive. It was certainly comprehensive enough that I'm capable of building a functional person from raw materials. But I wondered, then, what I was missing. Martine used phrases I'd never encountered, ideas that I now recognize as being part of the attachment theory she'd read about in the books I brought her while we lived together. She'd studied ideas that I'd dismissed as infant-oriented, as too simplistic, as behavioral rather than physiological.

She asked me if I had ever explored the long-term effect of isolation on my clones in their earliest stages of cognitive development. She asked me if I had ever considered letting them meet each other in their first few hours out of sedation.

She asked me if I was sure that they never remembered their conditioning.

I asked her questions in return, and she answered them with a greater degree of patience than I'd ever shown her in the lab. She turned out to have studied harder than I'd realized. She described a vast labyrinth of interweaving parenting models to me, described the theories behind each, explained the logic behind several of the choices she'd made. "I never had parents," she explained, and hearing her voice was like listening to a taped version of one of my own lectures. She was confident, authoritative.

Certain.

"I don't have my own model to work from. I don't have any built-in ideas about what works and what doesn't."

She stroked the back of Violet's head through the swathe of cloth that held it upright. With her other hand, she held up a finger, then turned and vanished back toward the nursery. When she returned, she was holding a yellow notebook with her own name on the cover.

"Actually," she murmured, "I might be wrong about that." She tossed the notebook onto the kitchen island, the same one where she'd been cutting onions the night the original Nathan had died. "Nathan programmed me with ideas about what's important and what's not. He gave me my priorities." She drummed her fingers on the notebook cover, chewed her lip in a twitchy way that I didn't recognize. A new habit she'd picked up in the time since I'd last seen her. Her eyes had gone distant. I waited as she studied the cover, tracing the ascender in the letter M over and over. Finally, she nodded, her decision made. "I'm reading it," she said.

"Is that a good idea?" I asked.

She nodded again, and it was the kind of authoritative gesture that didn't leave room for disagreement. "Yes," she said. "It is a good idea. That's why I'm going to do it."

She didn't offer any explanation, didn't leave any spaces into which I could wedge doubt. I felt caught in a strange trap of my own making—I'd wanted to argue with her, wanted to undermine her certainty enough that I might then be able to change her mind. But she wasn't prepared to have her mind changed.

She wasn't talking like *her*. She was talking like *me*.

In that moment, she was subtly demanding that I treat her as though she knew what she wanted. As though she didn't have any need for my approval. On some level, I'd still been thinking of her as a child; she was asking me to extend her at least some measure of the respect I might show to a peer.

So I did. I asked her to help me understand her reasoning.

"I want to know why I'm making the choices I'm making," she said, stroking the long hummock of Violet's swaddled back. "It's about Violet, but it's also not. I'm just——" She peeked under the edge of the cloth, smiled at the baby's face, and let the cloth fall back into place. When she looked back up at me, there was something arranged about her expression. Her resolve was formal, practiced. "I know that I'm responding to my programming a lot of the time, but I want to feel like I'm deciding whether or not to let it guide me." She gave her head a tiny shake and tried again. "No. I don't just want to *feel* like I'm deciding. I want to *decide*. I have a choice, and I'm going to exercise it."

All at once, I understood why she was being so formal, so rigid. Why she seemed prepared for a fight.

She was going to do something that went against my work.

But I hadn't been the one to program her. I could have argued that it didn't matter what she did, because if she managed to make decisions that went against her programming, then it was a sign of Nathan's poor craftsmanship, and nothing more.

I would have been lying to myself.

Nathan had done good work in Martine, and if she succeeded in bucking off her programming, she would be proving that my methods weren't ironclad.

She was going to try to prove that she was her own person.

To agree with her goal was to admit that her aims were valid; to disagree was to admit that her very desire for self-realization was a threat to my entire body of work. If this was a contest of wills, then I had already lost.

She was being brave. I nodded to her, placed my own hand on the notebook beside hers. Our knuckles had the same topography, but her hands weren't identical to mine. They had more calluses than I did, more tiny scars. Shorter fingernails. Our hands were a reflection of the time we each spent sowing our harvests—her in the garden, with her fists in the earth, and me in the lab, protected by gloves.

She was a thing that I could so easily have been. I couldn't begrudge her the opportunity to find out who she was capable of becoming.

"Okay," I said. "Let me know if you need help understanding any of it."

She peeked under the fabric again. From my angle, leaning forward across the kitchen island, I could see the soft curl of the baby's ear, her white-blond hair. Her scalp was laced with blue veins, visible through the thin layer of down.

"Finally," Martine breathed. "She's out."

"Already?" I glanced at the clock on the oven, trying to remember what time it had been when I arrived. Martine had said, then, that we only had a few hours. How long had the baby been awake? How soon would Nathan be home?

"It's like this in the afternoon," she said. "She's usually only awake for an hour or so between naps. She'll wake up for longer later." She began the work of unwrapping the fabric that held the baby to her chest. "Normally I'd just wear her around while she sleeps, but we should fix the yard, yes? I'll put her down. It'll only take a minute. She'll cry a bit—she always does, when I put her down. But it'll only take a minute and then she'll be out again."

She disappeared to the back of the house. I eyed the notebook on the counter and listened to the muffled sounds of Martine putting the baby into the crib, the wail that rose and then quickly fell again. I was seized by a powerful urge to destroy the notebook, to light all four of the burners on the gas stove and hold the pages over it until the climbing flames reached my too-soft fingertips. I gripped the edge of the counter to keep myself from doing it, reminded myself that it wasn't my place to protect Martine from herself in this. She wasn't my responsibility. She wasn't even my *relative*.

I didn't bother thinking about the part of me that wanted the notebook gone so I could protect myself, preserve my research. There was no profit in that level of honesty.

It didn't matter what I wanted. Not now, not about this.

I had to let Martine choose.

I heard the door to the nursery open and shut, the latch muted. I knew Martine's method precisely—the way she would grip the doorknob in her palm before letting her fingers fall onto the backside of it, the smooth, careful turn. The way she would ease the door shut all the way before slowly, so slowly, turning the knob back. No snaps or clicks, no sudden sounds to draw notice or wake a sleeper.

I had perfected the method while my father was alive, to protect myself. Martine had perfected it since the birth of her child, so that the baby would stay asleep. The air around me shivered with the sameness of her, and with the absolute difference of her.

She was padding down the hall, her footsteps soft on the carpet. I forced myself to breathe deep and slow. I forced that doorknob out of my mind. Now wasn't the time to be thinking about my father, not with all those bodies in the garden.

Not that the bodies in the garden made it easy to stop thinking of my father.

Inhale four, exhale five, keep it together. Poise, Evelyn. That's the way.

By the time she got to the kitchen, I'd collected myself. I tucked my father back where he belonged, let the roots of my breathing grow thick around him until he was safely out of sight and I could think straight.

"Okay," I said as Martine entered the room, "how long do we have to get the garden back in order?"

She looked at me blankly. "As long as we want," she said.

I remembered the last time I'd underestimated her intelligence in this kitchen, checked my impulse to think of her as stupid and slow. "Well," I said carefully, "we had better get it done before Nathan gets home and, you know. Sees the bodies. He won't have a memory of them, and he'll probably freak out."

Martine laughed, a lovely fluting laugh that didn't have anything to do with my own. "Oh, that!" She shook her head and smiled at me. "We don't need to worry about that. We don't need to worry about Nathan at all."

"No?" I said, starting to smile a little too, unable to help myself, even though I didn't quite understand why she was laughing. Her certainty was contagious.

"Of course not," she said, reaching out to clasp my hands in hers. "Because the second he walks through that door, he's going to die."

TWENTY-NINE

I looked between Martine's fever-bright eyes, my heart sinking.
I realized too late how badly I'd misread her. I'd thought she
was handling things well, that her initial panic had given way to
practicality. At worst, I had thought she was staying calm for the
baby.

But that wasn't it at all.

She was calm because she had already decided what to do about
it all. She was calm because she had a solution in mind.

"We can't. Martine. That's not the right answer." I said it
slowly, trying to keep my voice clear enough to remind her that
I was rational. That listening to me was a good idea. I needed to
cut through her certainty, needed to undermine the comfort she
was finding in the idea of killing Nathan. "We can't just kill him."

"Yes, we *can*," she said, squeezing my hands in hers as if she were
giving me a much-needed pep talk. She was still smiling that serene
smile, the one that said not to worry, it would all be okay. "We
installed the killswitch, remember? We installed it for something
just like this. All I have to do is say the trigger phrase, and it'll
all be fixed. Right?"

"No, that's—we installed the killswitch in case he tried to
hurt you." She sounded so reasonable, so certain, that I found
myself scrambling for a foothold in my own reality. *That's why we
installed the killswitch, just to keep Martine safe,* I reminded myself
frantically. *She's wrong. This is all wrong.* "We installed it in case you
were in danger."

"We installed the killswitch in case I was in danger." She

dropped my hands. "Well, I'm in danger. He's a murderer. He's a . . . a murderer, he's a *serial killer!*" She took a step back from me and pointed toward the backyard. She wasn't shouting, not yet, but panic was starting to boil in her voice. "Or didn't you notice all the corpses in the yard?"

"Please be sensible about this," I said, folding my arms.

She shook her head. The finger that pointed to the yard began to tremble. "No," she said, "no, don't tell me to be sensible, don't tell me to be reasonable, don't tell me I'm *crazy*, I'm not—those are bodies! Those are bodies and they look like *me*, he's a murderer, he tried to—" Her voice broke, and she lowered her hand, wrapped her arms around herself. "He tried to murder *me*."

She looked around the kitchen, her eyes brimming, her lips white. I could imagine what she was seeing: *There is the knife block, there is the place where I was cutting the onions, there is the place where he put his hands around my throat and tried to squeeze the words right out of me. There is the place where I stabbed him the first time, and the second, and the third.*

There is the place where he died, and it was probably the place where some of them died, and it could have been the place where I died.

"It wasn't him," I whispered. I stepped toward Martine, and she stepped back, away from me. Her grip on her own arms was merciless. There would be bruises later, I was sure.

"It was," she said. She was still staring at the kitchen floor. There was no bloodstain, but I don't doubt that she remembered the contours of the pool as well as I did.

"It wasn't." I ducked my head to try to catch her eyes. "It wasn't him. It was the original. We can't kill this one for something he didn't do. Please," I repeated, "be *sensible*."

She was breathing hard and fast through her nose. There was a scream building in her, I could see it—but she didn't let it loose into the room. Instead, she spun on her heel and strode out of the kitchen, her steps so fast that she may as well have been running. I said her name, but she didn't turn back, didn't answer. I heard the back door open and close, and then I was alone in the house with the faint music that came from behind the closed door of the nursery.

By the time I got to the backyard, Martine already had the shovel in her hands. She was flinging soil hard and fast, covering the most-exposed corpse, the one with the helixed mandible. She finished burying that one briskly, stepped over it with one decisive stride, and got to work on the next. I stood on the back porch, watching her toss shovelfuls of earth over the second body.

It had been the worst wrong thing to say. Even then, I could understand that much. Asking her to be sensible was a mistake. It was the thing she least wanted to hear in her moment of terror— that her fear was baseless.

But it *was* baseless. The Nathan who would be home from work in just a few hours wasn't the same monster that had killed Martine's predecessors. As far as he knew, he was a man who had been dissatisfied with his wife, and had proven himself a brilliant scientist, and had successfully made himself a new partner. He thought he had someone better this time, someone who wanted a baby and a nice house with a lovely garden. A second chance.

He thought he loved her. He thought she loved him.

That was who Martine and I had thought the original Nathan was, and so that was who this new Nathan thought he was.

But Martine couldn't seem to see that.

I could understand, objectively. Her position was an exceptionally difficult one. But now was not the time for her to indulge in fear and irrationality. We just didn't have time for this.

When she started burying the third body, I crossed the garden to join her. I breathed through my mouth, shallow as I could, but the smell of turned earth was invasive, inescapable. I forced myself to wade through it. *Forward, Evelyn,* I told myself. *Always forward.*

"You don't care," she said, as soon as I was within earshot. "He's a murderer and you don't care at all." She dug the shovel into the loose soil once every few seconds, and the patter of falling earth punctuated her words. "You're probably glad. He'll take care of all your problems if you just wait long enough, right?"

I bit back irritation, reminded myself that these weren't just the hysterical antics of a petulant child. The original Nathan *did* try to kill her, after all. That had obviously traumatized her in ways that I hadn't considered after that first night. She had never processed any of it, not that she'd told me.

She had a right to be upset. I told myself that as if the telling could make me believe it too.

"You know I don't feel that way," I said. I reached out and grabbed the shovel. She didn't let go of it at first. She tugged hard, nearly toppled me over—but we were matched for strength, and after a tense few seconds, her shoulders went slack. She sagged to the ground, still clutching the shovel. I let it go. It fell across her lap as she sat, hard, between two of the still-open graves.

"I know you don't feel that way," she agreed. She looked up at me, her face as broken as a dropped egg. "But it's still *true,* isn't it? The first Nathan was a murderer. I lived with him for two and a half years, I trusted him, I—" Her grip on the shovel tightened. "I slept with him. I got pregnant with his baby. And the whole time, they were out here." She waved her hands broadly enough to indicate the whole yard, not just the graves. There were other holes scattered through the yard, shallow ones, and I realized that she must have been searching for the boundaries of her discovery— trying to see if her entire garden was planted on a necropolis. "They were out here and he was ready, all along. All that time, he was ready to put me out here too."

I looked down at her, kneeling there in the soil with the shovel across her thighs like a penitent. There was some comfort that I was supposed to offer her, some way I was supposed to absolve her of this terrible knowledge. She was looking up at me as though I could possibly understand what she was going through, and I didn't want to understand, I didn't want to join her down there.

But I did.

I knelt beside her, felt the dirt embed itself in the fabric of my pants the instant my knees touched the ground. The word "ruined" glowed bright in my mind. I told myself that it didn't matter.

Things get ruined sometimes. That's just how it is.

"I know," I said. "I know how you feel. He was going to kill me, too. Remember?"

She slumped forward over the shovel. Then, quiet as a dying breath, she asked, "And would you be able to live with him, now? Knowing that?"

My face went numb at the thought of it. Of moving into this house with the new Nathan, knowing that the man his DNA had come from had planned to kill me, to plant me in this garden bed beside his other failures. "That's different," I said. It tasted dishonest before it even left my mouth.

Martine didn't bother to argue with me. I think she knew that I knew the flavor of that particular lie just as well as I did. She let the shovel fall to the ground in front of her, and she sank her hands into the earth on either side of her knees. "You couldn't do it. You couldn't live with him, knowing what you know. And I can't either," she said.

"But this version of Nathan," I said desperately, "he . . . he doesn't even *know*. If we bury these bodies, and we put the rose-bushes back, he'll never *have* to know. We didn't program him to think of murder as a solution. He's never killed anyone before."

"But he has killed before," she said. "On some level, he has. It's stamped into him somewhere. It's got to be." She made fists, compressing palmfuls of soil and dropping them, scooping up more loose earth. "This kind of thing doesn't just leave a person, even if you make a new version of them. He can't just be fresh and clean. It's not fair to them, is it? For him to get to keep going as if he didn't do anything wrong?"

I shook my head, resisted the urge to reach out and brush dirt from the fabric of her skirt. "How is this different?"

"Different from what?"

I reminded myself again—and again, and again—that she

wasn't stupid. She wasn't slow. Still, I could hear myself getting impatient, could see her registering the irritation in my voice. The more I spoke, the more I needed to speak, and the more I spoke, the more defensive the set of her mouth got. I couldn't stop myself, though. I couldn't hold it back.

And maybe I didn't try very hard.

"How is this any different from the way it was before? You *knew* he was a murderer, you knew he wanted to kill you. You knew he was *awful*. You can't say that it's just because he was awful to someone other than you, either, because you knew that part already too." Anger, hot and biting, flooded the back of my throat like a bolus of morphine—because this at last was the real thing. This was the splinter lodged beneath my thumbnail. This was the thing I could not stand. "You knew that he was awful to *me*. So why is this different? Why does this suddenly make it so you can't be here anymore?"

She clenched her fists in the soil a few more times before she answered me. She cocked her head, looking at me, her face hardening into grim lines I'd never seen her wear before. Finally, she let out a breath before saying, "Because they didn't deserve it."

I rocked back on my heels. "What?"

"None of them deserved what they got," she said. She brushed her palms against each other, raining dirt. "They failed because *he* failed. But me and you, we failed all on our own, didn't we? We failed on purpose."

I wanted so badly to rage at her. I wanted to push her down onto the ground, wanted to grind her hair into the dirt and scream *how dare you how dare you how dare you*—but I couldn't, because hadn't I thought the exact same thing a hundred times? Hadn't I sat on the floor of my town house with an open bottle of wine, thinking that I'd let Nathan down just as much as I possibly could?

I couldn't answer her with anger, because the anger died before I could even fully feel it. Instead, I tried to answer her the way I wished I could answer myself.

"No," I said. "We failed him because there was no way not to. I would have broken myself if I tried to be the thing he wanted me to be. You would have broken yourself if you had kept on trying to ignore the things he wanted you to ignore." She shook her head ruefully, but I kept going. "It's not just that we didn't deserve what he did. It's—I think we would have been dead either way. Even if we were still breathing, even if we were still aboveground, we would have been dead. *I* would have been dead. And I'm pretty sure you would have too."

Martine wilted. She lifted her hands as if to bury her face in them, then stopped with her palms a few inches from her face, seeming to notice for the first time how filthy they were. She let them drop again and hung her head.

She looked exhausted. I thought of her exacting sleep schedule, wondered how often the baby woke her in the night. There was no catching up, for her. This was just how tired she was going to have to be.

"I can't even be what I was made for," she said softly. "He put all that work in, and I still can't be a thing that he would have been satisfied with. If I can't even get that right, then what am I *for?*"

I didn't know how to answer her. She wasn't technically incorrect. She was a made thing, and she had failed to fulfill her purpose, but that was all wrong. She needed to hear something different. I couldn't sort out why it felt backward, couldn't figure out what I was supposed to say to her. It hit me afresh how absurd this situation was—I was comforting a specimen about the fact of its own existence. I was talking to Martine as if she were a person.

I had started to think of her as a person.

And I couldn't stop.

I tried to tell myself otherwise. I reminded myself of the truth about every specimen I had to dispose of: it's like a stopped watch, it's like an apple with a worm in it, it's no good and there's no use for it the way it is. But Martine's tears were making soft divots in the soil in front of her, and I wanted to reach for her, and it made me dizzy because she was just a thing, she was just a *broken thing*. But she was a broken thing that looked and sounded exactly like me.

"This Nathan doesn't know that you're a failure," I said at last. Maybe I should have argued with her, told her that she wasn't a failure, but it would have been a lie, and it didn't matter, anyway. "He doesn't know that there were ever any attempts before you. He doesn't know about any of this. You can have a perfectly good life with him."

"Or," she said, "we can killswitch him, and it will look like he died of natural causes, and I can have a perfectly good life here with Violet."

I couldn't do this part anymore. I couldn't sit and argue with her, couldn't comfort her, couldn't keep breathing in that loam-smell. It was suffocating, all of it, and it felt like my mouth and throat and lungs were slowly filling with rich, dark soil. It was going to kill me.

So I stood up, trying fruitlessly to brush the dirt from my legs. I held out my hands and she took them, pulling herself to her feet. "We can't kill him," I said.

"Why not?" she asked simply, stooping to grab the shovel.

I didn't have a ready answer. *Because murder is wrong* didn't fit; by my own rationale, he was a clone just like any other. If he'd come out wrong, I wouldn't have hesitated to encourage Martine to use the killswitch. *Because he didn't do anything wrong* didn't work, either—Martine couldn't hear that, wouldn't accept that he wasn't a murderer at the cellular level.

I tried for another angle that might work, one that would leave her feeling whole when she climbed into their bed next to him at the end of the day.

"If we kill him," I said slowly, "how are we any different from the original Nathan?"

She stared at me, holding the shovel in a loose, slack grip, as though she'd nearly forgotten it. After a moment, she turned and started reburying the third body. She was moving more slowly now, less frantic. She wasn't burning off panic; she was tidying up. It seemed somehow reflexive, self-soothing. This time, I didn't stop her from her work.

"I don't think you want me to answer that," she said. "Not really. I think you're hoping you'll change my mind, but I don't think you want me to answer your question."

I shoved my dirty hands into my pockets, feeling clumsy. She was right, which was bad. I could feel the situation slipping away from me. She had my motives pinned down, and she knew what button to press to derail me.

I didn't care for that feeling at all.

Worse, it was going to work. I knew what she was doing, but I couldn't fight it. "Tell me the answer," I said, knowing that hearing the answer would only make things feel more wrong.

She hesitated, then shrugged, still shoveling soil over the third body. "I don't think you're different from him," she said. "I think you make people and you dispose of them when it suits you, just like he did. I think that if this had all taken place inside a lab, and if his victims didn't look just like you? You wouldn't be conflicted about it at all. You wouldn't think he'd done anything wrong."

She used the back of her shovel to tamp down the earth over the body, then turned around and began working on the fourth. I didn't have an answer for her, didn't have an argument. She kept saying things that were true and I hated her for it, hated her with the reflexive venom of a child who's been tattled on. But there was nothing I could say. She knew me better than I knew her. She knew me so much more than I wanted her to.

Since there was nothing for me to say, I went to the garden shed, and I grabbed the second shovel, the small one Martine had used to help me bury Nathan. I got to work on the fifth body, and then we buried the sixth together, and then the seventh. We didn't speak until we were at the eleventh. I stepped carefully, trying not to let my feet land too close to the last, most-exposed corpse.

"If you think we shouldn't kill him," Martine said evenly, "then you must have a better idea. He'll be home in, what, four hours? And I can't stay here with him tonight. I'll do what I have to do, but I won't sleep next to him again."

I paused in my shoveling, because I didn't have a better idea. I didn't have a solution that could beat out murder for permanence and efficiency. She knew that, just like she knew everything else.

I was so tired of arguing that part of me thought maybe we *should* just kill the new Nathan. I could pretend to be stopping by for some reason, act like I found him, cold. I could tuck Martine and the baby away while the police took away the body. I didn't know what would happen to the house, but——

"He hasn't done anything wrong," I said, and I was flooded with relief, because it was so much more clear than I'd been telling myself it was.

It was selfish, but it was clear.

And I knew how to be selfish. I knew how to protect my own interests, how to treat myself as my own chief priority. This thing with Martine, it didn't have to be a moral dilemma. It didn't have to be a struggle between her opinion of me and my opinion of myself. It didn't have to be about right or wrong.

I drank that clarity down like cold champagne. It didn't have to be about right or wrong. I didn't have to figure out what was right.

I just had to make it about me.

"I haven't done anything wrong either," Martine replied coolly. "But this still——"

"No, you don't understand," I interrupted. "We pulled off something impossible, making him. We shouldn't have succeeded at this. It was such a long shot, such a reach, and it *worked*. We did it. I might not ever be able to publish a paper on it, I might not ever be able to tell anyone, but I won't let you kill him. He's my best work."

She laughed, a sudden brittle laugh. "Your best work," she said, incredulous, almost giddy. "Of course. What was I thinking? We can't possibly undermine your progress that way."

"I mean it," I said, tossing a shovelful of earth over the lifeless, slack-skinned face of Nathan's eleventh attempt. *Katrina,* my memory whispered. *Her name was Katrina.* "He's the pinnacle of—stop laughing." I used the back of my shovel to tamp down the loose soil of the grave. Martine moved toward the twelfth corpse, Laila, the one that still had eyes and lips, uneaten by the beetles and worms whose work it would have been to work away at the softest parts of her. I moved in front of her, stood in her way so she had to stop. I leveled a stare at her that I usually reserved for lab assistants I was about to fire. Cold, logical, direct, merciless. *That's the way.*

"You're serious," she said. She folded her arms across her chest, but there was only so much fight in her.

If I pushed just a little harder, I knew she would topple.

"I gutted myself making this version of Nathan for you," I said, trying to summon the cold, ruthless certainty with which my father had eyed the cast on my wrist. "I'll never be able to tell anyone about him, and I'll never win an award for him," I said, "but I will not let you destroy him the way you destroyed everything else I've spent my life building." Then, lower, letting her hear that note of quiet danger I'd used to keep her from leaping out of my car: "This isn't up for any further debate. I'm not asking you, Martine. I'm telling you."

It was enough to break her budding defiance. She kept her arms crossed, but her shoulders rose into a protective hunch. I felt a sense of cold satisfaction. I'd won. I'd crushed her just enough to remind her of the person she'd been before she met me, before she'd killed her husband, before she'd learned the details of how she was made.

It was power. I had given her that independence, and I could take it back.

Guilt came fast on the heels of that rush of power, but it wasn't the time. I pushed the shame into my cheek so I could talk around it. I could feel remorse later. For now: victory. That was all that mattered.

She looked past me to the last unburied body. Laila. Her face was turned away from us, one cheek resting on the inside of that plastic bag. I was thankful that I didn't have to look at her empty eyes. I couldn't avoid seeing the narrow collar of bruising that ringed her throat, though. It was stark and purple, set high. The place where the bottom of the bag had been, where she'd struggled against it as she suffocated.

"We should finish," Martine murmured. "We should bury her before he gets home. If I'm going to have to stay with him, I don't want to have to answer questions from him about this. I need that, at least."

I chewed on the inside of my cheek, and the guilt was there, I couldn't dodge it, but there was something else there too.

An idea.

"Actually," I said slowly, a plan coalescing in my mind like flesh in amnio, "I don't think we should bury her. I think there might be a way to let Nathan live, but get you out of here."

Her eyes didn't brighten. She looked at me as though looking at me were a responsibility, just another item on an endless list of tasks, and she might as well check this one off now.

The cold satisfaction I'd felt at my victory curdled. It was rotten, all of it. All my callous resolve, all my stern determination, all the ends that I used to justify the means.

This was not a victory. There was no triumph in reminding a broken thing that it was broken.

I wanted more than anything in that moment to hide in my bedroom with the door locked. I wanted to hunch over a pile of brochures that promised an escape from the person who knew that I had my father in me. My mother, at least, had offered me that exit.

But there was no escape from this. I couldn't run, couldn't hide, couldn't stay away over the holidays just in case. I couldn't turn away from Martine.

I had done precisely the damage I set out to do. I'd wanted the advantage badly enough to let the monstrous seed of cruelty in me push up shoots, and now that I had that advantage, I needed to use it.

I could fix her later. When there was more time.

"We need to get her inside," I said, tossing my shovel to the ground. Martine nodded, dull-eyed. She waited for me to move before she stepped toward the open grave. I forced myself to pay attention to the task at hand. *Forward.* "Get her ankles," I instructed, looking only at the band of purple around Laila's throat. "We don't have much time."

CHAPTER
THIRTY

I was not unused to bathing lifeless specimens. It was a standard part of the autopsy process. In fairness, it was a task I most often left to my assistants—the work of rinsing congealed amniotic gel from the cooling skin of a corpse was never going to be the best use of my time—but I was familiar with the strange work of it, the gentle practicality required to move a limp body without breaking it in the process.

Having that experience made the process of washing Laila familiar. Once we finished maneuvering her into the tub, it was almost comforting, doing this work I already understood. We cut off her half-rotted clothes and tossed them into the sink to keep the dirt from scattering. I used the handheld showerhead extension to rinse her down, sluicing water over her skin until the water running down the drain between her feet was close to clear.

Martine helped me to lather Laila's limbs with the same sweet-smelling vanilla soap I'd used to wash Nathan's blood from my hands. I used a lot of it, sweeping my hands in tight circles over her skin, trying to lift the death away from her.

When I rinsed the soap away, she almost looked new. She hadn't been conditioned any more than Martine had. Her skin was smooth and pale, unfreckled, unscarred. She didn't even have calluses on her fingers.

I wondered how long she had lived before Nathan decided that she would not suffice.

I didn't usually wash the hair of specimens who were ready

for autopsy; that, I think, was the strangest part. I was accustomed to rinsing their hair, usually before shaving it off, to make it easier to examine their skin and bones and brains. But I never washed it, never combed it out. I couldn't remember ever having done that work for anyone, alive or not. It felt wrong, too intimate. Too close.

But Laila's hair was matted with dirt, and the water simply wasn't enough, so I had no choice but to figure it out. I clumsily lifted her head a few times, trying to figure out how to work shampoo into her hair. Her neck was loose and her skull was heavy and it was all too cumbersome. I dropped her, and her head hit the bottom of the tub with a resonant *thunk*.

"May I?" Martine asked softly. I moved aside to make room for her. She leaned into the tub and cradled the back of Laila's head in both hands, letting her fingers tangle in the clone's damp hair. She leaned down, and it looked for all the world like she was going to kiss the dead woman. Then she slid one of her hands down under Laila's shoulders, using the other to support the head, and lifted her smoothly into a sitting position.

I remember thinking, irritably, that this wasn't a solution. That I wouldn't be able to reach around Martine to wash Laila's hair. That she was solving the wrong problem.

But then, Martine climbed into the bathtub and sat down behind the woman who had come before her. The fabric of her skirt began to darken as it wicked up water from the bottom of the tub, from Laila's skin. She splayed her legs on either side of Laila's hips, used her palms to prop up the clone's limp shoulders. "There," she said. She didn't look at me, just kept her eyes on the limp forward-sway of Laila's head. "That should be easier."

I swallowed hard before continuing. Martine was as tender with Laila's body as she had been with Violet. I worked a palmful of shampoo into Laila's hair—it was longer than Martine's, and I remember making a mental note that we would need to trim it. Her chin rested on her chest, and the lather ran down into her face. I flinched when it flooded across the lids of her closed eyes, then shook my head at myself for reacting as though she might tear up at the sting of it.

Rinsing out her mouth was the hardest part.

I couldn't bring myself to ask Martine to do it for me—couldn't explain to her why it was so hard. So I didn't ask. I just swallowed bile and panic, and I reached into Laila's mouth with my fingers and scooped out soil from between her teeth. Her tongue was dry under my touch, as dry as the skin of her face. Dirt rained down into her lap, just as it had rained down from Martine's palms in the garden. As it met the water that had beaded up on Laila's legs, it turned to mud, and I scolded myself for not having done this part first.

But I could not have done it first.

When her mouth was empty at last, I used the showerhead to rinse her teeth and tongue. It wasn't enough. There was dirt stuck to her gums, between her teeth. I kept rinsing and rinsing, but I knew that this was a waste of time, and after a few minutes of trying, I sat back on my heels.

Martine looked at me, waiting. Her eyes were still flat, but they sparked a little when I asked if she had a spare toothbrush.

When we were finished washing Laila, we toweled the body dry as gently as we could. Her skin wasn't in nearly as good condition as Martine's was, obviously, and her neck was awful. But her face had been preserved well by the plastic bag, and the rest of her was in excellent condition. That, of course, was when I decided that it was necessary to commit more time to studying the effects of telomere financing on decay. All the time we spent washing Laila's body, as I combed conditioner through her wet hair and flooded her mouth with water so the toothpaste would foam on her teeth and patted her eyelids with the corner of a towel—I spent all that time mentally structuring the research grant I would write, outlining a proposal. I spent that time calculating how many assistants that project would need.

I did not spend that time thinking about the work that I was doing. I did not spend that time wondering how different from

Laila I would look if I had been in the ground for three years, my face protected only by a plastic bag. I thought about the research instead.

When we finished, we had two hours left to prepare.

"I have a question about this plan," Martine said as we worked. She waited for me to nod before she continued. "Won't—when they find her, won't they know she's been dead for a long time? She looks okay on the outside, but as soon as anyone looks too close . . ."

I picked up a pair of scissors, eyed Martine's newly short hair. As I started to comb and cut Laila's hair, I nodded. "But no one is going to look too close. Nathan will panic. He'll try to hide her. You're illegal, remember? You aren't supposed to exist. He's not supposed to have you. He knows that, and since he doesn't know that he's ever killed one of you before, he wouldn't know what it looks like when one of you dies. For all he knows, the instant a clone dies, it liquefies."

Martine glanced back and forth between the loosely knotted rope in her hands and the scissors in mine. "I hope this works," she murmured.

"It will." I said it as though I could be certain.

We dressed Laila in Martine's clothes. Martine stood with her hands under Laila's armpits, lifting her to eye-level, and I reached my arms around from the front to fasten the hooks of a nursing bra behind the clone's back. We put her in one of Martine's nicer dresses, green with pale yellow flowers, because the sleeves were long enough and the neckline was high enough to cover the lividity where blood had pooled in her arms and back. She had been buried in her clothes; I didn't foresee Nathan trying to strip her naked this time, either.

We pushed aside the coats that hung on the sturdy wooden dowel in the front-hall closet, pushed them all the way to the sides of the closet. We stood back-to-back in the middle of that closet, each of us pushing at the coats with both hands, crushing them as flat as we could.

Martine hung the noose, and I looped it around Laila's neck. We lined it up until it matched that narrow ring of purple, tightened it hard so it would stay in place. Martine made a small, high sound when the rope dug deep into Laila's skin.

For reasons I still don't understand, that sound made me want to loosen the rope. Everything else, I had been able to stand—but that sound, that small aborted whimper, made me want to cut Laila free.

"This isn't fair to her," Martine said. "None of this is."

"I know," I said. The part of me that was willing to see Laila as a person—as a woman, as a part of a peculiar estranged family I'd never known I had—felt the terrible injustice of this. Laila had been born, hidden away, murdered, and buried, and she still wasn't finished. She still wasn't free.

I tried hard, so hard, to listen only to the part of me that saw her as a specimen. A specimen is born to serve a purpose. It dies when that function is fulfilled, or if it can't do its job. What happens to it after it dies doesn't matter, doesn't carry moral weight.

But in that moment, with Laila on the floor in front of the coat closet? *It doesn't matter* felt less like an objective fact, and more like a thing I told myself to justify the life I led, the work I did. I couldn't swallow back the way it felt wrong. I couldn't tell Martine to let it go, to forget it, to just get the work done. Because we had dressed up a corpse that looked just like her, had dressed the body in her clothes, had used her shampoo to make sure that it smelled the way she did. Because that corpse had my genes.

Laila was dead, and Laila had our face, and Martine was right: It wasn't fair. It wasn't fair to any of us.

Martine hauled Laila upright. She wrapped her arms tight around the clone's thighs and, panting, held her up high. I stood on a stepladder and tied the loose end of the rope to the dowel in the closet. One knot, then two, then three. As sturdy as I could make it.

Martine eased Laila down slowly, lowering her until the rope was taut. She was breathless, her forehead beaded with sweat. I wasn't sure if I could have lifted my own bodyweight the way she just had, not alone. Where had that strength come from?

Laila's toes nearly brushed the floor.

The dowel creaked ominously, but it held, at least for now. If it broke, so be it—he would find her on the ground.

There was something dreamlike about seeing her there. Over the course of the months I worked with Martine to make Nathan, I had grown accustomed to seeing my own face wearing unfamiliar expressions. Sleeping, eating, vomiting. The corpses in the ground had been uniquely terrible, but they were wrong enough that I could separate myself from them.

But this—this was different. Laila looked so much like me, so much like Martine, and her face was peaceful, and she was unmistakably dead.

I told myself that there was no time for reflection, and I turned my back to her.

There was still so much left to do.

We threw Laila's old clothes into a trash bag, swept up the dirt that Martine had tracked into the house before my arrival. We slipped out to the backyard, finished filling in the last open grave and the shallow, halfhearted holes in the lawn. We righted the rosebushes. We planted the apple trees over the graves, so that Nathan wouldn't question the tilled part of the garden. We even watered them, so they would grow. We did it all as Martine would have done it, were she committed to completing every item on her itinerary before sending herself away into the dark.

It would have been an impressive afternoon's work, all by itself. But the sun was low in the sky, and Nathan was already late getting home, and there was no time left to admire our handiwork.

"Okay," I said. "It's time to go. Are you ready?"

Martine stared at me, then walked into the house. She came back out a few minutes later with Violet wrapped tight against her chest, the box of yellow notebooks in her arms.

"Oh," I said, because I had forgotten. How could I have forgotten? But of course I had——I focused on the work, and I paid attention to my goal, and I forgot about the baby.

"Martine," I said, looking at Violet and wishing she would figure it out on her own. But she didn't, and I had to tell her. There was no time to soften it. There was no time to hesitate and flutter and be gentle. Still, I tried to be kind. I tried to tell her without cruelty. "Martine. We can't take Violet with us."

She looked at me blankly. "What?"

"We can't take her," I said, and I remember it like I remember the deep aching *crack* of my wrist breaking when I was a child. That moment, when Martine's face fell as I told her that she would need to leave her baby behind——that was the moment when I began to hate myself. Not before, not even when I'd been cruel to her, not even when I'd broken her for my own convenience.

When I told her that we had to leave Violet behind, it was obvious to me that she didn't understand yet why the baby had to stay behind. She looked sad and confused and a little angry. But she didn't look surprised. She didn't know why we couldn't bring her child with us, but she didn't seem surprised that I would tell her something so painful and, to her, unnecessary.

I couldn't blame her for expecting that from me.

"Nathan's going to expect the baby to be there when he gets home," I explained. It wasn't possible to explain this to her in a way that wouldn't hurt her more, because the more I explained, the more she would see that I was right. I walked toward her slowly, like she might spook and run off if I startled her. "Even if you're dead," I continued——then, seeing her face, I quickly amended that to "even if he *thinks* you're dead. When he finds Laila's body, the first thing he's going to do is run to check on the baby. If she's not there, he'll know that something doesn't add up."

Her eyes darted around the backyard as though she would be able to find something there that might prove me wrong. But, of course, there was nothing. I was right, and she knew it. The baby had to stay behind. There was no reason for Violet to be gone, and there was no chance that Nathan would decide not to go looking for answers.

Our plan relied on him deciding not to look for answers. And, although I didn't need to mention it to Martine, it struck me that leaving him to raise a baby on his own would help our cause. He would be exhausted and overwhelmed. He would decide it wasn't worth his time to investigate what would look to him like a simple suicide.

I eased the box of yellow notebooks from Martine's arms.

"You should put her back," I said. "You should put her in her crib, and you should probably say goodbye. And then we *have to go.*"

I will not try to describe the way her face crumpled before the first of her tears fell. I will not try to capture the way it felt, knowing that no matter what I did, some part of her would always blame me for this feeling.

I will not try to explain it.

I will never forget it, either.

I let her go into the house on her own. A minute or two after she walked inside, I heard Violet begin to cry. It was the same kind of wail as before, when Martine had put her baby into the crib as I stood in the kitchen and contemplated destroying the notebook that contained her blueprints.

But this time, the wail didn't die down. It rose, siren-like. It seemed to grow in size and weight, and as Martine walked back through the door into the backyard, it became grating, panicked, oppressively loud.

It was almost loud enough to cover the sound of the garage door opening.

"I left her," Martine said. Tears streamed down her cheeks continuously, and her voice was raw, but her face was placid. She wrapped her arms around herself and dug her fingernails into her skin, hard, deep, cruel. "I didn't—I couldn't stand it, I couldn't stay in there and get her to go back to sleep, I couldn't sing to her, I just had to—"

Inside the house, a door opened and then closed again. Just under the sound of Violet's howls, I could make out Nathan calling a greeting to Martine.

We didn't have much time. He was in the house, and it would only be a few seconds before he found Laila's corpse.

"Martine, we have to go. We have to go now," I said. She looked at me with wide, numb eyes. "He's home," I said, and she nodded slowly, and I knew that she wasn't hearing me at all.

I grabbed her by the elbow and dragged her behind me to the side of the house, to the garden gate. We slipped out and I pulled her with me, down the block to where I had parked my car. I put her into the passenger seat and leaned across her to buckle her in. The whole time, I could still hear Violet crying, crying, crying.

Then, just as I opened the driver's side door to get in, the crying stopped. He must have found the body, and then he must have gone to the baby. Violet was not alone anymore.

She was with him.

We drove away from that terrible sudden quiet, and Martine did not speak, and neither did I. There were too many things that we could never say, and so we stayed silent. We stayed silent the whole way home.

CHAPTER
THIRTY-ONE

It only took a week for him to come to me.

That week was hard, with Martine in the house. It was hard in ways that it never had been before. That first day, I couldn't move her from the bed, couldn't get a word out of her. I was frustrated that day by her silence, her immobility, her refusal to recover as quickly as I told myself I would have—but the rest of the week made me miss having her curled in on herself, crying silently and continuously into one of my pillows. She wandered aimlessly until I directed her, did as she was told with the listless apathy of a picked scab.

She haunted my house, filled the rooms with her grief until I thought I would suffocate. I found myself opening windows just to get air. I slept on the couch to avoid being next to her in the bed, as though her anguish could seep into me, poison me, leave me as broken as she was. But I couldn't avoid her entirely. I went to work during the day and stayed as late as I could, but when I got home at the end of the day, the oppressive fog of Martine's sorrow was always, always waiting for me.

I resented her more than I can say. I had rescued her. I had helped her get away with murder, and I had gotten her a clean escape from Nathan, and every time she drifted into a room I was occupying, with that lost look on her face, there was something in me that could only hiss the word "ungrateful" over and over again until I could think of a task to occupy her. It was as though she missed her baby too much to even see the magnitude of work I had taken on to help her, the amount of risk.

There was nowhere for me to send her, no boarding school I could stash her away in to rid myself of the constant reminder of the empty place in her life.

She was just *there*, always, staring at the walls with tears dripping from her chin. I remembered wondering if Nathan had programmed her to be able to cry. After seven days of her grief, a vicious part of me wished he hadn't.

I began to turn over the idea of telling Martine that she needed to find some other house to haunt. There was nowhere for her to go, of course—there was no one else she *knew*, other than maybe Seyed, but I somehow doubted that she would turn to him in her hour of need. I didn't savor the idea of putting her up in her own apartment, keeping her like a mistress, but it felt like the most humane option.

I will not pretend that it did not occur to me to kill her. I have wished, in the time since then, that there was any way for me to get credit for dismissing that notion out of hand.

I couldn't have killed her, any more than I could have turned her out of the house. Any more than I could have shouted at her for crying. All of it occurred to me—again and again, during that week, I had to swallow my father's voice to keep it from rising up out of my mouth. He was close to the surface in those days, bubbling under my skin like a blister. The taste of turned earth, the roses digging their roots into grave mud, the house flooded wall-to-wall with things that couldn't be said—it was too familiar, and Martine was endlessly fluttering her hands and drifting silently down the stairs, and a marrow-deep part of me knew my role. She made a space for a thing the shape of my father to fit into, and the gravity of that space was so, so powerful.

But I didn't. I didn't do it. I didn't shout at her, or level cold cruelty at her to bend her spine, or demand her silent obedience.

I didn't kill her. I didn't kill her, and there is no one in the world left who could ever tell me that it was an admirable thing for me to let her live.

I was turning the problem of Martine over in my head, trying to decide how I might go about telling her that we needed to find a different set of walls for her grief to drain into, when my doorbell rang. By the time my hand touched the front door, she had hidden herself away upstairs. That was a habit she'd developed during the spring she spent with me, or maybe one she'd developed during her time with Nathan and brought with her—going into the bedroom when the doorbell rang, just in case. I told her again and again that it was absurd: we went outside together, had been seen in public, in my car and in the lab and at the store. I wanted her hidden, but it was easy enough to hide her in the places where people didn't bother to look, in the eye contact people didn't want to make. But something about being home made her afraid, and I couldn't stop her from running off.

This time, I was relieved by her caution. Because this time, when I opened the door, Nathan was standing on my front step.

He had Violet in his arms, and his face was desperate.

———

After he left, I picked up my phone and dialed a number that I wasn't sure was still in service. I had to check it three times as I punched the numbers into my phone. I chewed on the pad of my thumb as it rang, a habit I'd broken in my first week at boarding school, and I waited, half hoping I'd have to leave a voicemail.

But she picked up.

I didn't bother with many pleasantries, after the *hello* and the *so nice to hear from you* and the *yes, it's been a while, longer than usual*. She was almost always the one to call me, and she was plainly jarred by this reversal.

I could hear in her voice that she was trying to figure out a way to get off the line. It was a mercy to both of us when I told her that I wouldn't waste her time.

"I need the house," I said.

"Oh."

That's all my mother said, the same sound she'd made when I

showed her my first lost tooth, told her about my first kiss on a dare, failed to conceal my swollen arm.

"I assume you haven't sold it?" I said. "I need it. I'll buy it from you, if you—"

"No," she said, "no, that won't be necessary. It would go to you anyway, if I died, and it's probably silly for it to be empty until then."

"Good." I sank my teeth into my thumb, too hard. Normally, I would have hissed at the pain—but my mother's voice was in my ear, and her voice always did make me default to silence.

She was quiet for a moment. I heard soft clinking noises on the other end of the line—her fidgeting with something, no doubt, clicking her fingernails against a glass or running the pendant of a necklace up and down the chain. *A human fucking twitch,* my father had sometimes called her, and as I remembered that phrase I experienced a vicious spasm of something that directly opposed nostalgia. It was a hatred for everything that had ever passed between my parents, for the people they had been together, for the way they had trapped me with their fear and their anger and their desperate need for everyone in the world to think that they were fine, that I was fine, that the walls of our house were built on steady ground. The fact that I could never forget that place, that life—it was so bitter that I very nearly spat to get the poison of it off my tongue.

"Well, good, then," she said. "I'll mail you the key, and I suppose that's all you need."

I thanked her, checked to be sure she had the right address for me. That's how simple it was. We said goodbye, and I hung up, and I went upstairs to let Martine out of the bedroom. Halfway up the stairs, I paused, looked down.

The side of my foot was pressed flush to the wall.

With immense deliberation, I lifted it, set it down again in the center of the step I was standing on. The step gave a soft creak under my foot. A few seconds later, the bedroom door at the top of the stairs opened.

"Come downstairs," I said to the sliver of Martine's face that peeked around the door. "We need to talk."

There were still two teacups on the table, and a little puddle of spilled milk from where Nathan had fumbled Violet's bottle. Martine sat in her usual chair and drew a finger through the milk. "I never bought a pump," she murmured.

I cleared away the cups, threw a dish towel onto the table to soak up the milk. "You what?"

"I never bought a breast pump," she said. "He must be using formula now." She pressed the heel of one hand to the place where her left breast met her sternum, massaged it hard. "I hadn't planned on weaning her so fast. I've been expressing manually for the last few days, but I suppose I should stop soon, or I'll never dry up. The books said it would hurt——"

"Yeah," I said, impatient. "Do you need anything for that?"

Her eyes lifted to mine slowly, as though they were weighted at the bottoms. "No," she said. "Sorry. I'm fine. What did you want to talk to me about?"

I swiped the dish towel across the table a few times, threw it into the sink. She flinched at the clatter the teacups made when it struck them. I forced myself to smile at her, a close-lipped attempt at offering her comfort. I sat down across from her and folded my hands on top of the little dining table.

I waited for her to smile back.

When she did, I began to tell her what Nathan had asked of me.

———

He held Violet wrong.

I didn't know how to hold her correctly either——I couldn't have held her any better than he was, to be certain——but I could tell that he was doing it wrong. She squirmed and cried in his arms, twisting her body, wormlike. She wore one sock, the other foot bare and fat and strangely smooth on the bottom. Her toes curled and stretched, and her face was snarled up into a red knot, and her misery was a palpable thing.

The lines of Nathan's face spoke to profound exhaustion. He cupped her neck in one hand, gently but with obvious discomfort. He didn't seem to like touching her, this baby that he had killed a dozen clones and destroyed a marriage—destroyed our life together—in order to get his hands on.

I watched him more closely than I had ever watched my own husband. The man in front of me moved and spoke like an adult, but he was just a handful of months old. There were so many things he had never seen or experienced, things he only thought he knew. He had no idea that he wasn't the man he thought himself to be.

He was treading water far out of his depth, and he thought he was just a few feet from shore. Martine and I were the only ones who knew exactly how lost he was.

He sat down at the dining-room table as I boiled water for tea, sat as though he'd never been off his feet before. This edition of Nathan was weary. Remembering Martine's sleepless nights and napless days, I could not bring myself to pity him. He looked as out of place as if he'd walked through my front door and somehow found himself standing on the surface of the moon. He glanced around, taking in my kitchen, patting Violet's back ineffectually.

I watched him taking it in: my mugs and wineglasses in the drying rack by the sink, my dish towel hung on the handle of the oven door, my magnetless refrigerator. After an awkward minute, his brow furrowed.

"It's funny," he said, "but I can't remember what our old kitchen looked like."

"Mmm," I said, hoping he would impose a suitable meaning on the noise. Of course he couldn't remember that—it wasn't a memory I'd handed him. It hadn't felt important, when we were mired in the programming process, that he remember what our home had looked like. It had never occurred to me that he would have cause to remember, that he would ever be in a position to draw a comparison between the rooms we decorated together and the rooms I decorated on my own. "It's good to see you," I added.

And it was good. I was glad to see this version of Nathan,

this slightly simpler, slightly better man who looked like my ex-husband. Some part of me had been sad at the knowledge that I couldn't observe him, couldn't watch his development as it progressed. But here he was, and I could see the way that he was settling into himself. He moved like the old Nathan had, spoke with much of his same inflection. It was like meeting an old friend at a high school reunion: he was different, but also, he was exactly the same. I didn't want to talk to him, but I couldn't help feeling obscurely happy to see him. Familiarity, is all. Familiarity and the satisfaction of my own curiosity.

"I have to share some . . . unfortunate news," he said, shifting the baby's weight from one arm to the other.

"Oh?" I brought him a cup of tea, a licorice blend that the original Nathan hadn't liked. I had always wondered if he *really* didn't like it, or if he was pretending to dislike it to be ornery. It was a petty indulgence, but I intended to have an answer one way or another.

He took a sip. He did not shudder or grimace or narrow his eyes. I counted myself victorious: he liked it. *I knew it.* Then he set his mug down, looking at it curiously—perhaps "liked it" was too strong a sentiment—and cleared his throat.

"It's about Martine," he said.

And then he told me.

He told me about how he'd come home and found her dead. A month ago, he said. Natural causes, he said. She'd had a heart condition. The lie flowed out of him as smooth as cream. He held my eyes as he told me his story, as he gently criticized himself for the flaws he'd given her. He spun a tale of himself heroically trying to handle the baby on his own for an entire month before breaking down and coming to me, and he didn't trip over a single word of it.

He lied to me with ease, and as he did, I saw the weave of the cloth he'd been cut from. This was the man I knew, after all.

I interrupted him before he could go into further detail about the "heart condition." I didn't want to make him dance for me, didn't want to see the routine he'd been practicing. I just wanted it to be over. "What do you need?" I asked, the words coming out sharp and abrupt. I didn't intend it to be cruel but it was, it was terribly cruel, and I saw how it hurt him.

"I don't know how to do this," he whispered. "I don't—I don't know anything about babies. I thought I did, but since Violet was born I've been learning it all fresh. Like this," he said, shifting the baby's weight between his arms again. "I don't know how to hold her right. I've been trying to figure it out all month, I even looked it up on—on my phone." He laughed. "Can you believe we don't have a computer in the house? I didn't even think about it, I always just use the one at work, but there's no computer in the house. Isn't that crazy?"

It took an effort to swallow the sip of tea that was in my mouth. It went down like an overlarge pill. Of course there was no computer in the house. The original Nathan wouldn't have wanted Martine to be able to use the internet, to learn about the way her life could be. He hadn't even given her books to read, and it wasn't out of neglect the way I'd assumed it was. He'd walled her up in a tower. The door wasn't locked, but he'd kept her trapped in her ignorance. It was by design.

This Nathan didn't know that—couldn't know. But the boundary between the original Nathan and the new one blurred together in my mind for a brief, furious moment, and I forgot that he truly had no idea. *He's lying again,* I thought, *pretending he didn't do this to her on purpose,* and I felt a buzzing rage deep in my bones and I knew that the original Nathan had been right about me. *A hornet,* he'd called me, full of hate and venom, and he'd been right because I looked across the table at the new Nathan and all I wanted to do was sting, sting, sting until he fell down swollen and dead.

I hadn't intended to be cruel when I asked this new Nathan what he needed from me. I hadn't intended to hurt him then. But I wanted to hurt him now. "Don't you have any friends you can ask?" I spread some butter on the "any," made it heavy.

It hit him exactly as I'd hoped it would. He looked down into his tea, took another sip, grimaced. "No one with kids," he said, lying again, lying the way he always had. He would tell me truths that were true *enough,* that weren't quite lies, and here he was, unwilling to confess his isolation to me.

Inside, I was smiling like a cat. I knew precisely how weak he was, knew the taste of his misery—but just at that moment, Violet let out a noise like the legs of a dining-room chair scraping against the floor, and reality clicked back into place. This was not the old Nathan. This was a new man, one who didn't deserve to be hurting, any more than he'd deserved to die when Martine wanted to kill him.

I'd put him there, after all. I'd made him into the man he was, and I'd put him into that house. It wasn't fair of me to be so callous. It wasn't fair of me to want him to hurt like this.

I tried to listen to him, this Nathan who had never been my husband. I tried not to interrupt, not to press. It was so hard, looking at this man who thought he had betrayed me, who thought he had ever loved me enough to stop loving me. Watching him hold his impossible baby the wrong way. I tried, but everything was fogged over by the shape of his mouth, the rise of his knuckles, the dip of his throat.

Everything about him was Nathan, and everything about me was a hornet, and I could not keep myself from hating him.

"Anyway," he said. "I don't know what I'm doing, and I need help. I know you never wanted children, but . . . I'm on my own, Evelyn. I can't do this on my own."

I shrugged. "Make another one," I said. "You did it right on the first try. Well, almost right, except for the heart condition." He only looked away from me at the last two words. Those were the only ones he knew to be untrue.

"No," he said slowly. "No, I can't make another one. I'll understand if this seems impossible to you, but . . . I loved Martine. I can't just replace her."

It hurt so much that it snatched the breath from my lungs,

hurt so much I wanted to turn into stone right there. But I wasn't made of stone, I was just bones and fingernails and undrinkable water.

Maybe that's why I couldn't stop myself from saying the weak, foolish, plaintive thing. "But you replaced *me*."

He shook his head. "Please," he said. "Let's not do this now."

The burn of tears struck my eyes like an open-handed slap. I blinked them back, telling myself that I could digest this later. I could save it in my snake-belly, the agony of the if-then with which Nathan had presented me: *If you are loved, then you cannot be replaced.*

"Sure," I said. "Never mind. It's not important." My voice came out raw. I slipped a hand under the table and dug my fingertips hard into the meat of my thigh, pushing bruise-deep until the muscle cramped. I swallowed a gasp at the pain, smoothed my face, dragged my gaze back to him. "What do you need, Nathan?"

He stammered his way through it, an entirely unreasonable request. One that was based in his constant certainty that I would, someday, change my mind about wanting children. He had always acted as though my decision not to have a baby were a temporary lapse, a delay. He had always assumed that all women came with an innate understanding of and desire for children—at least, the old Nathan had—and so it was not a surprise to me when he asked if I would help him raise Violet.

It was a surprise to him, I suspect, when I said yes.

THIRTY-TWO

When I was a child, the city felt endlessly far away. I would sit in my bedroom with the window open and strain to hear a car, looking out over the treetops and knowing that the city was beyond the distant hills that formed the horizon. I knew that my father worked in the city during the day, but I didn't know how long a commute could be—I only knew that he had one.

I didn't know, then, the precise duration of the drive from my parents' house to the city. And as an adult who lived in that city, I didn't have a sense of that distance either. Not really. I knew that it was about fifty miles, but I didn't know the way those miles would feel passing under me. I'd never driven them, never visited that house. I left it when I went to boarding school, and I didn't look back.

I never wondered why my mother hadn't sold it. I never encouraged her to, either. The risk of a new owner digging up the garden was simply too high. Just as she'd said on the phone, I was supposed to inherit the house. I might have been able to sell it, in the event of her death, or I might have simply had no choice but to keep it, to maintain it, to hold my parents' secrets in trust until my own death. I imagine I would have neglected the house, would have let the garden become overgrown and rotten. It wouldn't have occurred to me to live there, in the time before Martine.

But things are different now. I know the feel of those fifty miles, the way they disappear underneath me as the road goes from eight lanes to four lanes to two. The buildings shrink and the trees grow thicker as I near the place where *city* becomes *town*. The dominant color of the landscape goes from gray to green, until the corners I turn are bounded only by dense undergrowth.

If I make the drive while the sun is still up, I can see the way the light shines through the gaps where the trees don't touch. Crown shyness, that's called—the branches try not to touch each other, and their leaves grow to avoid competition for sunlight.

If I make the drive when the sun is down, I do it more slowly. The road, about twenty-five miles in, begins to curve wildly, and I never know which bend will reveal a deer or a rabbit. I drive more slowly, because if I brake too hard, the baby in the backseat will wake.

At first, I'd been prepared to deliver the killing *no*. I was going to refuse Nathan, and I was going to drink his failure down like cool water. He had betrayed me, betrayed our marriage, betrayed my *work* in order to get himself a baby, and I was ready to make him lie alone in the bed he'd made. That "no" may have been vindictive and venomous of me, but in that moment after he asked for my help, I could taste blood. I wanted more.

But then I'd heard a soft creak from upstairs, and everything came together all at once.

My agreement with Nathan is simple. I bring the baby to him for a weeklong visit, one week out of every five. That's as long as he needs, to feel like he's still involved, to feel like he's a good father. He still holds her awkwardly, still struggles to understand her development and her habits. I've taken to giving him the books that Martine finishes. He's catching up slowly.

I take no small satisfaction from the knowledge that she learns more quickly than he does.

Nathan thinks that I have found some deep well of maternal instinct. He thinks that I take the baby with me to my distant outpost, a lab in the country where I do grant-funded research.

He has never asked me for more detail on my work, but if he did, I would tell him the truth: I'm researching clone longevity. I'm looking into the reasons why their tissue decays so much more slowly than the tissue of a normal human. I'm looking into the ways one might alter a clone's programming, to let the subject take naps during the day.

I'm trying to find out how a clone could possibly change as quickly as Martine did, once the original Nathan was dead. She bucked some aspects of her programming far too easily, and now that I've had time to think about it, I can see that for what it is: useful data. It had never occurred to me that a clone could do that, and so I never looked into methods of making the programming process more ironclad.

I finally took that meeting with my lab director.

My research focus has shifted. My grant funding has increased.

And now, I have an entirely private lab in which to carry out my work. I never have to do anything for the sake of appearances, never have to appease a lab director or erect a screen to hide challenging visuals from a board chair. I can just *work*.

Thirty-five miles outside the city—fifteen miles from the house where I spent my silent, careful childhood—the trees are so thick that there's no parallax. The road is bounded on either side by a wall of green that rises up as dense and wild as a threat. I wonder if, when Violet is a little older, she'll be scared of those woods. For now, her visual acuity is too poor for her to even recognize the trees. I learned that from Martine: the baby can recognize faces, but she can't recognize forests yet.

She knows that I'm not her mother, too. She can recognize the difference between me and Martine. I'm not sure how—Martine could probably tell me—but she's different with the two of us. She sleeps on Martine's chest, laughs at the noises Martine makes. When I hold her, she's still, quiet, a little tense. With me, she perches on the edge of crying, but doesn't tip over into it.

She doesn't make sounds until she's in Martine's arms.

The trees thin out again forty-five miles outside the city. There's a little town there, mostly small houses. There's a grocery store and a gas station and a post office and a sheriff's office. The road straightens. There are stop signs, five of them, and then an orchard. We drive between rows of water-lined apple trees, their trunks scored at the place where the fields flood during irrigation, their branches twisted like something out of a children's book. Martine has designs on apple-picking, eventually. I tell her we'll see. I tell her that often.

I don't intend to keep her hidden away, the way Nathan did. I just don't have a plan yet for how to let her out into the world, for how to give her the freedoms she wants without endangering all of us. I'll get it figured out, though, in time. I just need to focus on my research for right now. She understands.

Past the orchard, the road narrows even further. It turns sharply left, then right, and then we're there.

We're home.

Violet almost always wakes when the car begins to crunch over the gravel of the long driveway. I drive over it slowly, passing between roses. Some of them are old and tangled, the bushes that my mother tended, but they've grown stubborn and leggy in her absence. Some of them are new, Martine's, grown from cuttings she asked me to bring her.

I try to bring her whatever she asks for, within reason.

Violet is always awake by the time I park the car, all the way at the end of the driveway. She doesn't cry right away, just makes little snuffling noises, soft vocalizations, like practice for talking. Once I lift her out of her car seat, she quiets, goes silent and watchful the way she always does in my arms. I carry her on one side, carry my handbag on the other.

I'm better at holding her than Nathan is.

It's the same every time I bring her back from one of her visits with the man who thinks he's her father. I park the car, and I get the baby from the backseat, and by the time the car is locked again, the front door to the house is open. Martine stands silhouetted there, waiting for us, her hands clasped tightly in front of her. She waits as we walk up the path to the door, white-knuckled, eager.

I give Violet to her right away. Regardless of what it is

convenient for Nathan to think, I am not eager to spend more time holding the baby than necessary. And Martine can hardly stand to be apart from Violet for an entire week; she frets and frays the entire time the baby is gone. It's better for everyone this way. I hand her the baby, and she smiles, occasionally cries a little.

Then we go inside, and we close the front door behind us, and we are alone together, the three of us.

Martine has made the house into a place I can bear to live. It's nice, the things she's done with it. I brought her here a month ahead of my own move, let her settle in and get the place ready while I wrapped things up at home and negotiated my transition at work. It was a relief, really, unburdening myself of incompetent assistants and nagging oversight and labyrinthine ethical reviews.

I used the same service to pack up my house that I had used a year before. They remembered me.

By the time I moved to the house fifty miles outside the city, Martine had turned it into something like a home. She'd uncovered all the furniture, rearranged most of it, beaten out the carpets and divested the rafters of cobwebs. She'd even gotten into the garden a bit. I warned her to leave the northwest corner alone, the part of the garden that came closest to the walls of the house, and she didn't ask me why. She just listened.

She doesn't touch that part of the garden, and she doesn't touch the study.

When I get home, I give her Violet. This is the bargain Martine and I have struck: While the baby is home, they can spend as much time together as Martine wants to take. Whenever Violet is awake, they're together, and I don't interfere, not much. I have my work to attend to, anyway.

And when Violet is asleep, or at her father's house, Martine's time is mine. That's what I proposed to her, when I found myself in a position to deny Nathan my help. "No more fugue state nonsense," I told her. "You'll snap out of this Havisham shit. You'll be a real person again, yes?"

She'd nodded, her brow knit, her fingers twisting together so tight that I looked away. "Yes, of course, anything," she said.

I'd folded my hands in front of me, because that was the word I'd wanted to hear. *Anything.* And it's worked out beautifully for everyone. Violet gets to be around her mother for weeks at a time, and Martine gets to see her baby. I get a tireless research assistant and a cooperative research subject all in one.

I'm going to figure out how Martine happened. I'm going to figure out how Nathan made a fertile clone, and I'm going to figure out how she broke her programming. We're already making great strides.

I walk through the bottom of the house while they greet each other. I listen to the soft noises they make at each other, the low conversation Martine has with the baby she thought she would never get back after leaving Nathan behind. The house smells like food, usually—Martine cooks while I drive to the city and back. She likes to have dinner ready by the time I get home, likes to have a fire lit.

The old couch in the living room is gone. There's a new one, a couch that I bought. There isn't a single memory attached to it. I don't think about it at all, and the not-thinking-about-it is a relief I cannot begin to describe.

I get home, and I walk through the bottom story of the house I grew up in, the one Martine has turned into a place for the three of us. At night, I walk up the stairs, planting my feet in the center of each step, and go to our bedroom to sleep. The baby is in my childhood bedroom, now a nursery, decorated to Martine's tastes. Martine and I are in my parent's old bedroom, a new mattress on an old bedframe, and at night, we sleep with our backs to each other. Sometimes I wake up in the night and hear her breathing; more often, I wake up and can't hear her breathing at all. I can't hear it because it's too perfectly synced with my own.

Between coming home and going to bed, though, I need to work. There's so much to do, so much to learn. I'm working on setting up an actual lab in the backyard shed—it won't be nearly the same quality as the one I fought so hard for, but it's mine, just mine, and it will have to do. Some of the hacked-together qualities of it remind me of my grad school days, the rickety old equipment and hand-me-down machines. It's romantic, really.

While I get the lab into shape, though, and while Martine and Violet are cooing at each other, there's still work to do. So much work. And so, once Martine has the baby in her arms, I proceed directly to my study.

I sit behind the desk, now, not in front of it. I've removed my father's things, replaced them with my own. His pens and note-pads and paperweights sit in a box in the corner of the room—I'll sort through them later, when there's time. When more pressing matters have been dealt with.

I sit in my study, and I close the door. Martine knows not to disturb me while I'm working, unless it's to bring me dinner. I try not to work through dinner too often—we sit at the dining table, eat together like a family should. But sometimes, I have no other choice, and Martine brings me a warm plate to keep me going as I work. She knows to be quiet while I'm working, too, and to keep the baby as quiet as she can. She knows I need to be able to concentrate.

There is one exception to this rule. Once a week—every week, no matter what—Martine puts the baby down for the night, then knocks on the door to my study. I tell her to come in, and she does, and she sits in the chair on the other side of my desk. She brings a notepad with her. It's filled with questions, every time. Questions about things she's been reading, things she doesn't un-derstand or hasn't quite put together yet, things I've done to her in the course of my research.

This time, once a week, is her time to ask those questions. I answer her as best I can. My father's hourglass is in the box in the corner. I have no need of the hourglass, because Martine gets more than an hour from me. I answer her questions until the answering's done, or until the baby wakes.

I'm not a monster.

It's a good life we've made here. I have my work, and my space. Martine has Violet. We may not know many people, but it's all right. We're happy here, in this home we've made.

It's better this way. We're better this way. We have everything we need.

The more I think about it, the more I'm sure that there's no reason at all why things should ever have to change.

ACKNOWLEDGMENTS

Traditionally, this section of the book is a place for expressions of gratitude. This book, I think, needs something different from gratitude—it needs acknowledgments in the truest sense of the word. There are things that need to be accounted for. As I look at the book I have written, I feel that it would be dishonest not to recognize those who brought it into the world. To say "thank you" to some of the people here would be wholly inadequate; to say "thank you" to some of them would be wholly fraudulent.

Here are the people without whom this book would not be possible:

The adult man who groomed and abused me in my teens and early twenties, who put his fingers onto the still-warm plastic of my brain and gripped tight as he could, who shaped me into someone who understood harm to be a form of love;

Those who encouraged him, covered for him, protected him, and benefited from his actions;

Those who helped me escape him when the time came;

Those who stuck with me, and those who could not;

The therapist who told me that I could have a self;

The pastor who shared a cigar with me and told me not to get a motorcycle;

The church community that welcomed me, loved me, drained me, and eventually left no place for me;

The incredibly kind man who I married, and those who loved and cared for us both when that marriage came to an end;

The friends who helped me navigate the time when I had no center;

The friend who bought me a last-minute bathing suit and inhaled a feather boa with me;

My literary agent and friend, DongWon Song, who loved this book when it was just an idea;

My brilliant editor, Miriam Weinberg, who gave that idea a home and made it richer than I ever could on my own;

The bartenders at Angel Face in Portland, who taught me to

love whiskey as I bulldozed my way through the first draft of a book about abuse and grooming and identity;

The therapist who told me that what happened to me was wrong;

The friends who read early drafts and middling drafts and late drafts, whose encouragement is my bedrock;

The entire team at Tor, who have nurtured and advocated for this book with unparalleled brilliance;

The friends who supported me when my body stopped working;

The health-care professionals who helped me to get on my feet again;

The partners who were kind and patient, and the partners who weren't;

The partner who tried to put his own fingerprints on my brain, and who showed me that I could be angry at someone for trying to hurt me;

The therapist who told me I could face memories I didn't feel brave enough for;

The writing community that has supported and critiqued me and my work;

The queer community that has shown me patience and kindness and stubborn compassion;

The booksellers and librarians who have put my work into the hands of readers;

The partner who showed me what kindness and family can be;

The beautiful home and family that's grown around us;

And more than anyone, the readers. All of it is for you.

Harm is not a form of love, and your home does not have to be a place of fear. If you or someone you know is a victim of domestic violence, there is help available 24 hours a day at the National Domestic Violence Hotline (1-800-799-SAFE) and the National Sexual Assault Helpline (1-800-656-HOPE). There are more resources available at https://ncadv.org/resources.